# ASHES ON THE EARTH

**SARAH ASHWOOD**

**Ashes on the Earth**

Copyright © 2020 Sarah Ashwood

Editing by Olivia Cornwell Editing Services

Proofreading by Fantasy Proofs

Cover art by Oliviaprodesign.

ALL RIGHTS RESERVED. Excepting brief review quotes, this book may not be reproduced in whole or in part without the express written permission of the copyright holder. The unauthorized reproduction or distribution of this copyrighted work is illegal.

This is a work of fiction. Any resemblance to persons, living or dead, real events, locations, or organizations is purely coincidental.

All Scripture quotations from The Authorized (King James) Version.

❦ Created with Vellum

## AUTHOR'S INSPIRATION

"Therefore will I bring forth a fire from the midst of thee, it shall devour thee, and I will bring thee to ashes upon the earth in the sight of all them that behold thee." —Ezekiel 28:18

"Thou art the anointed cherub that covereth; and I have set thee so: thou wast upon the holy mountain of God; thou hast walked up and down in the midst of the stones of fire." —Ezekiel 28:14

## AUTHOR'S NOTE

This series contains creatures from myth, folklore, and legend that I researched and gathered from around the world. I've tried in most cases to be as faithful to the prevailing mythology as possible. However, as you probably know, stories diverge and evolve over time, so there isn't always a general consensus of opinion. Furthermore, this is fantasy, which I felt gave me room to take a few liberties with the creatures I've showcased. I hope any variations from standard lore won't detract from your enjoyment of this series.

# CHAPTER ONE

"C'mon, c'mon."

Standing at the intersection beside Cook Children's Medical Center in downtown Fort Worth, Texas, I tapped my toe impatiently. It had been a long day. I was a third year nursing student, we'd been doing clinicals, and I'd just gotten off a twelve hour shift. Today, I'd cleaned up human waste, been vomited on and screamed at by patients, and reamed out by the RN I was shadowing.

I couldn't wait for this day to be over. I wanted to go home, take off these scrubs, hop in the shower, and then enjoy one of Mom's home cooked dinners. Unfortunately, the light at the intersection seemed to be taking forever.

"It's like the whole universe is conspiring against me today," I grumbled.

If I didn't make it to my car within the next few minutes and get out of the parking lot, I'd be stuck in unending lines of traffic on the way home. I desperately wanted to avoid that.

A small crowd had gathered behind me, comprised of other hospital employees getting off work and visitors leaving the hospital. Next to me, a sharply dressed young woman a few years older than me held the hand of a little boy about four years old. I noticed them—the woman, anyway—with a touch of envy. She looked classy in a careless sort of way, with her jeans, tank, ¾ sleeve jacket, and ballet flats. Her haircut had perfect beachy waves, her jewelry was bold, and her eyebrows were on point.

As a busy nursing student, I just didn't have the time or energy for fashion. My wispy blonde hair was usually pulled back in a sloppy braid or ponytail. My glasses tended to slide down my nose, and my favorite jacket looked like what it was: cheap. I wished I had the innate style, the money, and the time to look as pretty as the woman next to me, but envy wouldn't get me anywhere, so I switched my attention to the child she was with.

I was the oldest of three with two younger brothers, ages twelve and six. I was used to children, especially boys, and liked them. My upbringing had persuaded me to enter nursing school after high school and work towards becoming a pediatric nurse. At this point, I still lived at home to save money until I graduated, got a job, and could start paying off student loans.

The kid next to me was tugging on his mom's hand—I assumed it was his mom, anyway. She was looking down at her cell phone, sheathed in a pretty pink case studded with diamonds. Her perfectly manicured thumb nail clicked on the screen as she scrolled up, ignoring the little boy. He swayed towards me, bored, and our eyes met.

"Hi," I said, flashing him a smile.

"Hi. What's your name?" he asked.

"It's Ellie. What's yours?"

"Jackson."

"That's a nice name. I like it."

He frowned quizzically, studying my scrubs. "Are you a doctor?"

"Nope. But I am training to be a nurse."

"What's a nurse?"

"Leave her alone, Jackson," murmured his mom without glancing up from her phone.

"It's okay. He's not bothering me," I said. To the little boy, Jackson, I explained, "A nurse is sort of like a doctor's assistant. They help the doctor out."

"Oh." He opened his mouth as if to ask something else, then a flash of fur and color in the middle of the street caught his attention. "Look, Amy, a squirrel!"

"That's nic—" she started to say, disinterested, but even as she spoke Jackson jerked on her arm and broke free. "Hey!" she shouted, finally looking up.

My heart froze in my chest. It all happened in slow motion. Jackson jerked free. Amy looked up. Jackson darted into the street. Right into the path of an oncoming bus. The bus was slowing for the light, which was changing so pedestrians could cross, but it wasn't slowing fast enough. It was going to hit the kid.

I didn't stop to think. Sheer instinct propelled me. Before Amy could move, even as the gasps and screams of onlookers engulfed me, I dove for the little boy. I didn't try to grab him and pull him back. There wasn't time for that. Instead, I took a running leap and dove, shoving him forward. He fell onto the street and burst into tears. I fell onto the street, hearing the grinding and squealing of brakes. Jackson was out of the way. My legs weren't. There was a blur of color and sound. Gritting my teeth, my eyes squeezed shut, I waited to feel pain explode across my ankles and calves as bus tires crushed them.

Nothing happened.

For a second, it was like the world had gone silent or I had gone deaf. Then, slowly, awareness returned. Noise. Chaos. Confusion. People running. Feet pounding the area around me. I opened my eyes, my hand patting around for my glasses. I found them and slipped them on. There was a tiny crack in the corner of the right lens, but that didn't matter. I was okay. The tire had stopped centimeters from my legs. My legs were actually under the front of the bus, right next to the tire, but I hadn't been hit. I glanced over at the little boy. Amy had darted past me and dropped down to gather him in her arms.

"Jackson, Jackson, are you okay? Are you hurt?" she babbled. Her face had gone stark white. Her cell phone was dropped, forgotten. "Are you okay? What were you thinking? You can't do that! You can't run away from Miss Amy! You almost got killed. Oh, your dad's gonna kill me!"

I caught all that despite Jackson's wails. When I'd shoved him forward, he'd scraped his elbows on the asphalt. They were bleeding a little, which gave him cause to scream his head off.

"Hush, honey, it's okay, it's okay," Amy was saying. Her hand trembled as she ran it over his head. She looked at me, tears in her eyes. It was the weirdest thing, but for a split-second I swear I thought her eyes looked…gold. Like a shining bright gold. Then I blinked, and the illusion disappeared.

"Thank you," she mouthed. "Thank you."

I tried to reply, but my vocal chords were frozen. I didn't even realize how scared I was, that I was in shock, until legs and feet surrounded me. People were kneeling around me, talking all at once.

"Did you get hit?"

"Is she okay?"

"Her legs—watch out for her legs!"

A man in a uniform knelt next to me, the bus driver, peering under the bus.

"Her legs are fine, barely," he announced. His eyes were wide, and there was a pallor beneath his dark skin. "That was really brave, young lady. Really brave. I thought for sure I was gonna hit that kid, then you came flyin' out of nowhere—"

He swallowed hard and shook his head.

"Wow," he finished. "You're a hero."

At last I found my voice. "I'm not a hero," I said. My voice trembled and I laughed to cover the fact that I was suddenly so overwhelmed with emotions that I was about to cry. "I just like kids."

At this, the bus driver laughed. The people around us laughed. The tension was broken. A male voice said, "Let's get her out."

Several pairs of hands closed on me, including the bus driver. I clung to his arms as they drew me out from under the front of the bus and got me on my feet. I must've been more frightened than I knew. Once I was standing, my knees buckled. The bus driver grabbed me, supporting me.

"You sure you're okay? Here comes a wheelchair. Hey! Over here!" he hollered, waving his arm.

"I'm fine, I'm fine. I'm only scared."

I tried to brush off the care and concern, but nobody was listening. In the background, I heard Amy speaking over Jackson's wails, insisting on the behalf of her employers that I should be checked out. I wasn't sure what that meant about her employers. I knew I was fine and wanted to go home, but in the chaos and confusion nobody was paying attention to me, so eventually I quit trying to fight it. In short order, I was in one of the curtained off areas of the ER and Jackson was in the next. Someone had retrieved my purse and phone, which I'd dropped during my rescue attempt, and brought them to me. I typed out a text to both my parents.

*Got involved in something while leaving the hospital. Everything's fine, but I'm going to be late. Don't wait on me for dinner. Love you.*

That done, I settled in for the long haul until an ER physician could come see me. Machines hummed and beeped and blinked in the background as my vitals were monitored and recorded. Leaning my head back against the thin pillow, I shut my eyes. Instantly, I was overwhelmed with images of Jackson darting into the street and the bus headed straight for him, me diving for the kid and the bus almost hitting me instead...

"Hey."

A woman's soft voice broke into my train of thought. I opened my eyes. There stood Amy. She looked a little less cool and fashionable now, with her makeup smeared from crying and her face still pale. Gosh. If she looked that bad, I must've looked horrible.

"Hey," I said, pushing myself up on the bed. "Come in. How's Jackson?"

She stepped into the room, letting the curtain fall closed behind her.

"He's okay. He's finally calmed down. Our driver is with him, letting him play on his phone. I wanted to come see you for a second and thank you."

"You don't have to—"

"Oh, yes I do." She seated herself in the chair next to my bed. "I was too busy scrolling Instagram and not paying attention to Jackson. If you hadn't done what you did, he'd be…"

She stopped and tears filled her eyes.

"Hey, it's alright. It was an accident," I said, trying to ease the situation. "All's well that ends well. Nobody got hurt."

"Yeah, thanks to you," she said with a broken chuckle. Rising, she pulled a tissue from the box on the counter which she used to dab at her watery eyes, then her nose. "Anyway," she went on, resuming her seat, "I want you to know that I'll never forget this. Jackson's parents won't, either. I already called and told them what happened. Mr. Costas said I was right to insist on you getting checked out, and to tell you not to worry about your hospital bill or your glasses or anything. It will all be taken care of. He also said to expect a follow up from him in a few days. He wants to thank you personally."

"Mr. Costas? So you're not Jackson's mom?"

That made me remember her referring to herself as *Miss Amy*, which now made sense.

"Me? Oh no, no," Amy laughed. "I'm his nanny. We were here at the hospital to visit my cousin's kid for a few minutes who just had surgery. Not a place I'd normally bring Jackson, but I didn't want to wait for my day off. I figured we'd only be here a little while. No big deal, right? Guess you never can tell what's going to happen."

"No, you sure can't." I had to agree with her on that.

"Look," I said, "please tell your boss thank you for me, but he really doesn't have to—"

"Stop. Stop right there." Amy held up a hand. "You saved his son's life. I can promise you he will take this very seriously. There's nothing more important to Mr. Costas than family. You risked your life to save Jackson's. Mr. Costas will treat you like family now. You *are* family now."

## CHAPTER TWO

*You* are *family now*.

I didn't think too much about it when Amy said that, but she wasn't kidding.

I took the next day off from classes and clinicals. Mom insisted. She was really shaken when I finally got home that night and told my family what had happened. Shaken, and more than a little aggravated I hadn't called to tell her and Dad what had actually happened.

"I can't believe you drove yourself home!" she'd snapped. "What was the hospital thinking?"

"They checked me out, Mom. I was fine," I said. "Believe me, if I hadn't been okay, they wouldn't have turned me loose."

I think she half-guilted me into taking the next day off to rest and recover because she was so piqued that I hadn't called. Whatever. Mom was Mom, and there was no arguing with her. I spent the day at home, slobbing it up in faded yoga pants and a baggy t-shirt. I helped my younger brothers with their schoolwork, ate popcorn while watching sitcoms on Netflix, and did some light housecleaning. Honestly, it was nice to have a break.

By the next day, I was completely fine and knew it. I went

back to school, back to work at the hospital, and life got back into the swing of things.

Or, it was supposed to.

The invitation stopped all that.

Three days after the accident, I arrived home from the hospital.

"Hey, I'm home!" I called. Shrugging out of my jacket, I hung it on a peg behind the door and kicked my shoes off.

"Hey, honey, how was your day?" Mom asked, appearing around the corner from the kitchen into the living room. Without giving me the chance to answer, she went on, "Something came for you today."

She scooped up a package and an envelope from the antique side table, rescued from a flea market, and handed both to me.

"What's this?" I asked, flipping the package over to see the return address. "I didn't order anything."

"Open it and see."

I shot her a glance. Mom was practically bursting with curiosity.

"I bet it killed you to wait and not open this, didn't it?" I teased her.

She swatted me lightly on the arm. "Oh, hush. It did not."

I arched a brow.

"Okay, maybe it did. Go on, open it."

"Okay, okay."

She followed me as I moved into the living room and dropped onto the couch. I tore into the package first. Inside was a hard case. A hard leather case. Rich, expensive looking. I flipped it open. Nestled on a bed of soft black velvet was a pair of glasses. A little bit oversized, like mine, but with gold wire frames. Whereas my original pair, cracked during my dive to save Jackson Costas, had come from an optometrist at the front of a mega retail chain store, these were designer glasses. I recognized the name printed on the inside of the lid. And it was nothing I'd ever, ever dreamed of owning.

"Oh my goodness, Ellie," Mom said softly. Seated next to me on the couch, she reached out to touch the glasses almost reverently with a fingertip. "Those are beautiful."

"They are," I agreed, staring down at them. A weird feeling curdled in my stomach. "Amy, the little boy's nanny, she said her boss was going to cover my hospital bill and my glasses, but I didn't expect anything like this. I sure didn't expect it so soon. How'd they know my prescription anyway?"

"When they got your information to pay your hospital bills they got those records too?"

"Isn't that a little creepy? Medical records are supposed to be confidential."

"True," Mom agreed. "Are you going to accept them? I think you should. As a parent, I know I'd do anything I could for someone who saved my child's life. Buying someone designer glasses—I'm sure they feel like it's the least they could do. Still, they are very, very nice."

She was thinking the same thing I was: that this was something I'd never dreamed of owning. It was almost...too much.

During my childhood, we'd never had money to speak of. Dad had spent his career in the military, part of it as a Religious Affairs Specialist, or Chaplain's Assistant, meaning our family had moved from place to place, going where the Army ordered. Eventually, Mom had decided homeschooling us was a better option than constantly changing schools, so a dual income had gone out the window. Money was tight for a family of five. Nothing had changed since my father's recent retirement, except that he now worked at a center for vets with PTSD and other issues. Mom continued to homeschool my younger brothers. There was no way my parents could have ever afforded anything with this particular designer's label. There was no way I could afford it either, at least not for several years in the future when I had my nursing degree, a good job, and my student loans were paid off. Even then, I was too conservative by nature to blow money on something like this.

"I guess I can try them on," I said to please her.

I wasn't sure why I still felt funny about it. It was a nice gesture.

*And,* I told myself, *what is an expensive pair of glasses in comparison to their son's life?*

Placing my old glasses with the cracked lens on the couch beside my leg, I retrieved the new ones from the case and slid them onto my nose, hooking them behind my ears. They fit very well. Were extremely comfortable. The prescription was definitely up to date. They were nice. Too nice. I felt awkward.

"Aw you look so pretty," said my mom, reaching up to brush stray wisps of hair out of my face. "You deserve this, Ellie. You really do.

"Hey, go ahead and open the envelope next."

Quashing the weird feelings over the glasses, I laid aside the packaging and lifted the envelope. It was made of thick cream paper. My name, Miss Eleanor St. James, was printed in a rich black font across the front. Underneath was my address. In the upper left hand corner was the sender's name and address.

Mr. and Mrs. Sean Costas.

"Those must be Jackson's parents," I told my mom. "I remember Amy mentioning the name Costas."

"Costas?" She took the envelope from me, examining it. "Do you know who that is?"

I shook my head. "No."

"Ellie," Mom said, her reddish eyebrows pinching in a frown. "If it's the same person—and I bet it is—he's only one of the biggest businessmen in the whole Dallas/Fort Worth Metroplex. In the entire state of Texas. Possibly *the* biggest. He owns Costas Tower in downtown Fort Worth. Another in Dallas. No wonder he was able to get ahold of your glasses prescription." She took in my wide eyes and gaping mouth. "You really didn't know that?"

"Well, I mean, the name sounded a bit familiar, and Amy was a nanny and mentioned a driver and everything, but I never thought to put two and two together."

"Wow. I just—wow. I can't believe you saved the son of one of the richest men in Texas. Sending you expensive designer glasses probably really *is* the least he can do." Mom handed back the envelope. "Better go ahead and see what's in there."

I felt unaccountably nervous as I tugged at the flap, breaking the seal. The interior of the envelope was silver. I pulled out an embossed card, complete with a family crest or coat of arms at the bottom. With my mom leaning over my shoulder, I read,

*Miss Eleanor St. James,*

*The honor of your presence is requested at a dinner at the home of Sean and Ciara Costas on Thursday, November 1, at 6:00 P.M. A car and driver will be dispatched to pick you up at 5:15 P.M. and will return you home.*

The address at the bottom, above the family coat of arms, was some ritzy area of Fort Worth that people like me normally had no business visiting.

"Dang." I murmured aloud. I laid the invitation on my lap and turned to my mom. "I guess when Amy said her boss was going to treat me like family, she really meant it."

Mom shook her head, appearing worried. I was pretty sure I had a similar expression on my face. Looking at her was like looking in a mirror. People said we could almost pass for twins. It was from her I'd inherited my diminutive height, skinny build, pale complexion, and the light scattering of pale freckles across my nose and cheekbones. My hazel eyes, blonde hair, and darker eyebrows had come straight from my dad, though.

"I don't know about this, Ellie. I'm sure Mr. Costas means to be kind, but he does have a reputation."

"A reputation? For what? Rubbing elbows with the governor and president and hanging out at the swankiest golf clubs?"

Mom didn't crack a smile. "No, although he does all that too. He's sort of got a reputation as a mafia don or mob boss."

I would have snickered at the terms except Mom was so utterly serious.

"That—seems a little farfetched, Mom. Probably any rich businessman is going to be accused of shady business dealings."

"Well, some people think he's a little shadier than most."

"If he's breaking the law, then why isn't he in trouble with the law?" I inquired mildly, refusing to make myself more nervous than I already was at the idea of meeting this man and his wife.

"You know how people like that are. Money and connections can protect you from nearly anything."

"Oh yes, I know all about that," I joked, "and so do you. Honestly, Mom, I think you've been watching too many police dramas."

She didn't deny it but she didn't push the point, either. Instead, she said, "It's way out of our family's comfort zone. I don't know what your dad will say about it. On the other hand, we'd look like massive jerks if you didn't go, since they're having you over to thank you."

"Yeah...all mafia and mob boss stuff aside, I guess you don't really turn a man like Mr. Costas down," I agreed.

But as I gazed at the invitation in my lap, through the perfect lenses of the designer glasses they'd sent me, I wanted to. I felt anxious. Like Mom had said, this was way, way, way out of my comfort zone. Way out of my league.

## CHAPTER THREE

I felt even more out of my league a few days later sitting in the back of the car that was sent to pick me up. The sleek grey car—apparently some British sports car that made my twelve-year-old brother's jaw drop—had pulled up in front of our house right on time. A tall Native American woman, maybe around forty, dressed in crisp black clothes had gotten out of the driver's seat, came around and held the door for me.

I'd felt incredibly awkward as I said goodbye to my family, who were all gathered behind me in the doorway, staring, then bypassed the driver, thanking her as I climbed into the car. Now, on my way to the Costas' home, I sat in the backseat and fretted. My hair was already slipping out of its simple knot. My fine hair defied any kind of restraint, which was why I usually didn't mess with it much. I rarely wore makeup, either, except a little mascara and eyeshadow. Mom and I had made a special trip to the drugstore on the corner to buy foundation and powder and blush and other stuff I couldn't even name just for tonight.

Afterward, we'd scoured both of our closets, searching for something, anything appropriate. Neither of us really knew what you were supposed to wear to an event like this. Neither of us had ever been to an event like this. Finally, Mom suggested an ivory silk blouse from her closet paired with a simple black pencil skirt from mine. I'd buckled on my nicest pair of black heels, and we'd figured out jewelry. I hoped I looked presentable. I certainly looked Sunday morning church presentable, but what was that compared to dinner at the home of a man who owned freaking towers in downtown Fort Worth and Dallas?

To keep myself from fretting over my appearance, since there was nothing I could do about it now, I pulled the invitation from my purse and studied it in the dim light. The driver didn't seem inclined to talk, other than asking me how I was doing this evening when I'd first entered the car.

"Fine, how are you?" I'd responded.

"I'm well, thank you for asking."

"I-I'm Ellie," I'd said next, then felt foolish. Of course she knew who I was, since she'd been sent to fetch me.

"Nice to meet you, Miss Ellie."

She hadn't offered her name. Maybe she wasn't supposed to. Maybe she wasn't supposed to talk to me. Was I supposed to talk to her? Since I didn't know how any of this worked, I'd fallen silent and sat there fidgeting, hoping I wasn't sweating too much and that my deodorant would hold up.

I rubbed my thumb restlessly along the embossed frame bordering the invitation.

*Miss Eleanor St. James.*

It sounded so pretentious, almost like I belonged in the world of the Costas family. I'd never figured out why my parents stuck me with a name like Eleanor when I already had a pompous surname like St. James. I greatly preferred Ellie. It was so much easier.

I re-read the invitation, then skipped down to the bottom, to the family seal, or coat of arms. I'd always found coats of arms interesting, and was curious about both the blended coat of arms and the Costas's name. I'd googled the family after the invitation arrived, reading up on various charitable events and appearances, meetings with the governor, with senators and congressmen and women, not to mention golf with the president. A little about the different businesses Mr. Costas was involved with, which were too many for me to keep track of.

I didn't find much to verify Mom's warnings of the mafia or the mob, except Costas was a name of Greek origin, but both Mr. Costas and his wife had Irish first names—Sean, Ciara. Their coat of arms had a red shield, divided into four quarters. One quarter was a bull, one a mermaid figure, one some sort of stone-looking tablets, shaped like the Ten Commandments tablets in the old movie, and the last a quiver with a clutch of weapons: a spear, a rifle, a sword, arrows...

None of the items seemed to necessarily go together. Had they designed their own coat of arms? I didn't know, but puzzling over it was interesting enough to keep me from completely freaking out during the ride across the city to the Costas home.

My fears of being way out of my league were confirmed by the guarded gate, with actual guardsmen inside the hut. The wall surrounding their estate must have been a good ten feet high, at least. All I could see over the top was trees. The driver stopped the car and rolled down the windows, letting the guard glance inside before the gates were open and he waved her through. I leaned forward to stare out the windshield. In the fading evening light, supplemented by up-lights on the trees, I could see a winding, paved, tree-lined drive and manicured lawns underneath the trees, with boulders and fountains, seasonal flowers and bushes all perfectly maintained. I didn't spot the house until we'd driven a couple more minutes, the driveway was so long. We rounded the final bend. My breath caught when I saw the mansion at the end.

"Wow," I breathed.

The structure was white stone with black tiled roof and gables. A circular drive led to the front door—which also had two doormen. I caught glimpses of more buildings behind the main house. Quite a few of them, actually. The house itself was large enough to qualify for a small hospital.

*Okay, you're thinking like a nurse,* I told myself. *Don't think like a nurse. Think like a...a—*

A what? Somebody who belonged here? I sure wasn't that.

The car rolled to a stop, and one of the two men standing by the front door approached to open my door. Unfortunately, I'd already opened it and had started to duck out, so it turned into that awkward moment of me not knowing what he was intending and doing his job for him. Still, he was polite, keeping his hand on the doorknob as I climbed out and shutting the door closed behind me.

"Sorry," I muttered, wondering if I should explain that I wasn't used to people opening my car door for me. I kept my mouth shut. That seemed like the best thing to do. Say as little as possible and survive the evening until I could get back home and into a world I was familiar with.

"Not a problem, Miss," he said with a small smile. "This way."

He led me into the house, past a gigantic thick, wooden front door carved with the same coat of arms that decorated the invitation. Inside, everything was extensive space and white walls, dark furniture, and pops of color in the décor. Also inside, waiting in the vestibule, were my hosts.

---

"So, Ellie, tell us what you do," invited Mrs. Costas.

We were seated in a dining room that was bigger than the kitchen, living room, and dining area of my house combined. After introductions, Mr. Costas had led us here, pushing his wife's wheelchair, explaining with a smile that things were going to be a little more informal tonight. If this was informal, I would have hated to see their version of formal. The wallpaper was creams and golds, the dining room table was mahogany, the chairs had embroidered cushions, and the flower arrangements alone probably cost more than an entire month of groceries for my family.

I lifted my eyes from my plate, which I'd been staring at in an attempt not to stare at anything else. Ciara Costas was a beautiful woman, and, thanks to Google, I knew was consistently named to best dressed and most fashionable lists, despite living in a wheelchair. She was about fifteen years younger than her husband, so possibly in her late thirties. She was Irish, and had the lyrical accent to prove it. Her rich black hair was done up in a style that sort of reminded me of a Gibson Girl hairdo, but on her it looked fresh and modern. Her red lips and green eyes were a striking contrast to the darkness of her hair and eyebrows. Despite her wealth and beauty, she had a sweet look about her and was clearly trying to make me feel comfortable.

"I'm in nursing school," I replied. "Training to be an RN. Eventually, I plan to specialize in pediatrics."

"Pediatrics. You must love children, then."

"I do."

"Well, we can never thank you enough for what you did for our son," spoke up Mr. Costas.

I glanced his way. He was a powerfully built man in his fifties, with salt and pepper hair combed back, piercing grey eyes under thick dark brows, and a well-trimmed beard. Tonight he wore a pin-striped vest over a white button-up shirt. The sleeves were casually rolled to his elbows, and I'd been surprised to see that his forearms were sleeved in tattoos. The tattoos were strange, too. All kind of mythical looking animals and creatures, like bulls and mermaids (mermaids again) and winged women and skeletons in armor and even a medusa with snakes for hair. When we'd first sat down, I'd considered asking if he was into mythology or something, but figured it might come across as rude since my guess was based off his tattoos, and maybe I wasn't supposed to remark on them.

"It's fine," I said, feeling awkward, uncertain how to respond.

"I'm just glad I was in the right place at the right time. I'd never want to see a child hurt. How is Jackson doing?"

"He's recovered very well," my host assured me, picking up his coffee cup for a sip. "You know kids. They bounce back faster than adults. He acts like nothing ever happened."

"And Amy? How is Amy? She seemed pretty shaken up," I inquired next.

I was only trying to be nice. I wasn't prepared for the hard look that spread across my host's face.

"Amy has been relieved of her position," Mr. Costas said, setting the mug down with a clunk that made me jump. "When I hire someone to look after my son, I expect them to do exactly that. Guard my son. Amy's carelessness nearly got my son killed. She won't ever be allowed near him again."

"Oh." *Now you've done it,* I scolded myself. *You've stuck your foot in it for sure.* "I-I'm sorry. I—"

"You don't have to apologize. You didn't do anything wrong," spoke up Mrs. Costas, offering me a reassuring smile.

But I felt like I had. The atmosphere in the room had shifted. Mr. Costas had fallen to brooding, and his wife was obviously trying to ease the tension.

"Carter, would you fetch my husband some more coffee, please?" she said next, addressing the man hovering in the background, against the wall.

He'd been so quiet and so still I'd barely noticed he was there. I'd wondered if he was a butler or something, although he wasn't one of the people who'd been in and out, laying out dishes, serving food, and pouring drinks. This was the first time he'd moved at all as he stepped up to retrieve my host's coffee cup, carried it to the silver coffee pot on the side board, and refilled it. Our eyes met for a second when he stooped behind his employer's chair to set down the mug. I quickly glanced away, not wanting to be caught staring.

While he wasn't the handsomest man I'd ever seen, he had

sort of a striking appearance, with his olive skin and dark eyes. His black hair was cut close, and, like his boss, he wore a neatly trimmed goatee. The most eye-catching thing about him was how big he was. Not big as in tall—he wasn't much over average height. It was his build. He was wearing a dark suit, but the seams on the upper arms looked strained. His jacket couldn't hide the muscles in his broad chest and stacked shoulders. He looked more like a bodybuilder than a butler—if that's what he even was. Honestly, I didn't know if people still had butlers anymore, especially in Texas.

He stepped back into the corner, far enough behind his boss's chair to be helpful if needed, but to offer some privacy for conversation. Mrs. Costas, trying to keep the ambiance pleasant, asked a few questions about myself, my parents, and my family, starting with my mother. I explained briefly how Mom chose to be a stay-at-home mom and homeschool my brothers and myself, and why, hoping I didn't come across as some sort of weirdo. Mrs. Costas didn't bat an eye. She was smiling graciously and nodding, but I couldn't help worrying, especially since here I was the guest of a man some people claimed was a mafia don.

*He's not a mafia don. Stop thinking things like that,* I scolded myself, even as part of me wanted to study Mr. Costas to see if I could detect any truth to the rumors. Not that I would even know what a mafia don looked like, aside from gangster-type movies, which I wasn't a big fan of.

"How interesting. And your father? What does he do? Is he still in the military?"

"No, he's retired. He works with vets now, helping them transition back into civilian life."

*That sounded alright, didn't it?*

Did it? My throat was dry. I'd never felt more out of place in my life. Quickly, I retrieved my water goblet—and it was a fancy goblet, by the way, not a glass—for a sip.

"That sounds like a very worthwhile career choice," she

approved. "And homeschooling can be a viable option these days. Our Jackson is currently taught at home by tutors. We haven't decided yet which schools he'll attend."

"Plenty of time for that," his father spoke up. His voice was a little gruff, but I guess he was ready to return to the conversation.

"Of course," his wife agreed. "Ellie, you must let us know what nursing school you attend. Or if there's one you'd prefer to attend instead. We want you to know your tuition is completely covered. It's our gift to you."

"Oh." I'd thought the expensive designer glasses, which I was wearing, and the dinner were their thanks. "You don't have to do that," I said lamely. "Really, you don't."

"We insist. Don't we, dear?"

"We do. Absolutely," Mr. Costas affirmed.

The strength of his tone was final. I shut up and didn't argue any further.

At that moment, the door at the far end of the room opened. The main course was being served, and I was grateful for the diversion from the stilted conversation.

# CHAPTER FOUR

Standing in the background, hands folded in front of him, Carter Ballis observed the scene playing out in his boss's dining room.

The girl. Eleanor St. James. Ellie for short. Parents, Darryl and Susan St. James. Brothers, Andrew and Tyler. Father a former Chaplain's Assistant with a distinguished twenty years in the service, now an ordained minister and working at a center for military vets. Mother a school teacher turned homemaker turned homeschooling teacher. Ellie—twenty-one years old. Nursing student. Pediatrics the field she wanted to join.

Ciara Costas had known all of that information without asking. Nobody passed the threshold of the Costas home without being thoroughly vetted. The stakes were too high. As head of the Costas security team, and Sean Costas' personal bodyguard, Carter had had his people find out all there was to know about Ellie before she was invited in. Nothing had screamed danger, deceit, or her being a plant for the other side. Everything he'd dug up on Ellie and her family verified they were what they appeared to be: people minding their own business, living their own lives.

Ellie's social media accounts were non-descript, especially for a woman her age. Few selfies. A picture or two with her brothers. Talk about her studies, her work. Quotes she liked. Funny cat memes. Nothing controversial.

Watching her struggle tonight, Carter almost felt sorry for her. Her upbringing was showing. She was beyond her depth, and knew it. When dinner was served, she didn't know which fork to use. She chose the wrong one. Her hosts pretended not to notice. She didn't eat much; mainly pushed the food around on her plate. She should eat more. She was too skinny, too pale, in Carter's opinion. Cute, in a big-eyed, ingénue sort of way, with those freckles across her nose, but nothing that would stand out or catch most people's eye. There wasn't much about Ellie to really stand out or catch anyone's attention...

Except for the fact that she'd risked her own life, or at least a terrible accident, to save the Costas' son.

That kind of courage, of self-sacrifice, didn't grow on trees. Sean Costas wasn't the sort of man to forget it, either. Having the girl in his home might have been a little too much for her, but Carter knew he'd wanted to show her in his own way that she was a part of the family now. And nothing in heaven or earth or any worlds in-between meant more to Sean Costas than family and blood ties. Ellie St. James didn't know it, but that one brave act on her part had set her and her brothers for life. Whatever schools they chose—paid for. And that was merely the beginning.

Dinner had nearly ground to a halt. Miss St. James had apparently run out of things to say, even in answer to questions. Carter glanced at Mrs. Costas. She was smiling sympathetically at her guest, who looked painfully ill-at-ease. Clearly, Ellie was ready for things to be over, ready to get back to her own space, her own tribe, her own people. Taking pity on her, Ciara asked if she'd care for dessert or if she'd rather have it boxed up to take home with her.

"I'm guessing you probably have studying to do tonight, and might have to get up early for class tomorrow," she said. "I remember my college days."

Miss St. James' relief showed in the relaxing of her shoulders. "I do have an early morning tomorrow," she confessed.

"I figured. Well, we won't let dessert go to waste. In fact, we'll send some home with you for your brothers. I'm sure they won't turn it down, being growing boys and all. How about your parents—do you think they'd like some too?"

Carter didn't catch the girl's reply, because Mr. Costas crooked a finger, motioning him over.

"Get the car," he ordered quietly, and Carter nodded, slipping out of the dining room to do as ordered.

Outside in the hall, he texted Tracy, the driver, to bring the Aston Martin around front. Slipping his phone into his jacket pocket, he went back into the dining room. Mr. Costas was standing, and so was Ellie. Sean walked around the corner to get his wife's wheelchair, pushing her as they led their guest out of the dining room, down the maze of corridors, and into the foyer. Ciara maintained a light flow of conversation as they escorted their guest outside, into the cool autumn night, Carter following at a respectable distance. He hovered inside the foyer, behind his employers, as headlights flashed. Tracy was bringing the car around from the garage. For a split second, the headlights splashed over Ellie St. James, highlighting her ivory blouse, pale skin, and blonde hair. In spite of himself, Carter stared, distracted.

That was a mistake.

In that moment of distraction, of headlights' glow and a young woman's beauty, they went for it.

Nobody was expecting an attack. Not here at the Costas mansion, one of the most heavily guarded places in the state, if not *the* most. Probably why Nosizwe, his boss's arch-rival, had sent them, hoping they'd be caught off guard here on their home turf. And they almost were, but Carter Ballis was never fully caught off guard. Even as his focus was momentarily on his boss's guest, out of the corner of his eye he saw the dark shadow descending.

*Wings*, his mind told him.

There shouldn't be any wings here. They should be stationed elsewhere throughout the compound.

He reacted without thought. "Sean!" he shouted, even as a dark creature dropped from the sky onto his employer's back.

It all happened so fast. Sean roared in anger as talons pierced his skin, but his shapeshifter side took over and he changed so quickly that tender human skin was a Minotaur's thick hide in the blink of an eye. A human roar became a bull's bellow as he bucked, throwing off his attacker. Carter didn't have time to stop and see exactly what the creature was, but he thought maybe a griffin. Even as the Minotaur ridded itself of its assailant, a second winged creature, an itsumade with a snakelike body and human skull face, dropped from the sky with a screech, also aiming for the Minotaur. Carter leapt into action. He felt the ripple pass over his body, felt blood and flesh and bones swiftly alter to bronze as he shifted. Carter, the human, had been left behind. The Talos, a living, breathing, moving bronze statue, ruled now.

His roar could be heard across the courtyard, and the pounding of his feet shook the ground. In the back of his mind, he was vaguely aware of female screams, but the Talos had taken over, and his one instinct, to protect, was in full force.

He reached the Minotaur at the same time as the itsumade, and with a sweep of his bronze arm caught the creature, knocking it aside. It coiled like a serpent preparing to strike, but the Minotaur spun like a great bull, lashing out with its mighty fists, catching the monster in the middle of its chest, sending it rolling with an angry shriek. The Minotaur swerved around the hood of the car, chasing after it, even as Carter, the Talos, readdressed the original threat, the griffin.

It had taken to wing and was on him before he could react. Its eagle screech echoed in his bronze skull, but the talons that raked his shoulders did no more than create an annoying screech of sharp points against metal. Clothed in bronze, he felt no pain at the gouges. The griffin wasn't expecting him to. He wasn't its target. The talons scraping his shoulders were a mere distraction to throw him off guard as the winged animal flew at its real target: Ciara Costas.

Momentarily blinded by the griffin's wings and fur, the Talos spun as the creature streaked past. From across the courtyard, he heard a bellow from the Minotaur, a bellow in which he could hear Sean's wife's name.

"Ciara!"

Warm light spilled out from the vestibule onto the terrified faces of both Ciara Costas and her guest. Were Ciara in the water, she would be safe, but out of the water her ability to shapeshift, to change, was gone. She was stuck in the wheelchair, and as helpless as her very human guest. The griffin was coming right at her, ready to tear her apart. Even as it ducked, talons extended, there was a flash of ebony and ivory. Ellie St. James, looking small and helpless in comparison to the beast diving her way, had moved, throwing herself across the woman in the wheelchair. The griffin screeched, but didn't change course. Its talons ripped the back of the girl's blouse as a shot rang out.

Tracy.

Timewise, the Aston had screeched to a halt in the driveway, and the Minotaur had swerved around it to chase the itsumade. The griffin had raked Carter, the Talos, as it dove for Mrs. Costas in her wheelchair. The car door opened as Ellie St. James threw her body across her hostess, and Tracy had emerged, gun in hand. She hadn't taken the time to shift. Tracy was a Deer Woman from the Sioux tribe, which was not a creature that typically engaged in violence, fighting, or warfare. Her alter may not have made a difference in battle, but the sawed off shotgun in her hand did. She was never unarmed, usually driving with it under the front seat, which was a good thing for Ellie and Ciara.

The shotgun blast lit up the night, the sound echoing off the stone walls of the Costas mansion. Struck in the side, the griffin twisted, releasing an unearthly scream that was half bird, half human. Mortally wounded, it shifted as it fell, and what dropped onto the pavement right in front of the wheelchair was no mythological monster but a wounded man, naked from the waist up, his side blasted away, his blood drenching the paving stones.

The Talos ran forward as Tracy walked over, gun in hand. The man was twitching, writhing. Blood was everywhere, spattered on the wheelchair, the hem of Ciara's pants, and Miss St. James' ivory blouse. Pounding hooves approached and Carter, the Talos, whirled, but it was only his boss. Even as Sean slid to a halt next to Tracy, he shifted, resuming his human form. His shirt was torn and hanging in strips. There was blood on his back, but he would live. Releasing his alter, Carter shifted too. In the flash of an eye, the Talos was gone, and Carter stood next to his boss, his shirt and coat not merely gone but exploded into bits. Both men looked at each other.

"The itsumade?" Carter asked.

"I didn't kill it. Wounded it, but it got away," his boss growled.

Carter swore. His boss sidestepped Tracy and the bleeding attacker, currently gasping his last breaths, to approach his wife. He knelt next to her chair.

"Ciara, love?"

Miss St. James rose from off her hostess, but clutched the back of the wheel chair as if she was afraid to let go. Sean Costas glanced up at her.

"Are you alright, Ellie?"

She didn't reply. Just stared, her eyes huge and her mouth hanging open. Her glasses had fallen off into Ciara's lap. Even as

Ciara clutched her husband's left hand, murmuring that she was okay, Sean picked them up and handed them to his young guest. At first she stared blankly, like she wasn't sure what she was supposed to do, then slowly accepted them, letting go of the wheelchair to slide them onto her nose.

A gasp, a wheeze, a gurgle from the dying shifter seized all of their attention. Tracy stepped up, lowering her weapon.

"Want me to finish him off?"

Sean stood. "No, give it here."

Tracy passed the gun into his outstretched hand. Insensible to the blood on his clothes or shoes, Carter's boss knelt next to the fading man. Post-transformation, the griffin's human body was long and lanky. Shaggy dark hair framed a youthful face with glowing golden eyes. Eyes that were glazing over as blood bubbled from his lips, spilling down his neck.

"No one," Sean Costas said softly, to the dying man, "attacks my family. You can attack me. You can attack my people, my shifters. You can attack my business, my empire; anything that I am or have. But you do not attack my family. Nosizwe made a huge mistake. The pit itself can't compare to what I'm going to unleash on her."

Carter saw the wounded shifter's mouth work as he tried to speak, tried to say something. Too much blood. He was strangling on his own blood.

Sean Costas stood, looming over the once griffin.

"Go back to the pit from where you came," he said, and raised the gun.

But not to shoot.

Instead, he'd turned it, butt down, and brought it down with all of his considerable strength onto the attacker's skull. There was a loud crack. A groan from the shifter. A horrified scream from Ellie St. James. No one else reacted, Carter included, as his boss slammed the gun butt into his victim's face again and again and again. Teeth cracked and blood sprayed, splashing

Sean's skin, his beard, his face. Bits of bone, brains spattered everything within a few feet radius. To Carter, watching in the dim light from the foyer, between the fury on his boss's face and the blood streaking it, he almost looked like more of a devil than the nastiest shifter Carter had ever encountered. And that was saying a lot. Yet he watched without feeling, without pity. Like Sean had said, you didn't attack his family. Nosizwe should've known that. The skirmishes were over. She'd just unleashed war.

The dull whacks of the gun butt finally stopped. The shifter was long past dead. His body was limp, his skull more jelly than bone. He was barely recognizable as human. Sean stood over him, breathing hard, staring down at his handiwork.

"Carter?"

He stepped up.

"Call James. Tell him to get some fliers in the air and make certain this is all she sent. Then tell him to have this mess cleaned up and get the body ready to be moved. We're sending Nosizwe a message she won't miss.

"Tracy." He handed his driver the gun, looking her in the eye. "Thank you."

"Anything for you, Mr. Costas," she replied soberly, taking care to keep her feet out of the dark pool spreading across the paving stones in front of the house.

Pulling his phone from his pocket, Carter was about to make that call when a choking sound caught his attention. Everyone turned towards the Costas' guest, who'd been momentarily forgotten as Sean finished off the creature who had dared to strike at his wife. Ellie had retreated a few steps. Both hands were clapped over her mouth. Behind her palms, she was breathing hard, so hard Carter could see her chest heaving, despite the dim light. When he looked at her, her huge eyes behind her glasses caught his for a split second. Then she heaved, gagged. Spinning, she dashed towards a flowering bush, pruned down for the approaching cold season, and sagged to her knees, losing whatever dinner she'd managed to eat earlier.

Carter's attention switched back to his boss. Hands on hips, he was watching the girl also.

"Carter, we have a big problem here," he said.

## CHAPTER FIVE

That went without saying. The evening wasn't supposed to have gone like this. Ellie St. James, an ignorant human girl from a world of ignorant humans, wasn't supposed to know about their world, his world. Instead, she'd been introduced to it in the worst possible way. Shifters existed, and they tried to kill each other. Now that she knew, they couldn't simply let her go. More than that, she'd been seen by the itsumade. She'd thrown herself over Sean's wife to protect her from the griffin's attack. Nosizwe might not know who Ellie was now, but if she and her shifters found out, they'd assume she was aligned with Sean Costas and his mob. They would as happily kill her as any of them. Ellie had saved the life of both Sean Costas' son and his wife, and for that hers was now ruined.

"What do we do?" he questioned his boss, as both men stared at the young woman. She'd finally stopped retching and was working to push herself up off the ground.

"For now, you take her. Get her out of here to a safe place. You protect, you hear?" Sean turned to him, grey eyes flashing. "I'll send Ciara and Jackson to a safe home too, until we can check out the compound and make sure there are no more security breaches. You stick with Ellie and you protect her, no matter what. She's my family now. She stays alive and she stays safe. Get her somewhere separate and secure until we can decide what to do. Maybe they don't know who she is yet. Maybe they won't figure it out. Maybe she'll eventually be able to go home. We'll have to keep our ears to the ground and listen to the talk. But until we know, one way or the other, you stay with her and keep her alive. That's your one job now."

Carter nodded, accepting the orders. He was the Talos, created and designed as a bodyguard, to protect. His boss had just shifted the mantle from safeguarding him, his wife, and his son to Ellie St. James. Carter would do it. No monster would get to her while he lived.

"Go ahead and call James," his boss directed. "Grab a shirt, grab whatever you need, and get her out of here. Tracy and I will watch them."

Carter obeyed, heading into the house to do as bidden, thumb already pressing the button for James' number.

He was gone only a couple of minutes, grabbing a t-shirt from the room the Costases kept for him in case he stayed at the compound. Outside, Mr. Costas stood over his wife, hands on her wheelchair, while Tracy clutched the shotgun, eyeing the sky and surrounding area for any signs of danger. Ellie St. James had finally pulled herself together enough to get up and walk back, but she hovered in the darkness on the opposite side of the car like she didn't know where to turn or what to do, refusing to approach either her hosts or the body sprawled next to the front entrance.

Carter couldn't blame her. It was a grisly sight.

"Keys, Tracy?"

She dug in her pocket and handed them over.

"Good luck, Carter."

Nodding his thanks, he stepped around the car and walked over to the girl. She was huddled in on herself, both arms wrapped around her torso, staring, doubtless trying to come to grips with everything she'd seen. When he approached her, she glanced up, then shied backwards several steps.

"Get away from me," she breathed.

Carter stopped. "It's okay. I need you to come with me. I'm going to get you out of here. I'm not going to hurt you, I promise. We don't know if we're still under threat or not. I need to take you someplace safe."

He kept his voice level, his posture non-threatening, trying to reassure her. She was far from convinced.

"No. I'm not getting in a car with some bronze monster. Some freak. I want Tracy to drive me home."

He didn't bother telling her Tracy was a shifter too, or that she wasn't going home.

"Tracy has to stay here. I'm taking you. I need you to come with me."

She stepped backward again, shaking her head.

There wasn't time for this. Carter didn't like manhandling her, but standing there arguing or trying to persuade her wasn't a luxury they could afford. She didn't know it, but he was trying to help her.

"I'm asking you one more time to come with me before I make you go," he said a little more sternly, hoping she'd recognize the imperative and concede.

She just stared.

Shaking his head, he bit back a harsh word and surged forward, grabbing her upper arm.

"Sorry, kid, but we don't have a choice. You're coming with me, like it or not."

"No, let go of me!"

She reacted about like he figured she would, yanking against his hold. He was prepared for it, and hung on, hauling her across the courtyard and over to the car.

"Let go of me," she hissed, but Carter wasn't listening. He

opened the passenger door and shoved her inside, slamming it behind her.

"Hey!" she yelled, striking the glass with a fist.

Ignoring her, he strode around to the driver's side, nodding at his boss before opening the door to climb inside.

"Carter." Ciara's voice stopped him. "Be kind to her. She's terrified," his boss's wife said.

There wasn't time to say he didn't intend on scaring Ellie any further than she was already scared, or that he didn't mean to be a brute, but he had to do what he had to do. And in the process, she probably was going to be scared and she was probably going to hate him by the time it was all over. She probably already did.

He didn't say any of that. Just replied a simple, "Yes, ma'am," before getting in and shutting the door after himself.

He had to slide back the driver's seat, since his legs were longer than Tracy's. The car rumbled to life, dinging at him to put on a seatbelt. Swearing, he reached over his shoulder to grab it, wrench it across his chest, and buckle it on. As he did, he glanced over at his passenger. She caught his eye and scrabbled as far from him as she could go, pressing herself against the door.

"I'm not going to hurt you," he said. "I'm getting you out of here."

Her lower lip and chin were quivering. She looked like she was about to cry. She didn't respond. Carter put the car in gear and spun off. Away from the front of the house, night closed in quickly. Forewarned by James, who would assume Carter's duties for now, the guards had opened the gate when they saw approaching headlights and let them pass without a challenge. Carter exited the Costas compound, spun the wheel, and turned left. They slid out onto the road. He revved the engine, driving too fast, determined to get the girl away from here and back to his place, where she'd be safe, at least temporarily.

"This isn't the way we came."

He wasn't expecting her to speak. When he glanced over, she was still pressed up against the door, staring at him. The lights from the dashboard lit her skin and hair in blues and greens. She didn't look like much more than a kid, but she'd seen things tonight no kid—no human—should ever see.

"Yeah," he said gruffly, turning away, back to the road. "I know."

"Are you—are you taking me home a different way?"

He shook his head and didn't answer. He didn't want to deal with a crying, hysterical, arguing woman for the next twenty minutes.

She tried again.

"Where are we going? You're taking me home, right?"

Carter kept one hand on the stick shift and stared straight ahead. The tunnel of light created by the headlights lit up the paved road, surrounded by manicured trees. In a couple of minutes, they'd be past this neighborhood and back into the city.

A scuffling sound alerted him, and he glanced over to see Miss. St. James digging in the handbag at her feet. He didn't have to ask what she was doing. She pulled out a cell phone and held it up.

"I don't know what you're planning, but I'm not being kidnaped by some freak. Either take me home, or I'm calling the police."

Carter snorted. "Really?"

"Yes, really," she glared.

He waited a second to throw her off guard, then snaked out an arm, snatching the phone from her hand.

"Hey!"

With his other hand, he put his thumb on the window button and rolled it down far enough to chuck her phone outside.

"Hey, what're you doing?" she yelled. "That's mine!"

He slammed on the brakes, pitching them both forward. Ellie caught herself with an arm to the dashboard, righting her body even as he shoved them in reverse, watching the backup camera to aim the tire right over the phone.

"Hey!"

They both heard the pop, the crunch through the open window.

Ellie stared at him in dismay.

"You jerk! I saved two months for that phone. Why'd you do that?"

He could hear the distress in her voice.

"Mr. Costas will get you a new one. Whatever you want."

It was a cheap piece of crap anyway.

"I don't want a new one, I want that one! It's got my pictures and music and notes from class saved on it. It's got—"

Too late now. The phone was destroyed. Carter urged the gearshift in the opposite direction, put his foot on the pedal, and roared away from the mess in the street.

"Why'd you do that?" Ellie demanded again. She sat up straight in the seat, facing him, her body rigid with anger and fear, her hands fisted at her sides. "Why? Where are we going?"

"I'm taking you someplace safe," he finally snapped, turning, pinning her with a glare. "When we get there, I'll find you a burner phone so you can text your parents and let them know you're safe. Let them know you're not coming home for a few days. But for now, I can't have you doing something stupid like calling the cops or calling your family from your phone. I can't have you doing anything that will risk us being traced. We need to hide you for a while."

"Hide me?" she laughed in disbelief. "You're going to hide me? From what? Monsters like you?"

"Believe it or not, kid, there's way worse things than me out there," he muttered, turning his attention back to the road.

"Really? Like Sean Costas, who beat a helpless man to death? While you and everyone else stood there and did nothing? Worse than murdering someone on your front doorstep? No, I don't think so. Take me home."

She'd found her backbone, but her arguing was starting to get on his nerves. He almost wished she'd retreat back into the quiet, mousy, awkward person she'd been at dinner tonight. That she'd shut up and let him think, plan.

"You're not going home, okay?" He scowled at her, hoping to intimidate her into silence. "Not yet. You wanna risk bringing shifters like those that attacked us back there on your family? Is that what you want?"

"I don't understand. Why would things like that—shifters? I don't know what that means. I don't know what you are. And I sure don't understand why they would attack my family."

They were in the city now, weaving around the handful of cars —handful for this city—still out this late in the evening, avoiding the never-ending construction cones, orange lines, and detours, following a circuit to his apartment complex that Carter knew by heart. Ellie didn't seem aware of her surroundings. A little of her defiance had melted away. She was staring at him, at his profile, as if begging for answers. In Carter's head, he heard Ciara's voice.

*Be kind to her. She's terrified.*

Terrified. Overwhelmed. Didn't know what was going on. Didn't understand any of it.

Remembering she hadn't lived the last two decades in a world of shapeshifters and war, magic and slaughter, Carter softened his tone, even as he kept his focus on the road.

"What you saw, just now, back at the Costas home, that's only the beginning," he said. "There's an entire world of shapeshifters —people like me who can change into other...things."

"Shapeshifters? You mean like...werewolves?"

"Werewolves," he snorted. "That's the only shapeshifter humans are ever familiar with. Animal shifters are actually a fraction of the population."

"Then like what?"

"Everything. Anything. Almost anything you can think of." He stole a look at her. Behind the glasses, her eyes were wide in the dash lights, the streetlights as she stared at him. "Monsters from fairytales, folklore, mythology, and urban legend from around the world. Most of those ideas come from shapeshifters, like me."

She shook her head. "I don't understand."

"Humans never do." He looked back at the road. "That's why we keep it quiet. Why our world is a secret."

"Who's *we?*"

"*We* is people like Sean Costas who take in shifters and teach us to control our ability, to use it. People who give us a safe place, away from the rest of humans."

"A safe place from humans? Why? You're acting like we're the threat."

"Why?" Carter breathed a laugh, jerking the steering wheel a little harder than necessary to turn them right. "Look at you. You're sitting there staring at me like I'm ready to rip you in half, and you want to know why? Humans can't even put up with differences in each other, much less freaks and monsters like me."

He said it sardonically, but the twinge was there. It was always there, going back to his childhood, to the onset of early puberty, which usually happened in shifters. When he'd started to change and hadn't known what was happening in his body and mind or why. Back to the first time it happened at school and he'd terrified all the boys in the locker room. Only a partial change that day. They'd called him a freak and a monster then, too, even though he'd been as terrified of his body with its newfound abilities that he didn't understand as they were. That was when his parents had acted.

The recessive shifter gene had come from his father's side, skipping several generations before hitting him. His parents hadn't known, and none of his elderly relatives who might have known had ever breathed a word about his heritage until that particular day, hoping it would have skipped him too. No such luck. Instead, they'd ultimately been forced to explain to a terrified boy what was going on, and he'd wound up being sent from his native Greece to the United States, to a man named Sean Costas who everyone knew in the shifter world. A man who had taken him in and helped him, guided, taught, and mentored him. Like he had dozens of others from around the globe. But even though Carter had found a refuge there with the Costases, the taunts still stung.

Freak.

Monster.

"How do I know you're not?" she said. Her voice had softened. When he glanced over at her, thick strands of blonde hair had escaped her updo, falling untidily about her face. He could see she was trembling. Putting on a brave front to hide it, but trembling.

"How do you know I'm not what?"

"Going to kill me. Rip me in pieces. I saw that—that thing that you changed into. You could tear me in half without a second thought, couldn't you?"

He could, but there was no need to scare her.

"I'm trying to save your life here. Not hurt you," he said dryly.

"Save me from what? What is all this?"

Going into the background of tonight's attack wasn't high on Carter's agenda, but, considering what this woman had done for both Jackson and Ciara Costas, he supposed he owed her some clarification.

"*This* all boils down to a war between two shifter leaders with their own clans or gangs or mobs—whatever you want to call them. It's a rivalry that's existed for over a decade, a rivalry that involves ancient, magical artifacts called the Stones of Fire. The Stones of Fire are historically linked to shapeshifters and our abilities. Mr. Costas wants to keep the Stones, and us, secret and safe. His rival, Nosizwe, wants the opposite. They both have some Stones. They both want *all* the Stones. They've fought over them for years, and you just got shoved into the middle of their feud tonight. It's life and death and it's ugly and brutal. And that's why you can't go home. Because if Nosizwe—she heads up the other mob—finds out who you are, she'll come after you and she'll come after your family."

"Why would she come after me? I haven't done anything to her."

"Nope. You haven't," he agreed, slowing the car, making a U-turn into the drive leading to his gated apartment complex. "Not personally. But you were at the Costas home tonight and you risked yourself to protect Ciara. What does that look like to an outsider?"

She thought for a second.

"That I'm involved with the Costas family."

"Exactly. And nobody gets that close, that involved with the Costas family who isn't a shifter. One of their shifters."

He stopped at the wrought iron gate guarding the entrance to the complex, rolled down the window and punched in a code. The buttons beeped. The gate released with a slight screech. Carter left the window down as he rolled through and straight, headed towards the back of the complex.

"Ho—how would they know who I am?"

"They may not," he said, glancing at her again. She was hugging her arms around herself, still scared but handling this better than he'd thought she would. "We don't know for sure yet, so we can't risk it. We'll stay low for a few days, keep you hidden and safe until we know one way or the other and can figure out what to do with you."

"What about my family?"

"We'll figure that out too," he promised her, rolling to a stop underneath the parking canopy, aligning his boss's car next to his own. "For now, the best thing you can do to protect them is to stay away from them. If Nosizwe finds out who you are and decides to hurt Mr. Costas by coming after you, she may not stop at coming after your family, too."

Ellie St. James' face was panicked. It was a scary world she'd fallen into. She didn't seem to know how to respond.

Carter put the car in park, shutting off the engine.

"We're here. Let's get you inside."

## CHAPTER SIX

None of this made any sense. None of it. My mind was spinning, trying to grasp not only what I'd witnessed but what this man, this stranger was telling me.

Carter, I think I'd heard him called. Yes, Carter. It was hard to think straight, even about little things like someone's name. Wasn't he a butler? He sure didn't seem like a butler now.

Carter—who looked as normal, as human as me on the outside, but had the ability to change his entire body. To shift, he kept calling it. A shapeshifter. Like a werewolf, only he'd mocked the idea of werewolves. I didn't know what he was. One second, there in the Costas's driveway, he'd seemed like a regular guy, only a regular guy whose arms and chest and biceps were so huge they strained the seams of his coat. The next, something dark and fast and fierce had dropped from the sky. Mr. Costas had turned into a bull, a massive bull creature standing on its back legs, and, equally fast, Carter was…was something I couldn't even put a name to.

The closest comparison I could make was that big green guy from the superhero movies; when the human side got all mad, then the giant green monster appeared. Only Carter wasn't quite that big, that tall. When he'd shifted, he'd kept the same height, but the bulk he already had swelled, busting his shirt and suit coat. Even in the dim light I'd witnessed his skin turn a bronze color, his facial characteristics smoothing out until he more resembled a vaguely human statue than anything else. But a statue that moved and fought and spoke.

It was difficult to reconcile that statue with the man now facing me, telling me we were here and needed to get inside. I heard the words, but I didn't comprehend them. I just kept staring at him, trying to figure it out. Trying to figure out if this was a dream, or if I'd gone crazy, or if the Costases had slipped a hallucinogenic drug into my water at dinner.

*How does a normal guy turn into a bronze monster? How does a man change into a bull?*

Abruptly, it registered that he, Carter, was speaking to me again.

"Did you hear me? We need to get you inside."

His tone was sharp, cutting through the fog. I started.

"O—okay."

Satisfied that I'd responded, he opened his door and climbed out, came around to my side and opened mine for me. I stepped out into the cool night. Chilly November air touched my skin, reminding me of the griffin swooping over me after I'd thrown myself over my hostess. In that moment I'd braced myself, certain I was about to feel claws raking my spine. Instead, I'd felt the tug of torn fabric, then heard a blast as Tracy's shot took the monster right out of the sky.

All of those memories washed over me, and I glanced around uneasily.

"Where are we?"

My voice was shaky. I hated that my voice was shaky, but I was shaky too.

It was some sort of apartment complex. It didn't look fancy, but there was a wall and a gate. The place had some security features, which was probably why he'd chosen to bring me here, if anything he'd told me in the car was true.

"My place."

"Your place? I don't want to go in your place."

"Tough."

He put his hand on my elbow, started me walking. I tried to slide it out, but he wasn't having it and held on tighter. He probably thought I meant to run. I was thinking about it, glancing all around. Even if I did run, my mind reminded me, where would I go? If he wasn't lying to me, I couldn't go home. I couldn't risk bringing any of those things to my family. Could I?

*You could call the police?*

*That's a thought.*

He'd said he would get me a burner phone, whatever that was, so I could text my parents. Maybe I could use it to contact the police. Maybe I could...

He herded me up the stairs, moving me along faster than I wanted to go. I tripped, flinging out a hand to catch myself on the steps, but he caught me, the strength of his one arm bearing my weight like he hadn't even noticed. I recovered and he kept us going, up to the third floor. At his door, number 346, we stopped. He let go of me, but stood behind me, boxing me in between door and man as he reached around me to put the key in the lock. He was too close. I could hear him breathing, feel his body brushing against my clothes, the back of my torn blouse. My skin crawled, especially the exposed skin, at the idea of a strange man being that close to me.

A strange man who could change into something else.

A monster.

A monster who fought monsters.

A war between monsters, and I was caught in the middle.

*This is insane.*

I thought it even as the lock clicked open and Carter twisted the handle, pushing the door open so I could step inside. He followed, shutting the door behind us. It was dark. The only light was what seeped in around the edges of the blinds shielding the living room windows, and that wasn't much. I sucked in a breath when he moved next to me, putting a hand on my arm and pressing me gently against the door.

"Stay here a minute," he said. "Don't move."

All of the fear and terror and disbelief and horror of the last hour washed over me. My mouth went dry and my legs turned to jelly. I sagged against the door, helpless. What was going on? Had he been lying about trying to protect me? I didn't know him; I didn't know him at all. What if he was a killer too? A murderer? What if he'd brought me here to kill me? Or assault me? How did I know I could trust him? He hadn't saved my life. Tracy had. And I was suddenly wishing Tracy were here right now, Tracy with her gun and her dead aim, instead of this freak standing way too close in the dark...

I heard a noise and saw him draw something from his hip.

A gun, tucked into a black side holster. I hadn't noticed it earlier, since it would've been hidden beneath his suit jacket, and after the attack it was an inconsequential detail.

He gripped it with one hand while flicking a light switch that turned on the standing lamp in the corner, offering some illumination. My racing heart sped up.

"Going to check the place out," he said. "It should be safe, but we can't be too careful. Wait right there."

I don't remember saying anything. I think I tried to say something, but squeaked, like a mouse. He glanced over his shoulder at me, a frown between his brows, then shook his head and moved away. I watched him scope out the living room quickly, then he disappeared from my line of sight as he passed into the kitchen, then, I assumed, the bedroom down the hall. I waited, my mouth dry, hearing my heart pounding in my ears.

Something prickled in my brain.

*He's gone. Open the door. Run. You can get away. Hide, find someplace with a phone, call the cops. Just open the door. Do it. Do it now.*

But I couldn't move. I literally couldn't move. It felt like somebody had dunked my entire body in ice, freezing me into obeying Carter's orders. Funny how, twice, in the midst of a crisis, when it came to protecting someone else I had moved without thought. Instinct had taken over. At the hospital, I'd pushed Jackson Costas away from a bus. The attack at the Costas mansion had happened so quickly I hadn't been able to plan any escape, but when the griffin dove at my hostess I'd thrown myself over Ciara Costas in her wheelchair. Twice, when it came to saving others' lives, I hadn't hesitated. Now, when it came to helping myself, my mind was shrieking at me to move, to act, to do something, *anything*, and I was frozen. Frozen except for the tremors shaking my entire body.

*Griffins and bulls and bronze men and—and that thing with the snake body and skull for a head. People changed into those. People. Changed. Into. Those. He said there's an entire world of them, of people like him. He mentioned magic. He said they might be after me now. How am I supposed to fight things like that? How am I supposed to stay safe? How am I supposed to keep my family safe?*

Panic clawed at my throat. Tears filled my eyes, blurring my vision. I couldn't breathe.

*I can't, I can't. I can't do this. I've gotta get out of here. I've got to—*

"It's clear."

Footsteps heralded the man's approach, his announcement. He took one look at me, sagging against the door, crying without making a sound, and shoved the gun back into its holster, his expression softening a little.

"Don't panic now, kid. You're safe."

Even his annoying term, *kid*, didn't slice the haze this time. He came over to me, grasping me gently by the arm, steering me away from the door and toward the couch. If not for his support, my legs would've given out, but it was only a few steps from the door to the couch. He sat me down on it, reached for the throw on the back, took it and draped it around my shoulders.

"You're going to be okay."

Would I, though? I'd fallen into a nightmare, and I couldn't wake up. Even as I seized the edges of the blanket, clutching them tightly, not for warmth but as a shield, my roiling mind told me there was no way out of this. Even if this mess was cleared up. If Nosizwe, whoever and whatever she was, never found out who I was or decided I wasn't a threat, I'd still never be free. I'd seen too much. I'd caught a glimpse of an entire world that, an hour ago, I hadn't known existed. Now I knew, and it terrified me to death. How was I supposed to resume a normal life, knowing what I now knew?

For his part, Carter, whoever the heck he really was, just sat next to me. He didn't touch me. He didn't talk to me. He just sat with me. Several long minutes went by where I prayed and thought, tried to breathe, tried to drive the tears away, tried to get myself back under control. It took forever before the shivers racking my body slowed. Before my shoulders un-hunched themselves. Before I was able to sit up a little straighter, release the air caught in my chest in a shaky sigh.

Carter heard it and glanced at me.

"You okay?"

I started to nod my head, then shook it. Then shrugged.

"Yes, no. I don't know."

My voice trembled.

He stood. "Be right back."

My eyes latched onto him as he walked away. Onto the gun in its holster and the slacks with a t-shirt, the t-shirt I guess he'd thrown on after his dress shirt and suit coat had exploded during his change. The t-shirt was too tight, clinging to his muscular frame, revealing every line and outline and bulge of flesh that could turn to sculpted bronze in an instant.

I shuddered and dropped my gaze.

He was back a minute later, extending his hand, offering me a blue coffee mug. Inside was some sort of dark liquid that smelled faintly sweet.

"Here. Sorry I don't have a real wine glass."

Lifting my hands, I took it, eyeing it suspiciously.

"Is this wine?"

"Yeah. Not your finest vintage, but I like a glass every now and then."

"Why are you giving me this?"

He looked at me funny. "To calm you down," he said slowly, as if explaining to a child or a mentally challenged person.

That aggravated me.

"I don't need alcohol to calm me down," I said, turning and setting the cup forcefully on the end table.

I heard him snort as he lifted his own coffee mug of wine to his lips.

"Yeah, I forgot. Good little preacher's kid. Doesn't drink. Doesn't smoke. Doesn't do drugs. Doesn't have any vices like the rest of us mere mortals."

Despite my shock over the evening's events, despite my personal fear of him, I felt my face heat with a combination of anger and embarrassment. I was flabbergasted.

"Why would you say that? You take that back!"

"Sure, okay. Which part?" he taunted, dark eyes mocking. "The good little preacher's kid part? That is what you are, right? A Chaplain Assistant's basically a preacher, and your father is ordained, although he doesn't minister anywhere. Or the part where you don't drink, or smoke, or use drugs?"

"The—the...I drink sometimes!" I spouted defensively.

He rolled his eyes. "Oh, yes. The margarita on your twenty-first birthday, followed by the occasional glass of merlot during a nice dinner out. How could I forget?"

I had been hot with anger and embarrassment. Now I went cold with shock and even revulsion. Dismay. I felt my face freeze.

"How did you know about that? How did you know any of that stuff you said about me?"

"I'm head of Mr. Costas' security team. I know everything about you."

"*What?*"

The word came out as more or less of a shriek. As if, on top of everything else tonight, abruptly finding out this perfect stranger, this stranger who wasn't even human, who I didn't know *what* he was, apparently knew everything about me.

His phone buzzed in his pocket.

"No one gets into the Costas home without being thoroughly vetted," he said casually, reaching into his pocket to retrieve it.

"Vetted? Like—like people get vetted before they're allowed to enter the country and stuff?"

"Something like that."

His attention wasn't on me. He was tapping out a message on his phone.

I sat and stared, waiting for more. He finished, slid the phone back in his pocket, and glanced up.

"What?"

He must've noticed I was shaken, unhappy.

"What all do you know about me?"

"Like I said, practically everything."

He dropped to a seat in the recliner catty-cornered from the couch. Lifting his mug, he took another drink of wine, watching me all the while over the rim.

"I know your high school grades. I know when you graduated your home high school. I know what school you attend, and your field of interest. All of your grades in nursing school. What hospitals you're looking at for after graduation. That you don't have a steady boyfriend, but you've recently gone out for coffee a few times with that guy from your church. What's his name? Daniel?" He winked. "You and Daniel gonna hit it big time?"

I was so flummoxed I couldn't speak. I think I was staring at him with my mouth hanging open.

"Look, it's not that big a deal, really," he said, setting his mug down on the carpet. Leaning forward, he clasped his hands in front of himself. "You're nothing special as far as background checks go. Well, yours was a little more personal. We had to make sure you weren't a plant: too conveniently in the right place at the right time, you know?"

I didn't know.

"So, you think I—my trying to help Jackson was all a front?"

"I don't now. I didn't know until I had James run your intel for me."

"Intel? And who's James?"

"He handles all that stuff for Mr. Costas. I gave him your name. He took it to his geeks. He brought the printout to me. I read it. Double checked a fact or two. Made sure there was nothing suspicious. As far as we could tell, the accident with the bus really was an accident. You really were a stranger who was in the right place at the right time. So...you got invited to the Costas home."

His phone buzzed again. He leaned back to fish it out of his pocket, scroll for a minute, type another message. I waited, fingers on my temple, trying desperately to collect my thoughts, to deal with this latest sucker punch.

"If they were that worried about it, why invite me to their home at all? Why not stick with sending the glasses? I didn't want their thanks. I didn't do this to get anything out of anyone. I did it when I saw a little boy about to get hurt, and I didn't want that to happen."

"Maybe, but how could I know that? A man like Mr. Costas has lots of enemies—and I'm not even talking about just Nosizwe and her shifters. He's got business enemies, political enemies. People who hate him for backing politicians they hate. Rivals who hate him because he bought out a corporation they wanted or foreclosed on loans they couldn't pay. You name it, people hate him for it. Some folks will stop at nothing to hurt a man like Mr. Costas. I had to make sure you weren't working for them.

"On the other hand," he chuckled, "when I read your background, it was kind of funny to think of you being involved with anything like that."

This time, I felt not only my cheeks but the tips of my ears heat like they were on fire.

"Well, that's pretty good for *you* to say," I sputtered, anger finally consuming the fear. "You're not even human. You change into a walking bronze statue, and you want to make fun of *me* for being some kind of freak? Who's the real freak here?"

The room fell silent. Like dead silent, as if a heavy, sound-blocking blanket had been thrown over the two of us.

*Why did you say that?* my mind screamed at me. *He could crush you with one fist. Why would you insult him? You don't know him. You don't know that he doesn't have a terrible temper that makes him change when he's mad. You don't know if he'll lose it and kill you for fun. Are you trying to get yourself killed?*

Carter, head of Mr. Costas' security, stared at me quietly for several long seconds. My chest felt tight as I waited for him to explode back, to shift again into the bronze monster and come after me. Sweat beaded my palms as I mentally gauged the distance to the door, wondering, if he did, if I could possibly get outside before he caught me.

But there was no shapeshifting, nor any explosion. Instead, the hard, hard look in his dark eyes slowly faded, replaced by a gleam of humor. Picking up the mug from the floor, he lifted it in a salute.

"Touché," he said with a tight smile. "You win that round."

He took another drink. Then another, finishing off his wine in a couple of gulps.

The danger receded, at least for the moment, and my body relaxed as I slumped against the back of his couch. I didn't feel like I'd won anything. I felt like I'd dug whatever hole I was in even deeper.

## CHAPTER SEVEN

Carter's phone ringing came as a relief. It broke the stalemate between us, and gave him an excuse to walk out of the room as he answered it. While he was gone, I turned sideways into the couch, pulling the blanket even tighter about my shoulders. Closing my eyes, I tried not to think. My brain was overwhelmed by all of the horrible and mystical and frightening and even embarrassing revelations I'd experienced. I felt like I'd lived an entire lifetime in this one evening. I'd had plenty of mystery and adventure. I wanted to go home, and the fact that I couldn't, without potentially endangering my family, increased my misery.

Footsteps thudded back into the room. My eyes flew open and I bolted upright, staring at my host.

"You don't have to jump every time I enter the room and stare at me like I'm planning to eat you or cut off your head and keep it in my freezer," he said dryly. "Mr. Costas ordered me to protect you. That's all I'm trying to do here."

Before I could formulate a reply, he pulled out his phone, thumbed around a second and announced, "I'm gonna make a list. What do you need for tonight?"

"Tonight?"

"Tonight. I just heard from James. No static on you yet. You'll stay here tonight. We'll figure something else out tomorrow. Maybe we'll keep you here. Maybe get you to another safe house. Maybe back to the Costas compound. We'll see. Meantime, what do you need for tonight?"

I stared, blinked a few times, trying to list items in my head. The first thing I thought of was that phone he'd promised me so I could contact my family. Did I dare ask him for it?

I guess I took too long to answer. He glanced up from under his brows.

"Toothbrush? You can use my toothpaste, unless you have a problem with that. Face wash? Deodorant? Uh, I don't know what girls need. Something to wash your hair? Feminine products?"

"*What?*"

Again, the word came out as a cross between a yell and a shriek. He rubbed the inside of his ear with a fingertip, grimacing.

"Really wish you'd stop doing that. Hurts my ears."

"Why would you even ask that?" I demanded, mortified.

"I'm not trying to be a jerk. I don't have any around. What are you going to do if you need them in the middle of the night or something? Once we're in here for the night, we're in."

I barely even heard his explanation.

"I cannot believe some guy who's a perfect stranger just asked me about my period," I said through gritted teeth.

"Some guy who's really a freak that changes into a walking bronze statue," he corrected. I looked up, eyes wide, and he tipped his thumb and forefinger at me with a wink. "You forgot that part."

"Stop it!" Finally I'd had enough. Wrestling out of the blanket, I threw it onto the couch as I got to my feet, facing him. "Stop making fun of me! This has been the worst night of my life. I saw things I had no idea existed. Things I still don't know what they are. Something almost killed me. Look! Look at my blouse!" I half-turned, forcing him to face the slashes in my mom's silk blouse. "I saw a man beat to death by your boss. It was horrible. Horrible! Then I get kidnapped by you, who I for sure don't know, dragged here, and told I have to stay away from home because some woman I don't know and have no beef with might have an army of monsters wanting to kill me and possibly my family too. Then I find out my life's an open book to you, including really personal, private stuff you have no right to know, and you keep sitting there mocking me and making fun of me. It's not funny! Tonight's been *hell*, and I don't say that lightly."

To my utter humiliation, tears filled my eyes and my voice cracked on a sob. I spun around, pressing my fists to my mouth, trying again to keep the sobs at bay. Listing the events I'd survived tonight brought them all vividly to mind. For a few seconds I stood there, feeling like I was strangling on the tears that fought to break free. I was determined to keep them at bay. I'd been shamed enough tonight. I didn't want to give this guy the satisfaction of seeing me break down a second time.

"Hey."

A hand touched my shoulder gently. I shook it off fiercely and stumbled away a few steps, turning, glaring at him through wet eyes.

"Don't touch me."

"Okay, okay." He raised his palms in surrender. "I won't touch you, and I'll quit teasing you. Look, I'm, uh, I'm not very good at dealing with humans outside my realm, you know? Especially— especially women." He rubbed his hand over his short, dark hair. "It's not really something I do too much in my line of work. I mainly stick to the background. Make sure the Costases are safe. I don't have a lot to do with people like you out in your world. Especially nice girls like you. Guess I don't really know—know how to treat you."

His gruff, stumbling confession took me aback. I half-giggled, a little hysterically.

"I don't know how to treat you, either," I admitted, dashing away the moisture from under my eyes. "If you're not used to dealing with humans, I'm for sure not used to dealing with—with...whatever you are."

A grin quirked one corner of his mouth.

"Shifter," he said. "Thought I told you that. I'm a shapeshifter."

"Well, excuse me. I'm still having a hard time coming to grips with all this, and I'm not used to dealing with shapeshifters."

He nodded in understanding. "I know. This has been a crazy night for you, huh?"

I released a wobbly breath. "You can say that again."

Slowly, as if not to frighten me, he extended his right hand. "Since we're stuck together for now...truce?"

I switched from his hand to his face, trying to gauge his sincerity. If he was telling me the truth about any of this, we were stuck together, at least for the next day or two. He hadn't hurt me. Yet. He didn't seem to have any intentions of it. Not that I knew that for a fact, or knew him at all, but I'd seen what he could change into. In fact, he didn't even have to change. Regular human or bronze statue, he was clearly powerful. He could snap my neck without breaking a sweat. If he came after me, there was no way I could fight him off. Not to mention, he had a gun. I didn't. Despite all that, the fact remained that he apparently was looking after my welfare. I didn't want to trust him, and I didn't—not really. But I guessed it was time to make the best of this whole nightmare situation.

"Truce," I agreed, lifting my arm and setting my hand in his.

His hand was so much bigger than mine that it nearly swallowed it. The contrast between his olive skin, sprinkled with crisp black hair, and my pale-as-a-ghost complexion was intense. He squeezed my fingers gently, reassuringly, as I stared down at our hands, and all I could think was,

*He could crush my hand. If he squeezed hard enough he could snap every single bone in my hand and fingers. With just a squeeze.*

"Truce, right?"

I started, jerking my gaze from our hands to Carter's face. He was looking at me sideways, like he knew I was upset about something from the way I'd been fixated on our clasped hands, but couldn't figure out why. I didn't want to explain.

"Yeah—yeah, truce."

"Okay."

He shook my hand, let it go.

"Now that that's settled, tell me what you need for tonight. There's a little corner store a few blocks away. I'll run out and get it for you."

"You're leaving me alone?"

I was surprised. A little dismayed. A little dismayed to realize I was dismayed.

Mere seconds ago I'd been thinking how easily he could squash me, and now I felt a twinge of fear to think he was going. But his words still rang in my head: *There's way worse things than me out there.* I believed that, and I wasn't sure I wanted to be alone.

"I'll only be gone a few minutes. Why, you want to come?"

I wet my lips, shook my head.

*Don't be a chicken, Ellie.*

"I'll be fine. I can take a shower while you're gone."

It seemed better to get naked and vulnerable in the shower while he was gone than while he was here. I'd already showered today before I went to the Costas home, but that felt like weeks ago. My clothes were still splashed with blood and who-knew-what. My glasses were flecked with it. I felt icky, dirty. Maybe a hot shower would help soothe my roiling stomach, my nerves. Maybe it would help calm me down.

"Sure, that's fine," he was saying, calling my attention back to the present. "I've, uh, only got guy soap in there. Nothing girly. You're welcome to it, though."

I hid a smirk at his description of shower toiletries. "It's fine. I'm not too picky. All I want is to get clean."

"Okay, so all you need is a toothbrush then. Maybe a change of clothes?"

"Something to sleep in."

"Oh, right. Hang on a minute."

He walked out of the room and down the hall, toward his bedroom. I heard a drawer open and close. Returning, he tossed me a t-shirt.

"For after your shower. If you wanna get out of those clothes. Don't worry; it's clean."

I did want to get out of these clothes. They had a stranger's blood on them. They were ripped. My skirt hem was tainted with vomit. But I didn't want to run around in some strange man's t-shirt, either.

I held it up. "Um...can I get some shorts or pajama pants to go with this?"

He looked at me askance. "You know that thing will swallow you. You're tiny."

It was true. His upper body was huge and I was small compared to him. Nevertheless, I didn't know him, and it felt way too intimate.

"Please?"

I wasn't going to argue or explain, but I wanted what I wanted.

He seemed a little annoyed, but jotted it down on his phone anyway.

"I'll see what they've got, but I'm not making any promises. It's a corner store, not a mall. Anything else?"

"Feminine products. Unless you actually have some here."

I held his stare, refusing to blush or flinch. Why bother being embarrassed now? Unfortunately, his guess had been right. My period was supposed to start any day now, and I didn't want to be caught unprepared. Plus, it gave me a hint of vindictive pleasure to think of him having to go shop for them.

"Pfff. Yeah. I keep 'em around for all the women in my life."

I took that to mean there weren't many women in his personal life, but on a completely intellectual level, the whole shifter thing aside, I didn't understand why. He wasn't a bad looking guy.

"What do you want?"

"I don't care. You pick."

"Give me the hard job, why don't you?"

That made me laugh. "You work as head of security for one of the richest men in the entire state of Texas, who, by your own admission, has all sorts of enemies, human and non-human, and *this* is the hard job?"

"I'm a guy. I'm single. I don't do feminine products."

I laughed again. "What, you never had a mom, sisters?"

His face closed off. "Only child. Haven't seen my mother in twenty years."

"Oh." That was awkward. "I'm sorry."

"Nothing for you to be sorry about. Not your business, not your problem." He seemed ready to get off the topic. "So, that's it? Nothing else you need till tomorrow?"

"Not that I can think of."

"K. I'll make it quick. If you're hungry, help yourself to whatever you can find, although there's not a lot in the fridge besides condiments and beer."

"No, thanks."

"Didn't figure you'd be interested. Bathroom's first door on the left. Towels are in the hall closet across from the bathroom. Just—make yourself at home."

I nodded.

"One other thing. I'm going to set the house alarm from my phone. Don't open the window or the door. The alarm will go off, and I'll know. You haven't got the alarm code, so you can't sneak out. Don't try any dumb stunts. Don't go looking around for a phone to call your parents or the cops. I'll get you the burner phone when I get back."

I hid a guilty start. I hadn't necessarily been planning on calling anyone, but the idea had been half-forming in the back of my mind that maybe, maybe while he was gone, it wouldn't hurt to look around and see if I could find a phone...

"Be smart and stay put. Take your shower. Get cleaned up. I'll be back in a few minutes, okay?"

I guessed there weren't any arguments left. "Okay."

He headed for the door, unlocked and started to open it, then turned back to me.

"Do not open this door, Ellie. Not for anyone, not for any reason. There are shifters out there who can imitate every voice, noise, and sound. I don't care if there's a fire alarm going off outside and the fire department is banging on the door saying you need to get out. I don't care if your long-lost dead grandma resurrects and comes back and is out here talking to you, don't get all sentimental and open this door.

"The only person that's supposed to come through here is me, and I've got a key. This apartment is rigged with the best security features money can buy, but they won't do a bit of good if you do something stupid like open the door because you think your parents are outside. They aren't and they won't be. Keep it locked, and you'll be safe. Alright?"

His warning, the vivid picture he painted of shifters with the ability to imitate anything or anyone...reality came crashing back, erasing the half-hearted humor of a few minutes ago. A shiver rolled across my shoulders.

"Alright."

He nodded goodbye, opened the door and slipped out. The heavy door clicked shut behind him. I heard his key in the lock, saw both deadbolts flick up.

Carter was gone, and I was stuck, locked inside his apartment.

## CHAPTER EIGHT

I didn't stand there long staring after Carter or looking around his place. There wasn't much to see anyway. Top-of-the-line, giant, flat screen TV mounted on the wall across from the couch. Some kind of gaming console and controllers on the TV stand underneath. That struck me as ironic. I wasn't a gamer myself, but from what I'd seen my brothers and friends play, as well as the snippets I'd caught of the gamer shows they watched on YouTube, Carter's real life seemed more farfetched and warlike than any video game ever created.

Besides the entertainment stuff, there were a couple of lamps. A plain brown couch. Unremarkable but comfortable. Matching recliner. End table. No bookshelves or even stacks of books or magazines sitting around. No photos that might give me a clue into this man's life, either past or present. No artwork, except a framed sheet of white paper with writing on it hanging on the wall next to the TV. I walked over to study it. Someone, in neat, cursive handwriting, had written out a quote:

*We look not at the things which are seen, but at the things which are not seen: for the things which are seen are temporal; but the things which are not seen are eternal.*

I recognized it as a verse from the New Testament. 2 Corinthians, I thought, although I would've had to double check that. Why did a man like Carter have a framed Bible verse on his wall? Did he even know the quote was a Bible verse? What did it mean to him? The reference to being focused on the unseen instead of the seen—was that an allusion to him focusing on an unseen world of shapeshifters? Unseen, unknown by humans, but a very real and present danger to him and the people he worked for? Or was it something deeper?

I puzzled over it while I left the living room, skimming the kitchen with a glance as I walked through—clean, quiet, bare—and stepped into the hallway. I flicked on the bathroom light so I could see before opening the hall closet he'd indicated. Inside was a laundry hamper on the floor, half full, cleaning supplies on the top shelf, a couple of toiletry items on the shelf under that, and a few towels and hand towels and wash cloths on the shelf right above the hamper. Everything was organized, and the towels neatly folded. Not neat to the point of precision, like my mom being OCD about it and unfolding/refolding the towels the rest of the family hadn't folded to her specifications, but neat.

Whoever and whatever this Carter was, he wasn't your stereotypical bachelor with mounds of dirty laundry, dirty dishes, empty beer cans, and paper plates with moldy pizza slices flung everywhere. I supposed a man like him, who was smart enough to run security for the Costases wouldn't be a slob in his personal life. Probably too detail oriented for that. Also, judging from the sparseness of the place, he likely didn't spend much time here. I guessed the Costas mansion was probably his home away from home, basically his life as well as his job.

Picking up the towel and wash cloth on top of the pile, I closed the closet door and went into the bathroom, shutting and locking that door behind me. There wasn't much to see in the bathroom, either. Little to no décor, but it was clean. I hung the t-shirt he'd given me on a door hook and placed the towels on the vanity. Before taking off my glasses, I leaned over the sink to study my reflection in the mirror. I was a naturally pale person, who, much to my annoyance, couldn't seem to get a tan, but even I could see the pallor on my face tonight looked abnormal. Sickly. My hair was a mess, falling down everywhere. My mascara was smeared from crying. And on my cheek...

My fingers trembled as I reached up to touch the dark drops on my jawline.

Blood.

The griffiin-shifter's blood had spattered my face, my skin, my glasses, either from when Tracy had shot him or when Mr. Costas had used the gun butt to crush his skull.

I gaped at the drops on my reflection and felt my stomach heave as memories flashed in front of my eyes. My knees went weak and I sagged, gripping the countertop to keep from falling. Nausea surged. I lowered my head, trying to fight it off. In my mind's eye, all I could see was Sean Costas, a perfectly normal looking human one second, the next a shiver had raced over his body and there stood a bull-like creature. And Carter—Carter, whose apartment I was locked inside, a bronze statue. Meanwhile, from the air, two flying creatures that seemed almost a mishmash of animals put together, with wings and claws and talons and teeth, terrible, intending to kill. Diving right at Mrs. Costas, helpless in her wheelchair.

The bathroom's chilly air struck the exposed places on my skin, and I remembered feeling the talons shred my blouse, remembered thinking, "I'm going to die," right before Tracy's gun boomed.

"None of this is happening. This can't be happening. How is this possible? How is this happening?"

I came out of the memories, hearing me whisper the words to myself. I was rocking back and forth on my heels, still gripping the countertop.

"None of this is happening."

But it was happening. It was. Or else I wouldn't be here, in some strange man's apartment. I never went to strange men's apartments. That wasn't something I'd do. Yet here I was. About to take a shower and put on a stranger's t-shirt. That was definitely not something I'd do. But I was going to, because more creatures like Carter and Mr. Costas and those other two monsters existed. And they might want to kill me too, for being accidentally involved with the Costas family.

*No good deed goes unpunished.*

The quote echoed in my head, smacking me in the face with its irony.

*Ain't that the truth?*

My stomach calmed at last. Breathing a prayer for protection and comfort, I finally let go of the countertop, took off my glasses, and laid them on the vanity. To force away horrific, troubling memories, I focused on each tiny, specific act of undressing. Unbuttoning each button. Untucking my blouse. Pulling my arms through the sleeves. Taking off my skirt. Unbuckling my shoes. Stepping out of them. This helped distract me from the rips in my shirt, distract me from a new world that wanted to consume me alive. Finally naked, I turned on the water and adjusted the temperature, letting it warm before stepping into the shower. The warm spray rained down, soaking me, and I welcomed it, tilting my head back, letting it cleanse the blood and makeup from my face, wishing it could wash away memories and even reality as well. No chance of that, sadly, but there was definitely something soothing about the hot water and the simple, familiar act of taking a shower.

I stood there a long time—how long I didn't know—before opening my eyes to search the tub, see what was there. As I might have expected, there wasn't much. Some sort of men's three-in-one shampoo/conditioner/body wash, which struck me as funny, not only because it was so practical but also because Carter barely had any hair to wash at all. There was a razor, a bar of soap, a body scrub...and that was it. Nothing surprising, nothing outlandish. Reaching for the black body wash/shampoo bottle made me feel strange, though. It made me acutely aware of being in the personal, private domain of a man I didn't know. It made me feel self-conscious, like I knew I didn't belong and had no business being here, taking a shower where he took showers. It felt...intimate. Uncomfortable. All of the sudden, the hot shower that was so soothing before now felt like it was walling me in, trapping me in a place I shouldn't be.

*I need to finish and get out of here.*

I could probably breathe better with more space around me.

Squeezing some gel into my palm, I turned my back to the spray as I rubbed it into my hair, working up a lather. I soaped up the washcloth too, keeping my eyes tightly closed against the suds as I scrubbed my entire body, from head to foot, removing any physical traces that still remained of the shifter's attack, then death. Finished, I turned back around to let the water wash away the soap, working my hands through my hair, speeding the process along. As I did, I noticed the temperature of the water dropping. Dropping fast.

*Weird. There's no one else here running hot water.*

I was surprised in a nice apartment like this that the hot water would be used up that quickly, but it was dropping so fast the soap was barely half out of my hair and it was getting downright cold. Using my palm to swipe the soap off my face, I opened my eyes to check the shower head, seeking an identifiable reason for the change in water temperature.

There was, but it wasn't anything I expected.

Instead of a possible leaky pipe or clogged duct, there was a white, smoky film oozing out of the shower head along with the water.

*What is that?*

I stared at it, almost entranced, as it slid down the shower mist, mixing with the water, and glided down my legs to pool at my feet. My eyes dropped to my feet, only to see the milky film slowly congeal, alter, and shape itself into another pair of feet. A pair of feet right next to mine.

I gasped and my gaze flew upwards, up a pair of legs and a torso wrapped in a filmy, smoky, watery gown. A woman's chest and arms were forming from the water, from the smoky film. There was a neck and now a face.

*This can't be happening. This can't be happening.*

Panic choked my throat and stilled my body as icy-cold water sluiced over me. My wide gaze latched onto the face staring back at me. A winter-white face, smooth, almost featureless, formed of water and the milky film, strands of long hair drifting about it in the mist. The creature's mouth opened.

"Ellie..." it said, and its thin arms lifted, long, slender fingers reaching for my neck.

I screamed. I screamed and the sound of my own voice woke me from the cold, the stupor, the shock of seeing my shower transform into a living water creature. Another scream ripped from my throat as I clawed at the shower curtain, shoving it aside. I jumped out of the bathtub. My back foot caught on the tub's low wall and I stumbled, pitched forward, still screaming, but righted myself and dashed toward the door, grabbing the borrowed t-shirt off the hook. As I wrestled it on, I threw a glance over my shoulder at the creature in the bathtub who had turned, watching me.

"Ellie..." she said again, her thin, sinuous arms beginning to lengthen as she drew more water down into herself.

I screamed again, shoving the shirt down past my waist with one hand while fumbling with the lock with the other. My vision was blurry without my glasses and I was panicking, unable to think clearly. I'd turned into one of the idiots from horror movies who I'd always mocked that couldn't get their car door open, or couldn't get the engine to start, who made really rash, idiotic decisions when the psycho killer was chasing them.

From outside of myself, I heard my voice screaming, "Help me!" even though nobody was there to help me. Carter was gone. Cold water gushed over my toes and I turned again, a cry clogging my windpipe as the water-woman's body collapsed from the bottom down into a wave, a wave that, in half a second, had poured over the rim of the bathtub, flooded the bathroom floor, and was coming toward me. Even as I managed to release the lock and twist the door handle, the wave soaking my feet had materialized back into the water woman, who stood right next to me.

"Come with me, Ellie," she whispered, her voice rippling like the echoes of waves in an empty space. "Come with me."

Her hands grasped my hand, my neck. She squeezed. Water flowed upward, covering my nose and mouth as she drew me away from the door, toward the bathtub. I struggled against her compelling strength, whipping my head to the side. I caught a breath and screamed again, even as she kept dragging me back towards the bathtub, which was now overflowing with water. Past the toilet, the trashcan which had lifted and was floating.

"Come on, Ellie. I'll make it quick..."

I thrashed madly with my free hand, making a grab for the counter, shrieking until water surged back over my nose and mouth. She was heaving on my neck and right arm. I gripped the counter with my left hand, hanging on with all my might. She yanked harder—"Come on, Ellie," her tone almost impatient, like she didn't understand why I refused to get into the tub with her. I clawed at the counter, knowing if she succeeded she was going to drown me, kill me. More and more water flowed out of the tub, into her, strengthening her as she fought to draw me inside. I was losing strength as I lost air, but she must have felt it was taking too long.

Abruptly, she released my neck and arm. For a split second, the water receded. I gasped a breath, but deliverance was momentary. I felt the water rush down my thighs and draw back, like a wave on the beach receding for a mere instant before the next wave rushes in to take its place. The water retreated in a gush, but only to surge right back along with her hands. In a split-second's time, she'd morphed once more into the water woman and now knelt in the tub, her fingers around my ankles. She grabbed me and jerked, sweeping my feet out from under me. I yelped as I went down, splashing in the water on the floor, trying desperately to claw my way forward, kicking, shouting, but she heaved me backward again, then again. My knees struck the side of the tub. I felt her grip tighten as she prepared for the final heave that would draw me in with her.

If she got me in there, she'd win. No way out of it. Twisting onto my back, I kicked harder at her hands, but it was like kicking water. Nothing solid to kick. Ineffectual.

"Come on, Ellie," she said patiently and heaved. I felt myself hauled towards her and cried out in dismay as I went in, feet first. My butt caught on the rim. I heard a crash as my head struck the floor, hard. I thought the crash was from my skull striking the tile, but I was wrong. The crash must've come from behind me, because I heard someone bellow my name.

"*Ellie!*"

The creature glanced up and hissed in fury as, still helpless on my back, I twisted my head to look behind me.

Carter.

# CHAPTER NINE

The instant he stepped into his apartment, Carter knew something was wrong. He could hear the water from the shower, which meant the girl was still in the bathroom, but he heard other sounds too. Splashing. Knocking around. Then a scream.

Why she was screaming? She shouldn't be screaming. She was supposed to be safe here.

Those thoughts exploded across his mind. He dropped his keys and the shopping sacks, darting down the hall for the bathroom. Stopping to knock wasn't an option. The door was slightly ajar, and the thrashing sounds were louder. He heard a gurgling cry, a thud, even as he flung open the door.

"Ellie!"

She was on her back, and a water shifter, probably a Nakki, a water spirit, had her by the ankles and was trying to drag her into the overflowing bathtub.

When he shouted her name, her head twisted to look behind her. Naked fear, then relief passed over her terrified face.

The Nakki hissed at the sight of him, and Carter's blood boiled. Two steps into the room and he felt the familiar ripple.

Carter Ballis was gone. The Talos had taken over. It was the Talos that thundered forward, diving over Ellie's prone body, leaping for the tub. He ignored the Nakki. Water couldn't hurt bronze, but bronze couldn't hurt water, either. Instead, as he dove for the bathtub, he lifted his bronze fist high in the air, bringing it down with all his might against the drain. There was a crack, a groan, and the entire bathtub bottom splintered. He did it again, twice more, as fast as he could, and the porcelain gave way. A hole opened up and the drain dropped, as well as the tub floor surrounding it, along with chunks of the bathtub walls.

Instantly, water poured out. The Nakki hissed, trying to recoil in anger, but the hole was too big and the water was leaving too fast. The water shifter's grip was torn from the girl as its body went down the hole. It twisted, writhing, and tried to grab onto him with its top half even as its bottom half gushed down the hole. The Talos reared back with a roar, ripping away from the insubstantial arms. With nothing else to hold onto, the Nakki slid away. It flipped as it went down, and Carter caught a glimpse of it from behind. The benign female form was gone. Its back was hairy, lumpy, and scaled, showing a glimpse of its true nature. It flipped once more, large, flat, green saucer eyes staring balefully into his as it vanished into the pipes.

Quickly, the Talos shut off the water from the shower, then turned, crawling over to the girl. She'd pushed herself up on her elbows and was gasping for breath, her chest heaving. When he approached she scrabbled back, sloshing water everywhere, trying to get away, looking at the Talos with nearly as much fear as she'd looked at the Nakki.

Not good.

The Talos flinched, concentrated, and felt the ripple as his human form rolled over him again, transforming the bronze statue away.

"It's okay, Ellie. It's me. It's just me."

She stayed where she was, on her back for a split second, her hazel eyes huge, before abruptly pushing herself up and crawling forward, throwing herself against him. Her fingers dug like claws into the bare flesh of his arms.

"Get me out of here, get me out of here," she sobbed.

He did. Rising, Carter wrapped an arm around her, pulling her up with him, and half-dragged, half-carried her out of the bathroom and back into the living room. He fetched her over to the couch where she'd sat before and put her down, sinking next to her. Even then, she didn't let go, but still held onto him, clutching him like a drowning person might clutch a life preserver. Her fingers pinched so hard it actually hurt, but he ignored the pain, reaching behind her for the same throw blanket and slinging it around her shoulders. She wasn't talking, wasn't crying, but was still breathing hard, making a funny little half-choked, half-whimpering noise. It reminded him of a wounded animal, hurt and needing help, but not knowing where to turn.

Gingerly, he put his hands on her waist, tried to ease her back so he could talk to her, find out what happened, but she whimpered and clutched him even tighter.

"Okay, okay," he soothed, letting her be for a minute. "I'm not going anywhere anymore. You're safe now. You hear me? You're safe now."

He really wasn't sure what to do with this, but he didn't want her panicking further, so he kept still, letting her hold onto him while his mind raced.

A Nakki. A water shifter. Clever. One of the few things that could've gotten into his apartment without an army. The question was, had Nosizwe sent it for him or for her? There wasn't any secret who he was to Sean Costas, and he'd fought off more than one attempt on his life in the past. However, a Nakki against the Talos seemed like a pretty futile endeavor. Unless it had been sent for her, for Ellie, in which case Ellie and he were in real trouble. They'd waited until he was gone, meaning somebody was watching his place. The soundproof walls ensured neighbors wouldn't hear any struggle. They'd meant to take Ellie out, so Nosizwe already knew who she was and had determined Ellie was involved with the Costas family. Probably thought she was a shifter herself, making her fair game.

They needed to get out of here.

"Ellie?"

Her whimpers had quieted and her heaving breaths softened a little. Gently, he eased back from her. Her hands didn't fall from his shoulders, but this time she didn't freak out when he moved her.

"What happened, Ellie?"

Her eyes were still squeezed tightly shut. Her soaked hair spilled all around her face, dripping on her, on him. She was trembling, probably both from fright and the chill of the apartment air combined with the soaked t-shirt and wet hair.

"She—I—I was in the shower. And the water got real...got real cold, all of a sudden. And—and then I saw the...saw the white film. Like smoke, mixing with the water. And it formed into her. And she—she spoke my name. She called me. She said Ellie. She—she wanted me to go with her. She tried to kill me."

Finally, the girl opened her eyes. Tears pooled in the corners, and her chin quivered.

"She tried to strangle me. Drown me. I thought—I thought I was going to die." She paused, breathing hard for several seconds to regain control. "Then you came, and—"

She looked down, a shudder shaking her body.

"Sorry," she whispered. "I thought I was scared before. Back when—back at the C-Costas home. This was...I'd never felt so helpless."

Helpless. That's what she was. She was fully human, and helpless against a world of shifters that would use any means necessary to get to her.

"She said your name. You're certain."

The girl nodded. "She said it several times."

"Okay."

This had definitely been a hit on Ellie, then, meaning they clearly knew some things about her. If they knew that much, they'd know about her family too or would find out. Nosizwe might not go after them, but she might. They couldn't take that chance. He needed to put in a call to Sean. Have him tell James to put someone on Ellie's house to watch her family. No need to scare the family yet, but for Ellie's sake they shouldn't be left unguarded.

"Can you wait here a second while I call my boss? I'm not leaving the apartment. Just going in the bedroom. Okay?"

She nodded shakily, and Carter edged back so he could stand up. When he did, her head snapped up as if she were noticing for the first time that her hands were clinging to his upper body, and that his shirt was gone, exploded from the changing. She couldn't hide her embarrassment. Bright red stained her cheeks, even as she scooted away, grabbing the edges of the couch throw and pulling them tightly around her torso. Carter turned his head, pretending he hadn't noticed the way his wet t-shirt clung to every line and curve of her naked body underneath.

"I'll, uh, be right back," he said, clearing his throat, and rose to leave the room.

*Get a grip,* he told himself, angry that he would've noted such a thing at all, much less on a woman like her and during a situation like this.

He shoved aside the memory as he paused to check the bathroom, making sure all was quiet. It was a mess. Water a couple inches deep still on the floor. The bottom of the bathtub was cracked, shattered.

*Going to be fun explaining that to the landlord,* he thought, then shrugged it off.

Ah well. Wasn't like the Costases' pockets would be empty any time soon. Sean had said Ellie was family; any expenses incurred while taking care of her would be his. The landlord wouldn't squeak too loudly with Costas money shoved in his face.

The bath mat and most of Miss St. James' clothing lay scattered about in sad, sodden piles. Little seemed salvageable, but Carter spotted her glasses on the counter along with her bra. He took both. She'd probably be embarrassed he was touching her undergarments, bringing them to her, but she'd likely be even more embarrassed to run around without one. He carried both items into his room where he dressed and put in a call to the Costas compound.

Sean didn't berate him for what could have been construed as a lapse in judgment, leaving the girl alone. Like Carter, Sean would never have dreamed Nosizwe's people could have honed in on Ellie's whereabouts that quickly, or that they'd be able to breach Carter's home defenses. He simply told Carter, "Stay on it. Keep her safe."

Carter switched the call to James next.

By the time he hung up, Carter had a plan. He knew what he had to do next. He only hoped Ellie could handle it. She'd been through a lot tonight. A lot. And was probably going to go through a lot more before they could finally get her somewhere safe.

## CHAPTER TEN

Before returning to the living room, Carter took another shirt from his dresser, another towel from the hall closet. Miss St. James sat where he'd left her, braced on the edge of the couch like she was poised to run at the slightest provocation. She'd pulled the blanket down over her thigh as far it would go—which really wasn't far, and had swept her dripping hair around one shoulder in an effort to contain the mess.

Carter refused to let his gaze linger on her bare leg, or his mind conjure up images of her body underneath the sodden t-shirt. It wasn't fair to her, not after all she'd been through and her obvious embarrassment over it.

He handed her the glasses, bra, shirt, and towel without a word. She squinted up at him, and slid a hand from beneath the blanket to take them.

"Thanks," she said softly.

She didn't mention the bra, even though he'd half-expected a complaint over him touching it.

He grunted an acknowledgement before walking over to the front door to retrieve the bags he'd dropped when he'd heard her cries for help.

"Here's some stuff for you. I got you, uh, some kind of soft pants. Size small. Didn't know what you'd want, but maybe they'll work for now with the shirt I gave you. Get dressed. We need to get you out of here. Sooner rather than later."

"Wh-where are we going?"

She sounded shaky. When he studied her, she was shaking, visibly, beneath the blanket. Part of him felt bad for her terror, for how she'd already been traumatized twice tonight, dragged into a war she hadn't known existed and had no part in. Another part of him felt even worse, knowing the night was far from finished.

"I'll explain in the car," he said brusquely. "We really need to get moving. Go change, if you're going to."

"Where?"

"Where?"

"I can't—I don't want to go in the bathroom."

Ah.

"How about the kitchen? I'll wait out here."

She half opened her mouth like she wanted to say something. Shut it. Looked embarrassed, anxious. Carter took a guess at what was going through her mind.

"I promise I'll be good. No peeking."

He tried to say it like a joke, like he was teasing her, but she didn't appear convinced.

"Look, kid," he said, a little firmer now, "I didn't bring you here to hit on you, if that's what you're thinking. This isn't about you and me. This is about me protecting you because my boss ordered me to. All I'm going to do is keep you alive and reasonably unharmed. No more, no less, okay?"

She still didn't seem completely reassured, but perhaps her obvious anxiety had more to do with the death and mayhem she'd witnessed than actually being scared of him peeking at her changing. She didn't agree or disagree with his statement, but she did press her glasses onto her nose then stand, fumbling to gather up the towel, hold onto the blanket, and clasp the bags all at the same time. She shuffled out of the room, into the kitchen, and Carter heard the bags rustle as she dropped them on the table. More rustling, shifting of clothes, digging in bags.

While he waited for her, Carter thumbed through his phone, texting James, texting Sean, messaging three of his most trusted lieutenants, making sure the details were settled. That Miss St. James' house would be watched and he'd have backup tonight, just in case. That didn't take long, and neither did Ellie. Within a few minutes she'd reappeared in the doorway between the kitchen and living room, wearing the soft black pants he'd bought, along with his t-shirt, knotted at the waist. She must've toweled off her wet hair; it was no longer dripping. She'd condensed the other items down into a single plastic shopping bag, which hung from her hand.

"How're the shoes?" he asked.

She lifted a foot, showing off the women's slippers he'd thought to snag. He'd been trying to hurry, but when he saw the shoes he took a second to study them, in the back of his mind remembering that his guest had arrived wearing heels and thinking that wouldn't go over so well if they had to run. Which they might.

"Little small," she answered.

"Sorry about that. I was guessing at your size."

"It was a good guess. My feet are kind of big for my height."

"You ready to go?"

"I guess so?"

Her voice sounded as uncertain as she looked, but she approached him anyway, passing him by as she headed for the door. Carter followed her out, stopping to lock the door behind himself, making a mental note to call his landlord once the excitement had dissipated.

If they survived the remaining excitement.

Carter followed the girl down the outside staircase, keeping a weather eye for any signs of danger. A chill autumn breeze rippled across the parking lot; the back of his neck bristled. He couldn't see anything, didn't sense anything, but he was on edge, nonetheless, knowing what could be out there. He caught up to Miss. St. James, placing a hand on the small of her back, wordlessly hurrying her along to the car. She glanced up at the touch, startled, but seemed to notice how he was paying more attention to the sky, the walls, the surrounding area than her, and quickened her pace without him saying a word.

Carter made a swift perusal of the Aston's darkened interior before either of them climbed inside. He felt better once they were in. Smaller space. Walls. A ceiling. Safer than his own jeep, in case Nosizwe sent more fliers after them. The door clicked shut, the locks engaging automatically. Ellie put on her seat belt as he started the engine, backed out of the covered parking space, and spun them out of the courtyard, heading for the gates, then the city streets. She waited to talk until they were well outside the complex.

"Can we turn on some heat?" was the first thing she said.

Carter glanced over at her, huddling in the opposite seat. She had to be freezing, especially with wet hair. He hadn't thought to grab her a jacket or to buy her one. Idiot. He should have given her one of his, at least.

"Yeah, of course." Leaning forward, he flipped switches and pressed buttons, turning the heat on full blast.

"Thank you."

"No problem."

"So, where are we going? You said you'd explain when we got in the car."

"Did I?"

"Yes, you did. I wish you'd back up and explain everything. I need more information. I don't understand any of this. I really don't. Oh, and when can I contact my family?"

"Contact your family?"

This time he studied her from the corner of his eye,

wondering if she'd lost her dang mind. Did she not remember everything they'd just gone through?

"You said I could contact them, remember?"

Ellie raised her chin, looking stubborn. The gesture almost seemed funny, coming from her. Then again, she wasn't as frail as she looked. She was in nursing school, which couldn't be for the faint of heart. She hadn't thought twice about risking her life for total strangers, which was more than most people would've done. She hadn't fallen apart yet tonight, in spite of getting repeatedly slammed up against his world, against him. She was actually hanging pretty tough, and Carter couldn't deny a measure of respect for that.

"A burner phone?" she prompted, when he failed to speak. "You said you'd get me a burner phone, and I could—"

"Yeah, yeah, I remember." He waved off her explanation. "I'll take care of it when we get to our next stop."

"Our next stop? Why not now?"

"Because I may have the ability to shapeshift, but I don't have the ability to magically reach into my ass and pull out a burner phone for you, Ellie."

She shot him a dirty look.

"You don't have to be nasty about it. And stop cussing."

"Cussing?" He snorted a laugh. "Are you for real?"

A quick study of her face screamed that she was.

"Okay, okay, little Miss Goody Two Shoes. I won't cuss around you. That make you happy?"

The glare on her face remained at his mockery, but she said coolly, "It would be appreciated, thank you."

Carter turned his head to look out the window, muttering under his breath. If she heard the language he used, she pretended not to care. Instead, she hopped back on the original subject like a fox pouncing on a rabbit.

"So? Burner phone? Will you get me one so I can contact my

family? They're going to be worried sick. I hope they haven't already called the police when they couldn't reach me."

"What, you got a curfew or something? Are your parents that controlling?"

He was picking a fight to distract her from inquiring where they were headed or what he was planning, but it did seem like a case of over-concern for a twenty-one year old.

"You are an adult, after all," he added. "Old enough to smoke and vote and drink."

"They're not controlling and I don't have curfew," she responded, incensed, like he'd figured she would be. "They care about me. I don't do things like stay out all night with strangers. If I do stay out late, I let them know where I am. It's called being a family and being responsible."

"Sounds like the life. Aren't girls your age supposed to be out drinking and partying it up with sweaty frat boys?"

"Yes, *that* sounds like the life."

"Maybe you should give it a try. Loosen you up. Broaden your horizons."

Now she shifted to stare out the window. "My horizons have been broadened plenty tonight, and I'm too busy for that junk."

"Is that code for you're boring?"

She drew in a heavy breath. Released it. Refused to look at him.

"I don't need my life dissected by you, of all people, thank you very much. Not that it's any of your business, but I live at home because I have student loans and I'm trying to save money right now. Not because I can't live on my own. I don't party because, frankly, getting falling down drunk and pawed by sweaty frat boys doesn't sound fun, and I'd rather put my time into studying. But I'm sure you knew that already. If you're so interested in partying, why don't you go do it?"

"Nah, I'm too old. Never was any good at partying anyway. Don't know how to relax." Carter glanced over his shoulder, switching lanes as they circled past a couple of popular restaurants under the same family name—a Mexican and a seafood eatery—before exiting onto University Drive. They crossed the Trinity River, and drove alongside Trinity Park up to the Fort Worth Botanic Garden. "I'm only good at keeping people alive," he concluded. "People like you."

"Thank you for keeping me alive, but I'm also asking you to let me contact my family tonight like you promised."

Carter couldn't tell if she was being sarcastic. Her voice was a lot milder than he would've figured, given the direction their conversation had been headed, plus how she kept staring out the window. Like she was avoiding looking at him.

"Yeah, okay. I'll figure something out."

"Thank you."

Honestly, she sounded anything but grateful. She sounded like she was straining to hold herself together, but, hey, at least she was holding herself together.

A couple of minutes elapsed in strained silence, with her attention riveted outside at the empty park. It was broken when she glanced out his window and suddenly sat up.

"Hey, isn't that the Botanic Garden?"

"Yep."

He slowed the vehicle as they pulled into the circular drive in front of the main entrance.

"What are we doing here?"

Nervous, she glanced around the shadowy perimeter of the parking lot.

"Meeting someone."

He pulled up in front of the wrought iron gate. Parked. Shut off the engine.

"Wh-who are we meeting?"

She didn't like this. Carter didn't like it either, but this was their best chance of taking the fight out of the city, away from bystanders, and into open ground. Their best chance of getting rid of the initial threat, throwing Nosizwe off their scent for a bit.

"Someone who can help us."

He opened his door, got out, scanning the area. He didn't see them, but he knew they were close. Had to be.

It registered that he hadn't heard her door open and he ducked his head back into the Aston's interior.

"You coming or what?"

She started visibly when he spoke, and Carter realized she'd been staring at the steering wheel, the driver's seat.

"Uh uh, no. Just in case you get any bright ideas..."

He shoved the key fob in his pocket, nodded his head towards the outside.

"C'mon, kid."

"What if I don't want to go?"

Again, he could hear the tremor in her voice.

"You come willingly, or I carry you out over my shoulder. Your choice. Either way is fine by me. Carrying you might be more fun."

His goading worked, making her mad. Getting mad was better than being scared, which was why he did it.

Partly. She was kind of cute, all riled up, if he were being honest with himself.

Carter didn't like being *that* honest with himself.

"You're a jerk," she snapped, but she climbed out of the car.

"You've said that before. I'm flattered."

Carter leaned around her to shut the door. Again, she started at the noise.

"Don't be so jumpy," he reproved, taking her arm. "It's going to be okay. I told you, I'm not going to hurt you. Not going to let anyone else hurt you, either."

"Then why are we here?" she whispered, as he led her over to the low stone wall. The night had closed in around them, forbidding loud noises. That was okay. No point drawing extra attention to themselves.

Yet.

"Told you—we're meeting someone. Someone who can help us."

"Who?"

He didn't respond as he guided her into the darkness, past the compost outpost, the Texas Garden Clubs, over a stream, and into the Sister Cities International Grove. They pushed through the trees, breaking free in the narrow strip of the North Vista. The wind soughed through the half-bare branches behind and across from them, chilly and uninviting. The stars that should've been overhead were hidden by the city lights reflecting on the clouds overhanging the metropolis. This late in the year, there were no animal noises of croaking frogs or chirping crickets in the Garden. All was quiet, except for the wind rustling dry, brittle leaves.

"What's going on, Carter?"

Ellie was shivering, shivering hard, probably both from the chill and genuine fright.

"Trust me, Ellie."

"How am I supposed to trust you? I barely know you," she returned in a whisper.

"Except as the bronze freak?"

This time, she didn't rise to the bait.

"You said there are worse things than you out there. You've been saying I'm in danger. Some kind of water-creature-thing tried to kill me barely an hour ago, so you drag me outside, in the Garden, where there's no protection? Where nobody's around? What are you planning to do? If you want to kill me, go ahead and get it over with," she pleaded, looking genuinely distressed.

Carter sighed. "Don't be stupid. If I'd meant to kill you, I'd have done it already. I—"

"Carter."

Ellie gasped and they both spun to see someone emerge from the gloom, the bushes, a good hundred feet away.

"Blake."

Joab Blake. Ex US military. Special ops. Shifter, mercenary for hire to those who could afford his services. Most couldn't.

Sean Costas could afford anyone's services.

"Was hoping you'd still be in the area," Carter said.

It was too dark to get a good look at the newcomer, but Carter could tell he was studying the girl who had unknowingly pressed back against him at the other man's arrival.

Blake didn't remark on that. Said instead, "Costas said you had a job for me."

"I do."

"Why meet here?"

"So we could talk. No risk of being detected."

"What about her?"

"She'll wait."

Carter stepped away from Ellie and around her, intending to head to the other man, but Ellie grabbed the back of his shirt, tugging on it.

"Are you crazy?" she hissed. "You're not leaving me out here alone while you go off and have coffee with that guy."

Carter halted, turning to look down at her. "A minute ago you were scared of me and being alone out here with me. Now you don't want me walk off a few feet and talk to my business associate? Make up your mind, kid."

Before she could respond to the taunt, he gently removed her hand from his shirt. "I'll be right back. Just going over there to talk to Blake. Not leaving; only walking off for a minute. That okay with you?"

"No."

He half-chuckled. "You'll be fine. Stay there."

## CHAPTER ELEVEN

I didn't like it. I didn't like it one tiny bit. Nevertheless, arguing with Carter was futile. Before I could think up any more arguments he'd left to talk to that Blake guy, whoever and whatever he was, and left me alone, standing there in the cold and the dark, shivering and scared. I hated this. I hated it so bad. I wanted to be home. All I could think about was how desperately I wanted to be home. By this time of night, I'd probably be in my pajamas, up in my room, reading or studying for class the next morning. Mom and Dad might be watching TV downstairs. My brothers would probably be arguing over the Xbox in their room, and who got to play what before they had to go to bed.

Instead, no. I could picture Mom calling and texting my friends, classmates, acquaintances. Trying to get ahold of the Costases, if mortal peons like us could even reach people like them. I hoped she hadn't called the cops yet. No, I hoped she had called the cops. No, I didn't know whether I hoped it or not. I didn't know what to hope or want. I didn't know whether I trusted Carter, with his quips and smart-alecky remarks, or not. Carter, who could be such a jerk but had his kinder moments too, when he was almost human.

"Huh, almost human," I chuckled to myself. "Good one."

Because he wasn't human. Not fully, anyway. He was a shapeshifter. And I still didn't know what to make of that. On the other hand, his bronze alter ego—if it could be called that—had come in handy earlier when the water monster attacked me.

Thinking about him made me glance his way. I strained through the darkness to see him and whoever he was meeting. Only, when I glanced over their direction, the men had moved off. I couldn't see them anymore.

"Carter?"

Uneasy, I called his name. No response. I took a few faltering steps towards where I'd last seen him.

"Carter? Carter, where are you?"

I saw and heard nothing. Had he abandoned me? That didn't seem likely. However...

It was also my chance to run. To get away from him.

*And go where? You can't go home. Where can you run?*

Again, reason reinserted itself, but even as I dithered over whether to run into the unknown or to keep searching for Carter, the wind picked up, rustling more leaves that crackled and crunched in the darkness.

Wait, *crunched?*

The sound seemed at odds with the other night noises around us. I peered over my shoulder, wondering if maybe a squirrel was playing around, only to see a huge, shadowy form with glowing red eyes barreling towards me. I think my heart stopped. The world around me also stopped. I couldn't hear anything. I couldn't think. It was happening again. Again. Death coming at me, this time in the form of some horrific beast. I could see white fangs, hear the thunder of hooves. For a split-second I was frozen, then instinct took over. Self-preservation made me swing around, flailing my body out of the monster's path in the nick of time. I threw myself so hard I fell onto my back on the cold, brittle grass, flailing out a hand to keep my glasses on my face.

The monster thundered past a few steps, snorting in anger, before it was able to stop. Wheeling about, it stood there, glaring at me with baleful red eyes. I couldn't pick out its features, but I thought it was a massive boar with multiple tusks instead of fangs. Death was in its face: my death. I was panting so hard from fright that I could hear my own breath in my ears, but my vocal cords seemed frozen. I couldn't scream.

*Why can't I scream? Where are you, Carter? You promised you'd take care of me.*

Mentally, I was shouting all this even as the boar lowered its gigantic head—which was as tall as me—and pawed at the ground with a front hoof.

*Move, Ellie, move,* my mind shrieked.

Even as the boar took its first steps towards me I flipped over, pushed myself up off my knees, and tried to run. The ground was uneven and the night was dark. The hooves were pounding towards me so fast I knew I'd never make it to the trees. I glanced behind me, saw the creature right there, and screamed. It lowered its head to impale me with its tusks—

And was hit from the side by another beast.

The boar squealed in fury, the other beast answered with a roar. I didn't stop, but kept running towards the nearest tree, thinking, *Just get to the tree and climb.* If I were off the ground, I might stand a chance. Maybe Carter would show up.

*Carter, where is Carter?*

I reached the tree and jumped for the lowest branch. It was too high and I was too short. I jumped again. Missed. The roars, grunts, and squeals behind me caught my attention. Sick with terror, I looked back to see that a massive, simply *massive* creature with a vaguely human shape but covered in fur was taking on the boar. It was stupendously huge and strong, and also held weapons, two machetes, one in each hand. I gaped, so shocked by what I was witnessing that I momentarily forgot about getting away.

And that was when something dropped from the trees behind me. I whirled, yelped.

Even though it was dark, for once I knew what I was facing. I'd watched a movie about it with my brother. It was human sized, but with an insect's wings. More glowing red eyes. Claw-like hands instead of fingers.

A Mothman.

In my head, I heard Carter's voice: *Monsters from fairytales, folklore, mythology, and urban legend from around the world. Most of those ideas come from shapeshifters, like me.*

An American urban legend. The Mothman. Real, brought to life in front of me. Real, because shifters were real. And I was facing one.

This time, there wasn't anywhere to run, and there wasn't any time to do it. The Mothman had landed right in front of me. A soft thud alerted me and I spun to see another winged creature behind me. I couldn't be sure, but I thought it was the same thing that had attacked earlier in the courtyard of the Costas home. I recognized the skull-face, the wings.

Two winged creatures, me trapped between them, a tree at my back.

Dizziness washed over me. I was so terrified I felt hot all over. Both creatures reached for me as I lunged forward. The mothman had me first, grabbing me, wrapping me up in its long arms, disproportionate to its size. A scream escaped as it seized me, holding me in place while the other creature sprang. Its claws grabbed my upper arms, the teeth of its skull face brushed my neck...

And it was hit, like the boar before, only this time by a bullet, not a body. I heard the quiet bang of a shot fired from a weapon with a gun suppressor, and watched crimson explode from the skull-creature's chest. Three times it was shot before it let go of me, reeling backwards, mortally wounded. The Mothman, still clenching me, hissed and revolved about to face the attacker. The battle between the other two creatures raged on in the background, but I could see the taller, man-shaped shifter was winning. The machetes were going up and down, hacking relentlessly at the boar, which crumpled. At first, I couldn't see the attacker who had fired, but then I saw a flash of bronze and that thing Carter shifted into was there.

He was right there, like he'd been close all along. He didn't risk any more shots, possibly because the Mothman was using me like a shield. Instead, he charged, and his mighty, bronze hands grabbed the Mothman's arm, pulling it off me, twisting and snapping it like a twig. The monster reared back, recoiled, squealing even as Carter's alter ego tore me free, tossing me aside to the ground, away from immediate danger. I hit, rolled over once, and shoved myself up on my hands and knees. Blindly, I patted around for my glasses, which had fallen off, and was lucky to find them quickly.

As I searched, the bronze man was making short work of the Mothman. He gripped it by the shoulder with one hand, and with the other slammed his huge fist repeatedly into the other creature's face. Blood sprayed his bronze skin and the Mothman's head snapped back, its insect-like jaws opening and closing, opening and closing. Its massive wings, taller than itself, taller than the bronze man, beat wildly as it fought to escape, but there was no escaping that relentless bronze fist that smashed and smashed and smashed as Carter, quite literally, beat his opponent to death.

It sagged beneath the onslaught, its wings fluttering instead of beating, and still Carter continued to pummel it with his fists even as the Mothman drooped down backward to its knees. A ripple shuddered over it, and before my eyes the body transformed into that of a man, a very human man, a tall, once athletically built black man with a shaved head, whose face was barely recognizable as human anymore.

"Carter!" I gasped, horrified to see my assailant as human and not a mere monster. The bronze man pulled his fist back for a final blow that crushed the other man's face, sending him flat on his back in the dry leaves.

Behind me, I heard a final, ugly squeal from the boar and whipped my head to the side in time to see the fur-covered humanoid lowering his machete. The boar was lying on its side, and even as the machete came towards it, the body rippled. In an instant, the boar was gone. A huge man with a shaved head and multiple tattoos, wearing black leather, lay there—but in the next instant the machete had severed his head from his neck. The dull whack of the blade was followed by the soft thunk of the severed head hitting the earth. It rolled a few paces away and stopped, staring up sightlessly into the nighttime sky.

I stared. I stared at the severed head, trying to figure out what had gone wrong, and how, in one night, I'd been transported from earth to the very gates of hell. Then I turned to where the bronze man, having shifted back into Carter, stood over the dead once-Mothman. I stared at him, then pivoted and stared at the other flying creature Carter had shot. A woman. An Asian woman. I stared at the three dead bodies. Dead, because of me. Were they dead because of me? My mind was whirling, my thoughts in pieces. One thing stood out.

This had been a set up.

Carter hadn't come here, brought me here, just to meet this Blake. Blake, the insanely tall, fur-covered humanoid who had already shifted back into a tall human with longish hair and a long beard. Blake, with his bloody machetes. Carter and Blake had withdrawn into the night, leaving me open to assault from these other shifters. Monsters. I'd been bait, used to draw them out of hiding.

They'd used me as bait.

I was alive and uninjured, but barely. A half-second slower on the gunshots and the Asian-shifter would've torn my throat out. Or the Mothman would've crushed me to death. The boar would have trampled me, gored me. Death had been all around me, but somehow I'd survived.

I tried to pray a prayer of gratitude for having been kept safe, even as fury at Carter and this other man, Blake, bloomed in my chest for using me like that. Without my permission. Without my consent. Without warning.

I used what was left of my strength to push myself back on my heels, then, shakily, to my feet. I'd overestimated my reserves, even my burning anger, because I felt my knees crumple underneath me. I swayed, flailing for something to hold onto. There was nothing. I sat down again, hard, on my butt in the crisp grass and this time I just sat there.

"Stay down, Ellie. Don't try to get up."

Carter spoke from where he was picking up the Mothman-shifter's feet.

I opened my mouth to answer, to argue, to ream him out, to say something, anything, but my mind was so full and my body so numb and my mouth so dry. I couldn't speak. I simply watched, huddled on the ground, as Carter dragged my attacker's corpse over to the body of the boar-shifter. Blake had retrieved the head, picking it up like he wasn't bothered at all, and placed it next to its body. Carter bypassed me again as he went for the skull-faced creature's cadaver, also dragging her by the feet over to the other two corpses.

The bodies made a soft, funny thud when Carter tossed hers onto the top of the heap. Sickness twisted my stomach, and I turned my face away so I wouldn't see.

"Call Amy."

That was Blake, the other man, the stranger, who had fought off the boar for me tonight.

Amy? The same Amy who Jackson had gotten away from, precipitating my plunge into this dark, murderous world? Why did they want her?

I heard Carter's phone buzzing from where I sat. Then, "Amy. How far away are you? Okay. Good. We're waiting."

To Blake he said, "Three minutes. She's parking and leaving the car. Flying in."

"Good. Meanwhile, look around. No evidence left. No clothes, teeth, weapons, shoes, nothing."

"Yep."

Both men flicked on flashlights I hadn't even known they had, with small but powerful beams. Carter sidestepped me as he searched the area next to the tree, the area now stained with shifter blood, the area where I'd been held by a Mothman, a legend brought to life, and attacked by another type of creature that I still couldn't identify. Carter ignored me, the other man ignored me, as they both zipped their flashlights over the scene, looking for what I wasn't sure. Any evidence that might tie them, us, here, I reckoned. I watched, immobile, feeling numb. There had been too much terror tonight. I wasn't even afraid anymore. I was numb.

Next thing I knew, I heard the beating of wings. Maybe I'd thought I was numb and incapable of fear, but I'd heard that sound enough times in this one night to make my body recoil in terror. I jerked back from my seat on the cold ground, wrenching my neck upward, in time to see a winged figure with scales and a long tail, a vaguely human, vaguely female shape, descend from the sky. She landed lightly on the grass, next to Blake, next to the pile of bodies.

"Amy," Blake said. "Long time no see."

"Always a pleasure, Blake. *Not*," she added, and the man chuckled.

I recognized her voice. It was the same woman. It was Jackson's former nanny. She was a shifter too.

Her head swung around, and I saw her eyes. Golden. A memory leapt out at me, of something I'd dismissed at the time of the accident. Of her huddling over Jackson, and how I fancied

I'd caught a glimpse of golden eyes. Yes, I'd written it off as my overworked brain and fear then. I didn't write it off now, because she did have golden eyes. Golden eyes with slits. She was the most recognizable figure to me out of all the things I'd seen tonight.

She was a dragon. A dragon with a human-ish shape, but still a dragon.

Now it made sense, Mr. Costas's strange turn of a phrase at dinner hours earlier: *When I hire someone to look after my son, I expect them to do exactly that.*

Guard, of course. Amy wasn't merely a nanny, or hadn't been. She was also a guard. A shapeshifter. Knowing his secret, it stood to reason that Sean Costas wouldn't let a mere human nanny his son. Jackson had to be well protected at all times, and a woman who could shift into a dragon must've seemed the perfect choice.

Even as my brain struggled to accept all of this as fact, not insanity, I heard footsteps. I jolted again, but this time it was Carter stooping next to me, his flashlight pointing down and his hand on my shoulder.

"C'mon, kid," he said. "Out of the line of fire."

Line of fire? Did that mean there would be more shooting? More killing? I couldn't handle anything else. I really, really couldn't. I barely made it to my feet on my own. Seeing me struggle, Carter put an arm around my shoulders to support me as he walked me from the tree, the blood, the sight of death, and into the open area, well behind Amy and Blake, away from the pile of bodies. Under ordinary circumstances, I might've been embarrassed at being so physically close to a strange man with his shirt off, but under ordinary circumstances I wouldn't have been there at all and none of this would've happened. Instead, I did the extraordinary, something I never dreamt I'd do, and I turned into that shirtless man, hiding my face in his chest. The action knocked my glasses askew, but I found solace in how his bare arm around my back and upper arm was warm against the autumn night air.

"Hey, it's going to be okay," he said. I heard his voice like a distant thing in the far reaches of my consciousness. "We're going to clean this up and I'll get you out of here. No more attacks tonight. No more killing."

*No more...*

I shut my eyes and clung to that like I clung to him, letting him be my strength for a few minutes until they finished whatever they were discussing and we could leave. A sound like a massive whoosh, a blast of wind and air caught my attention, and I twisted to see what it was, straightening my glasses. I felt my eyes get big when I saw Amy, her back hunched as if physically straining, her jaws open wide, shooting a stream of flame from her mouth. The center of her scaled chest glowed bright red, as if lit by hot coals. The fire burst from within her, like a storybook dragon shooting flames, and landed on the three bodies of the shifters Carter and Blake had killed, devouring them with dragon fire, destroying the evidence.

I didn't want to think about burning bodies. I didn't want to think about those people lying there. Yes, they were shifters, but they were people too. What if they had husbands or wives? Maybe they had kids. What if they had kids? I raised my face to look up at Carter and say something along those lines. When I did, I glimpsed something dark in the air behind us, something hidden in the shadows pushed back by Amy's flames, something with a smooth skull and pointed ears, with fangs and claws, leathery wings, and a wicked expression. Something that had come out of nowhere and was barreling right towards Carter.

There wasn't time to warn him. His gun was shoved down the back of his jeans. I didn't wait. I didn't think. I simply reacted. I grabbed the gun, flicked the safety off as I raised it, and fired.

It all happened at once.

Carter spun as he felt me grab the gun. Grunted in surprise when I fired. The monster hit the ground as Amy and Blake's shouts of surprise rose.

Then everything was silent except for the ringing in my ears. It wasn't necessarily from the gunshot. The gun had a suppressor. It was shock, sheer shock at what I'd done.

I'd moved because my body took over, recognizing danger and reacting before my mind could even catch up. Now my mind had caught up, and it realized the body on the ground, morphing back into the figure of a middle-aged woman with jet black hair and long, brilliant red nails was there, motionless, because I'd put it there. I had pulled the trigger. I had shot someone. I had killed someone. My hands were still holding the gun. My arms were trembling. I couldn't look away from the corpse at the end of the barrel. Not until I felt Carter clasp my arm with one hand and with the other gently grab the gun, taking it away.

"Let me have it, kid."

I didn't protest. I didn't have any arguments or protests left. I couldn't stop staring at the body. I felt the heaves starting.

"I think I'm gonna be sick," I moaned.

Carter grabbed my shoulders, spinning me around.

"Don't do it on me," he snapped. "Try not to do it at all. We don't need to leave behind more evidence."

I tried to hold it back, but my stomach heaved, the vomit came, and I curved over as it poured out of me. Afterward, the spasms came, rocking my body from my toes all the way up to my head. I shut my eyes as Carter drew me back from the pile of vomit on the ground at my feet, but I kept seeing that monster, arguably the most terrifying shifter yet. I kept feeling my finger pull the trigger, kept feeling the gun kick, kept seeing the monster plummet and the woman lying there.

The woman.

Not a monster.

A woman.

A human being.

I'd been raised to believe human life was sacred. That was partly why I'd wanted to go into nursing. To help save lives. Now,

I wasn't a savior. I was a killer. I'd killed someone. Was I a monster too?

"C'mon, Ellie, pull it together." I heard Carter in the background, talking to me, sternness in his voice, trying to penetrate the fog and grab me, pull me back from the abyss. "This isn't the worst thing you've seen tonight. You didn't do anything wrong. We need to take care of this and get out of here before someone calls the police."

*Calls the police.*

"Yes, that's what we need to do. We need to call the police."

"What?" I heard Amy sputter a laugh. "Why would we do that?"

I straightened slowly and turned to look at them: Blake, Carter, Amy. They were all regarding me with various degrees of incredulity. I felt just as incredulous that they didn't understand.

"I just—I just killed someone," I stammered. "We need to call the police. Let them know what happened."

"Yeah, because the police react so well when you call and tell them you killed someone. Right," Amy said, rolling her eyes, the flames that still burned reflecting off the golden orbs.

"But—but he said I didn't do anything wrong. It was self-defense. I can't be charged for that, can I?"

"Do you really want to run that risk?" Blake challenged.

"I want to do the right thing," I whispered, feeling small and helpless and overwhelmed. So overwhelmed I didn't know if I was expressing this correctly, if I was making any sense.

Apparently I wasn't making any sense to them.

"You did do the right thing, Ellie," said Amy, a little kinder now. "You protected Carter. But you can't call the cops. What are you going to tell them? How are you going to explain being out here in the Garden at this time of night? What's your story for why the woman attacked? Are you going to explain about shifters to the police? What do you think that'll get you? I'll tell you what —twenty-four hours in a psych ward and a doctor insisting on medications. And that's before they arraign you and take you to trial for murder. Is that what you want to risk?"

"Yes. No. I don't know."

My head hurt. Somebody was pounding on the back of my neck with a hammer, and the pain was bursting rhythmically inside my skull.

I guess Carter could tell I wasn't in any sort of shape to be making decisions.

"Leave her alone, Amy. She doesn't need this," he ordered. Then, "Blake?"

"I'll take care of it."

I wasn't sure what he was taking care of until I saw him walk past Carter and me, stoop next to the body, and scoop it up. He carried the woman over to the pile of half-burned bodies already scorched by Amy's flames. Her pale arm flopped limply over his elbow. He didn't bother with any niceties or respect for the dead; simply dumped her onto the charred corpses.

"Alright. Finish it up, Amy, so we can go. Make sure you get the puke, too. No traces left behind."

Amy didn't respond verbally to Blake's directive, but I heard the intake of her breath, then that loud whooshing, the blast of flame, wind, air. I knotted my fists, squeezing my eyes shut against the light that hurt my eyes and exacerbated my headache, against the pain drubbing in my skull and the hideous reality of what I'd stumbled into, what I'd done. I'd seen sickness and death at the hospital, but not like this. I couldn't bear to watch these people burn. I stood next to Carter with my eyes closed until it was all over. Until the warmth on my side, the warmth of dragon flame devouring human bodies, had died down, until the crackling and popping and hissing of the fire had diminished and the smell of roasting human flesh drifted off into the night.

Dragon fire must have worked differently than regular fire. It only took a few minutes. When I finally dared to peek, I saw nothing more than a black, charred spot on the ground where the bodies of the shifters had been, along with piles of soot and ashes. Ashes on the earth that the breeze stirred and picked up and carried away.

Carter said, "It's over. Time to get you out of here."

And I went with him, because I had nowhere else to go.

## CHAPTER TWELVE

The hum of the engine was soothing as we drove, passing underneath alternating patches of darkness and light from the street lights. Holding my glasses in my hand, I leaned my head back and closed my eyes, trying to shut out the world around me. The heater in Blake's truck didn't work so well, and I was still cold, shivering. I didn't know where we were going. When I inquired, Carter said,

"Somewhere safe. I promise."

I wasn't so sure I believed him.

"You said that before. Then I got attacked at your place."

"Nosizwe found out about you much quicker than I figured she would."

"Uh huh."

I opened my eyes to slits, staring at his blurry profile.

"So you promised to keep me safe, and you did that by bringing me out to the Botanic Garden and using me as bait?"

He glanced over at me.

"You complaining? You're still alive. The shifters she put on your tail aren't."

"That's not the point. You used me as bait."

He didn't seem to get it. "Yeah. So?"

"You. Used. Me. As. Bait," I said louder, firmer.

I wanted to scream at him. It wouldn't have done any good. He continued to stare at me like he had no idea why I was upset. How can you argue with someone like that?

Heaving a disgusted sigh, I looked away.

"You could've told me what was going on. You could've warned me. You could've said something, but you didn't. I can't trust you, Carter."

"You can't trust me?" He laughed, mockingly. "Who just took out three of Nosizwe's best shifters? That Erymanthian boar that Blake decapitated? That was Turner, one of her lead lieutenants. We've been after him a long time. Nosizwe wasn't leaving anything to chance. You popped up out of nowhere, helping Sean's family, saving their lives, and she wanted you dead because of it."

"She's going to want me dead even more now."

"Nah, I don't think so." He slowed to take the off ramp. "Nosizwe isn't stupid. And she isn't wasteful. The Nakki's attack didn't work, and she lost four shifters tonight. Five, if you count the griffin back at Sean's house. She'll back off and regroup. She may decide you're not worth it. That's my hope. That's why I planned it out the way I did."

"Planned what out?"

He took his eyes off the road to look at me again. "Taking out your tail all at once. Using you as bait. Before we left my apartment, after the Nakki attacked, I knew she had a tail on you. James's guys picked up the chatter quick. I could've kept driving you from place to place, hoping to throw them off, but I decided to end it for once and for all, instead."

"Risking getting me killed to prevent me getting killed..."

He snorted. "You weren't in any danger. I was there. Blake was there. Nothing was gonna get to you."

"How about the one that almost got to you?"

My throat tightened as I recalled that moment, that horrible moment, of seeing the monstrous shifter, like a gargoyle or a demon, flying straight toward him. At making the decision to pull his gun and shoot. Only I didn't recall making the decision. Instinct had taken over where my brain hadn't yet followed.

I saw him wince. "That was a little unexpected. James' intel only had three tailing you, not four. Nosizwe's good. Her man Turner was good. Our intel isn't always perfect. But, hey," he shrugged, "one less of Nosizwe's gang to worry about."

He was so cavalier about it. So cavalier about life and death and all this horror and bloodshed and magic. It angered me, but it made me sad too. What kind of life had he led to bring him to this point? Where killing four monsters who were also four other people was simply another night's work? Where almost being killed by a demon-looking creature was something he could brush off?

"You know, earlier you told me Sean tries to keep your world secret from humans," I said slowly, replacing my glasses and watching him as he maneuvered the truck into the narrower lanes of the inner city slums. "You said humans can't put up with differences in each other, much less tolerate shifters."

"What about it?"

I raised one shoulder. "I don't get it. Seems to me you don't have to worry too much about humans. You seem to be doing a pretty good job of killing each other off all on your own."

There was a yellow light in front of us. He could've made it, but he chose instead to stomp on the brakes, sending me pitching forward against the seatbelt. I gasped and threw out a hand, catching myself on the dash.

"You don't know *anything*," he said, his voice quiet and low, ugly. There was no one behind us, not in this area and at this time of night, and he didn't move the truck.

"You don't know anything," he repeated. "Sean and Nosizwe— they battle each other, yes. Because the stakes are high. They're warring over something that could be the survival or the extinction of all shifters, the world over. They both think they're doing what's best for us. Sometimes, to win a war, you have to have a few casualties. That's just the way of it. Humans? Humans wouldn't care anything about protecting us. They wouldn't care what's best for us. Humans would hunt us out of fear, or capture us for science experiments, or put us in their zoos and freak shows."

"That wouldn't happen," I tried to object.

"It wouldn't? You really think that hasn't happened before? That throughout the history of the world we haven't been sideshow attractions, or accused of witchcraft, burned at the stake and drowned, kidnapped and sold on the black market, or dissected so they could try to discover what makes us tick? You really think that hasn't happened?"

I'd struck a raw nerve, and his anger, his bitterness against humanity were truly frightening.

"Maybe, maybe in the past," I conceded, "but it wouldn't happen now."

"You don't know what you're talking about if you think it wouldn't happen now," he sneered.

He pressed the gas, making the truck lurch forward, ignoring the fact that we'd sat there so long the light had switched back to yellow again.

"If the human world at large discovered us, there would be people after us. Trophy hunters. Scientists. Governments. Some wanting to use our abilities in their wars, and some wanting to take us out to keep the peace and protect their own population. We'd be decimated in no time. Destroyed. Burned out."

"Burned out like they were back there," I observed. "Turned into ashes."

He glanced over at me. "What?"

"Ashes," I repeated, thinking of the incinerated bodies, scorched to mere ashes and blown away by the wind. "Ashes, like the bodies Amy burned. Shifters turned into nothing but ashes. Ashes on the earth."

He gave me a funny look before turning back to the road.

"That's one way of putting it. Actually it's...a pretty good way of putting it."

I guess he was done arguing for now. Silence fell between us the rest of the drive.

---

He took me to a motel. Not a nice hotel, but a cheap motel in a rundown, crappy part of the city. Rusted bikes were piled in one corner of the weed patch that passed for a lawn. Bags of trash on another. Beer cans and bottles littered the alley behind the building. I shuddered. Hookers wouldn't be out of place standing on the street corner, and you could probably find any illegal drug you wanted. A woman in my condition wouldn't be looked at twice, meaning it was easy to hide, except for the car.

Blake had been the solution for that. We were in his truck for a reason. We'd left the Botanic Garden's driveway, driven to Blake's truck at Trinity Park, and switched cars. His truck was a couple decades old and didn't stand out in this part of the city like the fancy European car would. Amy flew off in dragon form, presumably back to her car. I'd heard Carter thanking her for her help, promising to put in a good word with Mr. Costas for her.

Now, I huddled in the truck while Carter went inside the office to check in. The neon lights of the sign overhead were broken, blinking and flashing in time with the pounding in my skull.

*Please,* I prayed. *Let me have some peace tonight. Just a little peace. No more fighting. No more arguing with Carter. No more killing. No more anything. No more, no more. Please let me sleep. Let me wake up tomorrow, safe at home, and have all of this be a nightmare.*

The sound of the truck door opening startled me. I bolted upright, but it was only Carter standing there next to me, wearing a grimy old shirt of Blake's that had been lying in the backseat.

"Let's get you inside."

I obeyed, moving stiff and slow like an injured or elderly person. Honestly, there wasn't anything physically wrong with me, besides a few bumps and bruises, but all the powerful emotions crashing over me had rendered my limbs practically useless. Carter had to help me down; Carter, who kept so calm under pressure. Unless he was talking about his people—shapeshifters versus humans. He showed more passion on that topic than anything else so far. Now, his hand cupped my elbow, lending me strength and support as he walked me to the door, using a key with a long tag on it to unlock it and get me inside.

"Sit there a minute," he said, leaving me on the edge of the bed as he went to flick on the lights. Again, he took the precaution of scoping out the room, although there wasn't much to scope out or see. One king bed, covered with a faded floral comforter from the 1980's. Nightstands with tiny, chipped lamps from the same era on either side. A chair. A TV on a scuffed dresser opposite the bed. A sink and mirror at the far end of the room, shower and toilet in the tiny, closed off room beside it. Still, he wasn't the type of man to leave anything to chance, and he came back from peeking in the bathroom, shoving his gun into his waistband, pulling the t-shirt down over it.

"You okay?" he asked, walking over and crouching in front of me, catching my eye.

I sat huddled on the bed, shaking. The tremors wouldn't stop. I didn't know if it was because I was scared, cold from the lack of heating in the truck, or from simply being overwrought, but I couldn't stop shaking.

"Hey, kid, c'mon," Carter said, laying a hand on my knee. "I know it's been a rough night, but you're still here. You're still alive. Don't fall to pieces on me now, okay?"

I tried to nod. I guess he decided that was good enough.

"Good girl."

Patting my knee, he stood.

"I'm going to move the truck and lock it up. Stay here. I'll be right back."

Again, I tried to nod. He took that for assent and left, shutting the door behind him. I heard the click of the automatic lock. Thought, *I should stay awake. I need to unlock the door for him when he comes back.*

Then I realized he must have the key with him, so I didn't have to worry about that, did I?

I couldn't worry about anything else. I couldn't think about anything else. That last conversation at the yellow light had done me in, expending whatever mental and physical energy remained. I crawled up to the head of the bed, took off my glasses and placed them on the nightstand, then pawed at the blankets and sheets to yank them free so I could climb underneath the covers. I should have checked for bed bugs or lice or stains on the sheets, but I was too spent to care. Part of me said I needed to shower. Again. I had blood on me. Probably vomit too. The other part of me remembered the creature Carter had called the Nakki, which had attacked me through the water of the shower. I didn't want to risk that again. And, honestly, I didn't have the energy for a shower, nor did I have any clean clothes to put on afterward. And I sure wasn't about to run around in front of Carter with no clothes on.

*Carter...*

I'd claimed in the truck that I didn't trust him, and I didn't think that I did. However, despite the fatigue dragging at my body and shutting down my brain, I didn't allow myself to pass out until I heard the key in the lock, heard the door click open, and saw him walk back into the room. He shut the door, turned the deadbolt. I thought,

*Okay, he's in. He's safe. But there's only one bed. Where's he going to sleep?*

It was a problem too complex for me to worry about. I couldn't decide. He'd have to figure it out for himself.

My eyelids closed and I went out.

## CHAPTER THIRTEEN

Carter glanced over at the bed as he re-entered the room. Ellie was huddled up under the blankets. His first thought was she was probably trying to get warm. Then he looked closer and saw her eyelids slide shut. By the time he'd locked the door, dropped the plastic shopping sack full of supplies he'd bought for her earlier on the floor, and sank into the chair to pull off his shoes he heard a soft snore. Surprised, he twisted in the chair to study her. In the yellow glow from the lamp, he could see her mouth was half open, and wild blonde hairs protruded all around her face

The snoring was funny for some reason, coming from a waif like her. He half-smiled as he bent to unlace his boots and kick them off. Bet if he teased her about it tomorrow she'd get embarrassed and deny it. Probably turn bright red. She was so pale she couldn't hide her embarrassment. He'd never seen anyone flush quite as brightly as her.

Rising, Carter walked over to the dresser and set his boots next to it. He took off his belt and emptied his pockets, removing wallet, keys, and phone, placing them next to the TV. He stripped off his shirt as he walked into the bathroom area, tossing it onto the counter next to the sink. He didn't bother removing the gun until he'd stepped into the combination shower/toilet stall, and even then he laid the gun on the back of the toilet, keeping it nearby, close at hand...just in case.

He didn't think there would be any more attacks tonight. Like he'd told Ellie earlier in the truck, Nosizwe wasn't a fool. There came a point when the best leaders knew it was time to back off. One of Nosizwe's most trusted lieutenants, Turner, was dead, taken out by Blake. That alone was enough of a setback for her to call off her forces, at least for the time being. Carter had called James outside, and there was no more chatter. Everything was quiet. Hopefully, they hadn't been tracked here. He'd move them again in the morning, but, for now, he knew Ellie had to get some rest or she'd lose her sanity. It was unimaginable what the woman had gone through tonight.

*Ellie.*

Carter stood under the hot spray of the shower, thinking about her. Measuring her up. His preliminary impression of her at the Costas house had been mousy and socially awkward. Ill at ease. In the car, their first car ride after the initial attack, she'd been angry. Scared at his apartment. There had been that moment in the bathroom, after he'd saved her from the Nakki, when she'd scuttled away from the Talos, every bit as frightened of him as the water-shifter. But when he'd reversed to human form, she'd clung to him. Clutched him. A lot like she'd done in the Garden a little while ago, after the danger was past and Amy was disposing of the bodies.

Or the danger was nearly past.

He still couldn't believe she'd pulled his gun and shot the gargoyle bearing down on him. Couldn't believe someone as frail looking and sheltered as her had had the presence of mind to reach for his weapon, click the safety off, aim, and fire. Clearly, she knew something about firearms. Dead shot too, despite the dimness. Her father was military. Maybe he'd trained her.

Whatever instincts she had for protecting other people, they were strong. Like with Jackson Costas, Ciara Costas, and now himself. She was made of much sterner stuff than she appeared. Carter had to give her that. And he also had to admit, as he climbed from the shower and toweled himself off, she may have had a sheltered upbringing that left her a little out of pace from the rest of society, but, then again, he was out of pace too. Boy, was he. They didn't see eye to eye on lots of issues, but...

He cracked the bathroom door, peeking out to make sure she was still okay, sleeping soundly, before he stepped back inside to get dressed.

She was growing on him. Whether it was the inner courage underneath the outward shell, or the fact that she'd felt...good... close to him when she'd held onto him, he didn't know. He shouldn't be reacting like this, especially to a human woman. It was stupid, and it irritated him. Downright stupid. But there was no denying he'd noticed the softness of her body, and how she'd felt so small next to him, making him feel like he wanted to gather her up and crush her close. Wrap her up and protect her.

*It's the Talos*, he told himself, exiting the bathroom. *Just the Talos. It's not me. It's certainly not her. She's not my type.*

The Talos was a creature created to protect and defend. Maybe the Talos' instincts were taking over Carter's human side too, as far as she was concerned. The Talos, as a bodyguard, was responding to her clear instincts to protect other people. The Talos understood that. Respected it.

But the mental images filling his mind of her in his wet t-shirt, of her bare leg sticking out from beneath the couch throw, and her body pressed up against his...the Talos had nothing to do with that. That was sheer, male attraction, an attraction he shouldn't be feeling. Images he felt like a dog for recalling at all.

Guilt wasn't something he experienced often, and Carter didn't like it. He tried to distract himself from the images, from the guilt, as he made a hasty final check of the room. He put the gun on the nightstand and switched off the lamp before peeling back the thin comforter, the sheets, and climbing into bed. Across the mattress, Ellie stirred, mumbled something, and buried her face deeper into the pillow. Carter shut his eyes and tried to will himself to sleep, but his mind was too full.

Mostly of her.

Every nerve in his body seemed fine-tuned to the fact that he was in bed with her. It was stupid, and he tried to block out mental awareness of her, but either his brain or the inner Talos wasn't having it. She was there, she was right there. He twisted his neck to look at her. It wasn't like he was doing anything wrong. He wasn't trying to seduce her. He wasn't touching her. She was on the far side of the bed, on a king sized mattress. They weren't in any danger of touching. She was fully dressed. He had jeans on, for Pete's sake. Wasn't like he'd come to bed naked.

But she still wouldn't like it.

Maybe that was why he couldn't relax, couldn't sleep.

Because he knew, if she knew, she would disapprove. She'd known him for one night, and a girl like that didn't get in bed with a guy after one night, not even to sleep.

*What she doesn't know won't hurt her.*

True, but he still felt like he was violating her space, her trust in some way, and no matter what arguments he used, he couldn't stop feeling that way.

Cursing himself for being an idiot, he finally pushed back the blankets and sat up, swinging his legs off the side of the bed. He sat there a moment, thinking, *What the crap have I gotten into? What am I doing?* Sighing, he rose to get a drink from the sink, wishing he had a bottle of gin to knock back a shot or two. Instead, there were little plastic cups wrapped in plastic film by the side of the sink. He unwrapped one, got a drink, and came back to the bed. This time, he didn't bother lying down, but grabbed the remote from off the top of the TV as he passed by, sat on the edge of the mattress, and powered the machine on.

He turned the volume down low, so as not to awaken the girl, and started flipping channels, seeking anything to distract himself or hold his interest. It was typical late night TV, meaning mostly infomercials, talk show comedians, and reruns of old shows he cared nothing about. The images flickered past his vision, nothing standing out, nothing sticking.

Carter scrubbed a hand down his face. He was tired. On a normal night, he'd be in bed asleep, either in his apartment or in his rooms at the Costas mansion. Not stuck in a roach motel with a woman he couldn't sleep next to, much less sleep with. There was only one reason to be in a room like this with a woman, and this sure wasn't it.

*You need to get laid,* he told himself. *Maybe that's your problem. It's been too long.*

Whether that was the root of the problem or not, he didn't know, but he kept flipping channels, finally finding some sports station discussing college and pro football stats and recaps. Okay, not bad. He liked American football. As a kid, coming to the States, it had taken awhile to get used to their version of the sport, but nobody could live in Texas and not be touched by the general craze for college football in that part of the country. Not to mention the fact that one of the most famous pro football teams out there, the Dallas Cowboys, were one city over in the giant Texas Metroplex.

How long he sat there, absorbing soundbites and reels, watching talking heads discuss tackles and kicks, sacks and passes, he didn't know, but it was long enough that his mind had finally quieted. Quieted until he started hearing shuffling from the bed behind him, along with little whimpers. Carter rotated to see Ellie, who was moving. Light from the television provided sufficient glow that he could see her curl up tighter into a fetal position. Straighten out. Curl up again. Her hand popped out from under the blanket and thrashed around. She grabbed a handful of the comforter, squeezed it, and moaned. Her jaw was clenched.

The snoring had stopped altogether, replaced by tiny moans and whimpers, sounds of distress.

Nightmares.

He wasn't surprised. Carter watched her a minute, uncertain if he should try to wake her up or leave her be. In the end, he shrugged and went back to the TV. She'd either come out of it on her own, or she'd wake up. Not much he could do, really. He doubted she wanted to turn to him again for comfort tonight.

She quieted, and he thought the moment was past. That she'd gone back to sleep. There were a few seconds of silence, punctuated by soft chatter from the screen. Then, the bed squeaked and the blankets swished as Ellie bolted upright behind him. Again, he turned to look and saw her sitting there, her chest heaving beneath his borrowed shirt, hair sticking out all over the place, gulping great swallows of air. She was staring dead ahead, then glanced around wildly, to the right, to the left. Her eyes landed on him.

"Carter?"

"It's me."

She squinted like she wasn't sure, like she didn't trust that he was the only one there and she was safe.

"It's me," he said again. "It's okay, Ellie. Go back to sleep. You're fine."

She swallowed, shut her eyes, ran a hand up over her face, her hair, down the back of her neck.

"I keep—I keep dreaming about it all. Nightmares. I just want them to go away. I just want to sleep."

Carter didn't say anything. He didn't know what to say. He could do a lot of things, but he couldn't magically make her nightmares vanish.

She dropped her hand with a sigh. "I need to go home."

Unfortunately, he couldn't do that for her, either, but the way she said it, in a sad, small voice, tugged at him in ways he wasn't familiar with, ways he didn't expect. He watched her shove away the blankets and get up. Like he'd done earlier, she walked over to the sink, unwrapped the other plastic cup, turned on the faucet and filled it up. She drained the glass in two gulps, set it down, and walked back to the bed. Carter turned to the television as she laid down again. Hopefully, she'd sleep now. But after several minutes of shuffling around, she finally gave up. Crawling back out from beneath the covers, she stood up again, this time walking around the foot of the bed to take a seat next to him. Not close enough to be in any danger of touching, but next to him, all the same. He gave her a sideways glance, a little surprised, but kept quiet.

She sat there in silence a few moments, watching the talking heads on the screen. She hadn't retrieved her glasses, so he didn't know how much she could actually discern. From the corner of his vision, he could see she looked abnormally pale and there were dark smudges beneath her eyes. Her hair was a wreck. Her freckles stood out against the pallor of her face. She looked bad. Or so his brain thought. Other parts of him noticed the curves beneath his shirt, the outline of her thigh in the soft pants. He wrenched his gaze away, disgusted with himself for being an idiot.

After several minutes, she sighed. Then said quietly, "Carter? Can we talk?"

Talking didn't seem like a good idea.

"Not in the mood."

He flicked the channel. Starting flicking through channels. Maybe she didn't like sports. Maybe he could find something else that would distract her. Distract her from talking to him. Distract him from noticing her. He didn't like noticing her. He didn't like noticing he was attracted to her, or that something about her was infiltrating his nearly lifelong dislike of humans in general.

"Okay."

She sounded tired and defeated. Discouraged. Like she'd been crushed too often tonight to fight back this time. Against his better judgment, he studied her again. Her shoulders had slumped. She looked disheartened. She probably needed to discuss what she'd witnessed tonight, what she'd seen and done. She probably wanted answers. An entire world had opened up before her. She had to have a million questions. He just didn't feel like answering them.

It was easier to discount her when she was angry and arguing. When she was livid, unwilling to cooperate, it was easier to see her as only a human, one of the enemy, incapable of understanding or accepting a creature like him. It was easier to goad her and make her mad than to ignore her while she sat there giving in, refusing to fight. Then, he felt sorry for her. Felt guilty that she'd been dragged into his world, his life, where she had absolutely no business being.

She shifted, glancing around, recapturing his attention. She was shivering all over. Her body still hadn't calmed down from the fright and terror. Mute, she rose and walked back to the head of the bed, grabbed the comforter and pulled it down towards the foot of the bed. She reseated herself, wrapping it around her shoulders. Only, when she did, she looked at him and seemed to notice, for the first time, that he was sitting there wearing only jeans.

"Aren't you cold?" she asked.

"I'm fine."

The room was a little chilly, but he was pretty sure her shivers were more from nerves than actual cold.

"I can't stop shaking. It's so cold in here. You must be cold."

She stood up and flipped one end of the blanket over one of his shoulders, trying to share, but anger surged through Carter and he ripped it off.

"I said I'm fine."

She retreated a step, her face falling.

"Okay. I'm sorry. I was only trying to help."

"I don't need your help."

"Okay. I'm sorry," she repeated, backing off.

This time, when she resumed her seat, he noticed that she sat several inches further from him.

Her shoulders hunched and she gathered the comforter tightly around herself, huddling inside it like armor. Possibly to protect herself from the cold, or else from him.

He felt like he'd kicked a puppy, but he didn't want her being nice to him. Didn't want to see the nurturing side of her that made her pursue a career as a nurse, ultimately a pediatric nurse, working with sick kids and babies. As long as he thought of her as only a job, he'd be fine. As long as he thought of her as only a human, someone he couldn't like or trust, he'd be okay.

If she'd maintained her initial fear of him, it would be easier to think of her like he, as a shifter, had always thought of humans. It wasn't okay to think of her as a desirable woman, no matter how his body shouted otherwise. And it sure wasn't okay to think of her as a person, an entire person, with peculiarities and flaws, but a good heart in spite of it all. Thinking of her like that was dangerous, because it removed the barriers between them. And right now, Carter felt like he needed all the barriers he could sustain.

## CHAPTER FOURTEEN

How long we sat in silence, I don't know. Now, along with the trauma and the fear and the crushing, overwhelming guilt at having killed someone, I felt bad for offending the man next to me, like I'd done something wrong when I was trying to be nice. Maybe he'd thought I was smothering him. Some men didn't like that, or so I'd heard. It wasn't like I spent tons of time with men outside family, church, school, and the hospital. I sure hadn't spent any time with a man like Carter, and I found him difficult to read.

I didn't focus long on having upset him, though. I was too worried about my family. I'd never stayed out all night without contacting them. Never. I knew my mom was probably frantic right now. I felt so guilty about that, knowing she must be worried sick. I wanted to call her, text her, reassure her—but when I glanced at Carter his jaw was set and he was practically punching buttons on the remote with his thumb. I was scared to ask him for any favors. Scared he'd bite my head off, like he had a second ago.

*Huh. Bite my head off.*

The irony of that made me smile, since one or more of those

creatures tonight might actually have bitten my head off. If not for Carter. Carter and his allies, his meticulous planning, his ability to alter forms into a bronze statue.

Okay, so he might snap at me, but he wasn't going to hurt me, right? After all I'd survived tonight, I could handle some grumpiness. Grumpiness was the least of my problems.

I pep-talked myself for a while before finally daring to speak. Even when I did, I started with a lesser request.

"Carter?"

"What?"

His tone wasn't friendly. I had no idea what I'd done to irritate him so badly, unless he was still mad from our argument in the truck. Or possibly at this entire situation and at being trapped here with me, protecting me.

"I know this sounds really weird right now, but...I'm hungry."

"Well, why don't you call up room service, then, and have them deliver something from the five star dining room?" he said, not even bothering to look at me.

Resentment surged, coupled with a thread of hurt.

"You don't have to be nasty. I didn't ask to be put in this situation. If you hate me this much, and hate being here with me this much, then send me home. My family and I will pack up and move. We'll get out of here, if that's what it takes. Then your job is done and you don't have to worry about me anymore."

"Hmmmph." He snorted through his nose.

"What?"

"Go home and tell your family. Get them to move. Yeah. What're you planning to tell them, Ellie? Tell them about the big, bad scary shifters? Tell them about the one that's dragged you around all over the place tonight, the one who turns from a man into a bronze statue? They gonna believe you, gonna pack up and leave their lives here and move you away to keep you safe? Good luck, kid."

I stared at his profile, the short, black hair, the close-trimmed dark beard, the olive skin, wondering how bones and flesh and blood and cells could unloose and re-knit and change and re-fashion themselves into skin and flesh of bronze. In the world of science, the world of reality, they couldn't. Things like this didn't happen.

So what would my family think if I came home and told them about Carter, about Sean Costas, about Blake and Amy and all the rest?

They wouldn't believe me. They would think I was high or drunk, which wasn't me, but how else would they explain it away? Maybe they'd think I had a brain tumor or brain injury. They'd take me to the hospital to get evaluated. The more I insisted on what I'd seen, the more they'd know something was wrong—but they'd probably think that something wrong was with me.

"Fine. You may be right," I allowed, "but you don't have to be a jackass about it."

"I'm not trying to be an ass," he replied, his tone half-apologetic.

I shot him a glare, which he caught.

"What? That's not a cuss word. You said it first."

"I did not. I said jackass. That's a male donkey. It's different, and yeah, you were too."

"I really wasn't," he disagreed. "But we are stuck together for now, like it or not. You can't tell your family about this. That would be stupid, as well as dangerous. I've got a couple of people on your house. Best thing you can do is stay away. Nosizwe might know your name, but there are other folks with your family name in this city. She might not have figured out about your family yet. Her intel's never been as good as ours. Anyway, keeping away makes it look like they're not your weakness. Which means you're stuck with me for the time being."

"Does being stuck with you mean I have to starve?"

It was easier to ignore my true plight by focusing on the small things, like the fact that I was hungry. I couldn't believe I was hungry, but I was. I wanted something warm, something with cheese and hot sauce. Some junk food that was horribly unhealthy but comforting and familiar.

"So, what do you want me to do about it, Ellie?" He twisted, tossing the remote on the bed.

"One of those food delivery services?"

"They won't deliver in this part of town. Not this late at night."

"You could go get me something." His eyes narrowed in the darkness of the room, lit only by the flickering of the screen. "And while you're at it..." I swallowed to wet my dry throat, nervous even to ask. "You could get me a burner phone."

Now his scowl darkened.

"You promised," I said, refusing to wilt. "You promised when we got to our next safe spot that you'd get me a burner phone so I could contact my family. Well, we're here. And I want to contact my family."

I didn't mean for my throat to swell and my voice to crack on that last word, but it did. Quickly, I turned my face away. I wanted my mom. I felt like a little kid for admitting it, but right now I wanted my mom more badly than I'd ever wanted her in my life.

As I sat there battling myself, trying to get my emotions under control, I heard a quiet sigh from the man behind me.

"What do you want to eat?" he asked.

"Huh?"

I turned back to him, scrubbing the traces of moisture off my cheeks.

"I said, what do you want to eat?"

"Um, are you going to go get it?"

He shook his head, pointed towards his cell phone.

"I can't leave you here alone, but put in a quick call and I can get anything delivered. Mr. Costas has people for everything. Believe me. Everything."

"Oh, I hate to wake someone up and put them out just for me—"

"Stop it, Ellie," he snapped. "Stop being self-sacrificial. That's what got you in this mess in the first place. You wanted it, you're getting it. It's their job. Tell me what you want, I'll put in a call. I'll have them bring a burner phone too. You can talk to your family, but only for a few minutes, okay? And no telling them where we are or what's been happening. You're only allowed to tell them that you're safe. That's it. Tell them you're safe, and you'll be home when you can. Try to do more than that, and I'm ripping the phone away. Got it?"

I nodded. I didn't doubt he meant every word he said.

---

Forty-five minutes later, a car pulled up into the hotel parking lot. Carter rose to part the curtains and look outside.

"That's him," he said to me. "Stay here."

And he went outside, without even bothering to throw on a shirt or put on shoes, to meet the car's driver. I obeyed, remaining on the edge of the bed, where I'd sat for the last while.

Earlier, he'd gone outside to place the call to—whoever he called. Someone in his extensive network of colleagues and flunkies, I supposed. He'd stood right outside the window, shirtless and barefoot like he was now, hunched slightly against the cold. I'd stared at him through the frayed, filmy curtains, simply stared and tried to figure out who he was and what made him tick. He could be such a smart-aleck. Such a jerk. Condescending and rude. Bitter. Seemingly at me and the world around us.

Then again, as soon as I'd sniffled over missing my parents he'd caved and contacted someone to bring me both food and a phone. He'd let me cling to him after the attack in his bathroom, when his bronze alter ego had crushed the bathtub floor, sending the Nakki back to wherever it had come from. He'd let me cling to him again in the Botanic Garden, after rescuing me from the Mothman and the other shifter, after I'd shot the gargoyle or the demon—whatever it was—to save him. He'd gone shopping for me and brought me clothes, personal products. Even thought to grab shoes. What kind of guy does that?

*I killed someone to save him*, I'd thought, gazing at him outside. I was still having trouble wrapping my mind around that fact. *I killed someone. Someone is dead because of me. I killed them to save him. Why? Why did I do that?*

As if my thinking about him somehow snagged his attention, Carter had glanced up from outside the window and looked in. Our eyes had met through the dirty glass, the faded curtains. His dark gaze narrowed, pinning me for a second before he turned around, hunching in a little further, finishing up his phone conversation. Was he aggravated that he'd caught me staring at him?

Since his back was presently turned and he wouldn't know, I sat there studying him. Every line and outline was taut with muscle. He looked like a bodybuilder, but was that him or was it because of the thing he turned into? He was already big, but when he shifted his upper form became simply massive. Every time he'd shifted his shirt had been ripped off. His power, both as a human and a shapeshifter, was undeniable, daunting. Frightening. But he hadn't used that strength against me, only to protect me.

So far.

Yes, so far. Clearly, he resented something about me. Possibly the fact that I was a human and he didn't seem to care for humans at all. There seemed to be something underlying that, something when he'd said, *Sean and Nosizwe—they battle each other, yes. Because the stakes are high. They're warring over something that could be the survival or the extinction of all shifters, the world over.* I didn't understand that. I wanted to know, but when I'd asked if we could talk he'd shut me down quick.

Earlier, after he'd finished his call and returned to our room, I'd noticed he sat in the chair instead of on the end of the bed, next to me. He didn't say a word, just slumped there, arms crossed, kind of glaring at the screen. The silence was so heavy, so awkward, that out of sheer desperation I'd finally picked up the remote and started changing channels. Finally, I found a sitcom from the 90's, *King of Queens*, that never failed to make me laugh. Some channel was hosting a weekend long marathon, so I sat the remote down and tried to distract myself with humor.

It hadn't worked very well. Nothing was funny tonight, but at least it gave me somewhere to pretend to focus instead of on the man in the chair. The minutes had dragged by until the car pulled up outside and Carter rose to fetch our delivery. Now, I observed through the smudged glass as he leaned into the car to talk to the driver for a minute before finally straightening, hands gripping two fast food sacks and a plastic grocery sack, hopefully containing my phone.

A phone.

Excitement swelled in my belly over finally being able to contact my parents, hear my mom's voice. By the time Carter walked back in our room, I was standing, the blanket dropped onto the bed behind me, waiting expectantly. He entered the room, nudged the door with his hip, then transferred all three sacks to one hand so he could lock the deadbolt and the sliding bolt.

"Did they bring a phone?"

He turned around and approached the bed.

"Yeah, yeah they brought a phone."

He placed the bags down on top of the thin floral comforter. Opened one, peered inside, slid it across the bed towards me.

"This one's yours."

"Thanks. But...the phone?"

He gave me an impatient look. "Would you chill? It's going to take me a minute to get it set up for you. Go ahead and eat. You're the one who was starving and couldn't wait."

I felt like a kid being reprimanded by their parent for asking the dreaded, *When will we get there?* Carter had this way of talking down to me that made me feel young and naive. I couldn't tell if he did it on purpose. Maybe he didn't know he was doing it at all, but it really aggravated me. It wasn't like he was that much older than me. Maybe eight or ten years. Maybe.

I didn't argue with him, though, mostly because I didn't want to make him mad enough to change his mind and refuse to give me the phone. Instead, I took the steaming sack of food and retreated to the far corner of the bed. Spreading a couple of paper napkins in my lap, I unwrapped a taco and ripped the corner off two hot sauce packets, dousing the taco's interior. Before eating, I paused to bow my head and silently give thanks—not only for the food, but for being alive tonight in spite of everything, and to ask for my family's protection.

And that the phone would work and Carter would cooperate so I could talk to them.

When I opened my eyes, it was to see Carter staring at me from across the bed. He had a half-unwrapped taco in one hand, and the package with the phone in the other.

"Did you pray over your food?"

I blinked at the sarcasm in his voice.

"Yes." I felt defensive. "Why are you surprised? You knew about my religion. Does saying grace bother you?"

He raised his eyebrows and looked away. "Doesn't bother me. Just don't see it often, even among religious people. Your business, not mine. You have a right to your beliefs."

"That's right, I do," I said, and started in on the tacos to forestall a debate on religion.

I couldn't believe how hungry I was. I'd vomited twice tonight, sick from watching violent death before my eyes. I'd killed someone. Food should've been the last thing on my mind. Even though I felt anxious and full of pent up nerves, my stomach was growling with hunger. Comfort eating, stress eating. Some people shut down under bad circumstances and don't eat at all. I was the opposite. Stress made me want to eat, and I devoured three tacos without stopping while watching Carter deal with the phone: opening the package, turning it on, pushing buttons, setting it up for me. He was eating too, but slowly, indifferently, because it was there, not because he had any interest in it. His entire focus at the moment seemed to be the phone. When he finished and looked up to hand it over, he saw the pile of wrappers next to me on the bed and the plastic dish piled with nachos in my lap and smirked.

"You ate all that already?"

My mouth was full of chips and cheese. I shrugged.

"As a nurse, you'd think you would know better. That crap stunts your growth. You better slow down."

I chewed and swallowed, grabbing a napkin to wipe yellow cheese sauce off my fingers. "Ha ha. I'm young, I'm human, I'm a Chaplain Assistant's kid, I was homeschooled, I pray before I eat, and I'm short. Anything else you want to make fun of me about? How about my freckles? Or my glasses?"

"No, I kind of like those. Give me some time. I'll come up with something else."

I glowered at him, but this time he only laughed. "I'm kidding, Ellie. Relax. I am surprised, though, that you can pack that much food away."

"Stress makes me eat."

"Apparently. Here." He handed the phone over.

"It's ready?"

I sat the nachos aside and retrieved it.

"Yep. You can call home. Remember the rules, though."

I nodded eagerly, already dialing my home phone number. I felt Carter's eyes on me as I stood, pacing while it rang. Once. Twice. On the third ring, my mom answered.

"Hello?"

She sounded like she'd been crying.

"Mom? It's me, Ellie."

"Ellie!" she practically shrieked, then I heard her hissing at my brothers. "It's Ellie. Quick, go get your dad!" Back to me, "Ellie, Ellie, where are you, honey? Are you okay? We've been worried sick! I couldn't find a number to call the Costas home. I couldn't reach anybody there to find out where you were. I was afraid there'd been a car accident. We called your phone a million times. Ellie, what are you doing? Where are you?"

Now that she'd heard from me, knew I was alive, I could hear a smidge of anger creeping into her voice that I'd dared to do this to my parents.

"Mom, I—I can't explain right now. I need you to trust me. I'm okay. I promise. I'm really okay."

But I wasn't okay. I was in a mess that defied belief, a mess that I had no idea how to get out of. I was depending on someone who goaded me at every turn to keep me safe, and I was helpless without him against the host of monsters that wanted me dead. I had killed someone and let them burn the body to cover it up. I was potentially running from the law, as well as an army of shapeshifters.

Tears filled my eyes and choked my voice as I lied through my teeth to my mother. I swiveled around so Carter, sitting on the bed, watching gravely, waiting for me to slip up, couldn't see.

"If you're okay, then you need to come home! Wait, here's your dad. Honey, talk to Ellie." She pushed the button to switch to speaker mode. "Tell her to come home right now."

"Ellie?" Dad's voice sounded calmer. "Where are you? What are you doing?"

"Daddy."

I didn't mean for it to, but my voice cracked on a sob.

"Ellie, what's—"

"Daddy, please. Please listen to me." I gulped several breaths to stop the tears. "I can't—I can't explain what's going on right now, but I promise I'm okay. Trust me. Please trust me. I'll be home as soon as I can. Try not to worry about me, okay? I love you guys. I love you all."

I heard the bed springs creak as Carter stood, walking towards me, extending his hand for the phone. He tapped the watch on his wrist, telling me it was time to get off.

"Mom, Daddy, I have to go. Wait, Mom, can you call the school and hospital for me? Or email them? Tell them I won't be in class for a few days. The names and numbers and email addresses you'll need are all in the red binder in my room."

"Ellie, this is ridiculous, no, I—"

Carter made a move for the phone. I shoved his hand away, retreated a few steps.

"Please, Mom. I love you guys. Tell the boys I love them too. I have to go."

"Ellie, don't you dare hang up—" Mom started to say, speaking on top of my father's, "Ellie, hey—"

It hurt too much. I punched the red button to end the call, surrendered the phone to Carter, and sank down on the floor, my back against the dresser and my bottom on the worn carpet that smelled faintly of cigarette smoke. I buried my face in my knees, and I sobbed. The floodgates had been unleashed. There was no more bridling the fear and horror, no more trying to be strong, no more attempts to hide my tears so Carter wouldn't see me fall apart.

Who cared what he thought? He was a stranger. He was here to protect me, but he was still a stranger. I'd never felt so alone in my life, never mind his presence, as I did then, pouring out my heart in sobs that wouldn't stop. I cried like my heart was broken, and maybe it was. I cried until I was physically exhausted and couldn't cry anymore. The knees of my pants were soaked and my nose was overflowing. When I finally lifted my face, Carter was there, handing me some napkins from the fast food bag.

"Here, kid. Blow your nose. Calm down. It's gonna be okay. I'll get you back with your family. I promise. Somehow, we'll make this right, okay?"

I didn't say anything, just blew my nose noisily, still breathing down shaky sobs. Carter's hand touched my back gently, almost hesitantly.

"Go back to bed, Ellie. You've got to get some sleep. Tomorrow's another day. We'll figure something out."

With his help, I managed to get on my feet and slump around the end of the bed. I took off my glasses and handed them to him. He set them on the nightstand as I more or less collapsed into the bed, face down in the pillow. It was Carter who went back to the foot of the bed and removed the remnants of the meal. Carter who drew the covers back up over my body. Carter who pushed my hair back from my face so he could smooth the blankets up over my shoulder and around my neck.

"Get some sleep, Ellie," he said again.

And I did. My eyes shut, and this time I dreamed the deep, fathomless sleep of the utterly exhausted.

# CHAPTER FIFTEEN

Fort Worth Police Department, Investigative and Support Command

Police homicide detective Candace Ewing pushed open the double glass doors of the Fort Worth homicide division and stepped inside. The smell of burned coffee, stale food, and bodies packed into too small a space assaulted her senses. It was too early in the morning for this, but that was the life when the homicide force was always in need of manpower. She was supposed to be off for the weekend, but she should've known better.

Maneuvering around furniture and fellow officers, Candace made her way to her own desk, slung her purse across the back of the chair, and plopped down. Shutting her eyes, she braced her elbow against the desktop and started rubbing her forehead, trying to get rid of the headache. There was a creak from the desk across from hers as her partner and fellow officer, Gary Tozzi stood up. Footsteps as he approached. Through the corner of her vision, Candace watched him take a seat on the edge of her desk.

"Morning."

"It's not a good morning," she mumbled.

"I didn't say it was good, I said it was morning."

"Can it really be called that yet?"

Gary chuckled. "Well, you do look nice this morning, if that's a comfort to you."

Candace raised her face to shoot her partner a glare. "Is that supposed to be a joke? I'm wearing last night's makeup and I didn't touch my hair before leaving the house."

He shrugged. "I think you look nice. That color suits you."

She glanced down, unsure what she'd even pulled on before leaving the house. A violet-colored blouse that contrasted well with her deep sable skin tone, grey slacks, a black leather jacket. Her hair was a sleek, chin length bob, with the ends angled towards her mouth. Technically, she had touched her hair this morning, running her hands over it a couple of times this morning on the drive in, trying to get it presentable for the day. The rest of her look, she wasn't so sure. Nor did she really care.

"Did you tie one on last night?" Gary now asked, dark eyes twinkling as he teased her. Gary was a morning person. Candace wasn't to begin with, and she sure wasn't on a morning like this.

"I was supposed to have the weekend off," she said, finally raising her head to squint at her partner. "I've worked thirty-eight straight days. Captain Hollands said he was going to make sure I didn't get called in today. So, yeah, I went to a party with my cousin. I should've known better."

Gary chuckled. "Yes, you should have. You know Fort Worth can't do without you."

Candace groaned, shielding her eyes again with her hand.

"One of these days, I swear I'm going to block his number on my day off so he can't call me."

"Nah, you won't."

"Why won't I?"

"You're too good a cop to do that."

"Being a good cop is why I'm always here with you instead of having a life outside the department."

"That's the nature of the beast," her partner replied, rising and walking away.

Candace didn't know where he was going and didn't bother checking. She and Gary got along because they understood each other. Gary, at nearly twenty years her senior, was tall, thin, and single with tan skin from his Italian heritage and prematurely white-grey hair. He had two failed marriages, mostly due to giving his life to the city and the force instead of his family. He had no kids, and no plans to remarry. Meanwhile, at thirty-four, Candace seemed stuck in a never-ending cycle of meaningless dates and the inability to develop deep relationships. There wasn't time to foster anything beyond a casual interest, not with murder victims and their families needing her attention at every turn.

A minute later, her partner was back, a cup of coffee, nearly white with creamer, in hand.

"Here, drink this. It'll make you feel better."

Candace's lower lip curled as she stared at the mug, embossed with the Fort Worth PD's logo.

"You know I can't drink that stuff on an empty stomach."

"I know. That's why I brought you this."

In his other hand was a donut. A frosted donut with red sprinkles, wrapped in a paper napkin.

Candace lifted an eyebrow. "Really? Offering a cop a donut? You're a walking cliché, you know that?"

"Yep. And for every cliché, there's some truth. Cops love donuts. Everyone loves donuts, and this one's your favorite. Go on, take it."

Reluctantly, she did. Gary placed the mug on her desk while she lifted the donut to her lips, trying to decide if her stomach would put up with it or not.

"While you're mulling over that donut, you want to hear what's landed in our laps today?"

"Hit me with it."

"Okay." Gary resumed his seat on the edge of her desk while Candace carefully took her first bite of the sugary treat.

"So groundskeepers at the Botanic Garden went in early this morning to do their thing before the park opened for the day. Over at the North Vista they found something strange. A big burned out patch, roughly eight feet by eight feet. Someone was in there last night setting a fire. They swear it wasn't there yesterday, so it had to be during the night."

"That sounds like a case for the fire department, not us," Candace mumbled around a mouthful of frosting and fried dough.

"You'd think. Hold on, though, this is where it gets interesting. When they searched a little further, they found traces of what appeared to be blood under nearby trees, along with a human tooth. CSU is out there now, canvassing the area, but they're thinking something went down there last night. Something ugly. Possibly a homicide. The Garden has been shut for the day so we can get out there and do our work, but management is already clamoring. They either want this investigation cleared up as soon as possible, or else that part of the park closed and the rest opened."

"They open the rest of the park, and some skeezeball's going to be over there slipping under the crime scene tape to take pictures and potentially destroying evidence."

"Exactly. That's why the captain called you in. We're supposed to get out there ASAP and look around. If a homicide has been committed, it falls on us. It's in our precinct. Everyone else is dealing with last night's shootout at Vickers Apartments."

"Lucky us."

"Yep, lucky us. So finish your donut, and get a few swallows of coffee."

"I can bring the coffee in the car."

"Not in my car you can't. Not without a lid."

Candace scowled at her partner.

"One accident, Gary. One accident."

"One accident and my carpet was stained forever."

"You stomped on the brakes!"

"To avoid rear-ending a semi! You're welcome for saving your life, by the way."

"You shouldn't have been driving so fast."

"You should've been paying more attention. Looking out the windshield instead of at your phone."

"Hey, that spill didn't do me any favors either, remember? I had a dry cleaning bill after that to save my blouse."

"Then that's another reason not to take open coffee cups in the car."

"Uuuuh," Candace groaned. "I'm done with you. Get out of here and give me a minute to drink this coffee. Find me something for this headache while you're at it, why don't you?"

"Yes, ma'am." Gary mock saluted as he stood.

He walked away as Candace devoured the rest of the donut. Her coffee had cooled to the point that she could gulp it, and she did, standing, trying to mentally prepare herself for the day. By the time Gary returned with a bottle of water and a couple of pills, her mug was half drained and her eyes were fully open. The headache wasn't gone yet, but at least she was functional.

"Ready?" Gary handed over the pills and water.

She cupped them in her hand, threw her head back and tossed them down, finishing with three long gulps of water.

"Ready."

Screwing the cap back on the water bottle, she set it on her desk, then checked her piece in its side holster, patted her pockets for her key, and slid her phone into her jacket pocket.

"Let's go."

The November morning air was still brisk and Candace was grateful for the leather jacket as she walked the perimeter of the North Vista, scouting out the scene. Yellow crime scene tape was strung between trees and stakes in the ground, marking off the burned area, which was visibly at odds with the rest of the crisp grass. Winter hadn't yet taken hold in Texas, and there was still some green to the grass, which may have helped prevent the fire from spreading. There hadn't been any recent rains to make the ground soft enough for capturing footprints, but the grass in the enclosure was matted and trampled. Scuffed up, actually. Like someone or something had been rolling around. There was also traces of what appeared to be dried blood both here and beneath the trees, several yards away.

She absorbed all of this through sunglasses; the darkened lenses kept the brightness from exacerbating her headache. Actually, getting outside into the nippy autumn air was easing her stomach and headache. She felt better. More awake. Finally alive. Gary stooped several feet away, staring at the dark spots where blood had seeped into the ground. Flies buzzed around spatters on trees, bushes. Samples had already been taken by CSU to test for DNA. Candace finally dared to walk over and hunch next to her partner, careful to keep the hem of her slacks out of the way.

"What do you think?" she asked.

"Burned bodies says someone who had an idea of what they were doing."

"Yeah, I don't know..."

"What don't you know?"

She shoved back the edges of her angled bob, tilting her head as she glanced at her partner.

"Burning usually isn't a good way to get rid of a body. You know how long it takes a body to burn? People don't realize it takes as long as it does. And there are usually bone fragments or teeth left behind."

"True, and there's nothing left here. Meaning some kind of accelerant must've been used. That says somebody who knew what they were doing. A first timer? There'd be something left. There's nothing left."

She stood, and Gary followed suit.

"Fire chief's already been sniffing around. He couldn't label any accelerants, but he took traces of the ashes—what they could find—for testing."

"That's right, there aren't many ashes, are there?" She studied the grass nearby. "It wasn't particularly windy last night, was it?"

"No more than usual. So whatever was used to get rid of the body, or bodies, must've burned it down very small. To nothing. Enough that what wind there was blew it away or scattered it."

"What kind of fire does that? Fire always leave something. Bones. Coals. Ashes," she listed, harkening back to her earlier observation. "There should be some bones here."

Twisting, she canned the area. There weren't. There was absolutely nothing, nothing except a scorched area. Traces of blood. One tooth, so far, although they were looking for others, and it had been found beneath the trees, not by the scorched spot.

"Detectives?"

A young CSU tech approached from behind, holding a bullet casing between two gloved fingertips.

"We just found this."

Gary and Candace exchanged looks.

"Well, that's interesting," Gary murmured, even as Candace drew her own gloves from a pocket, slipping on one before taking the casing. She held it between her partner and herself, turning it round and round, studying it in the early morning light.

"Where did you find this?"

"Right over there." The young tech indicated the area behind them.

"It's a 9 mil," Gary said. "Maybe a SIG, Beretta, Glock…?"

"Yeah…" Candace murmured. "Hmm. A 9 mil and a big burned spot. Looking more and more likely that somebody was killed last night."

"Possibly more than one?"

"It's possible. Not to mention the tooth way over there…" Both detectives swung to look at the area where the blood, the tooth had been found. "Blood on the far side of the burned spot, and then the burned area itself," Candace summarized.

"Fire that burned everything, leaving behind no traces of the victim. Or victims."

For some reason, her partner's remark sent a shiver down Candace's spine. Or maybe it was the sly morning breeze that snaked its way down the slight gap between jacket, blouse, and neck.

She and Gary exchanged glances from behind their sunglasses.

"This is a weird one."

"Yeah," her partner agreed, scratching his bearded chin. "It is. Gonna be hard to make a case without any bodies. Maybe impossible."

"We have the tooth."

"That proves one person was here. Maybe not even the vic. Maybe the killer? Defense could argue it belonged to a visitor from the park. Someone had an accident, lost their tooth. We can't prove they're wrong. Really, there's just nothing here."

"We have the blood."

"Again, could be vic's, could be killer's. Could be some kids tried to climb trees and scratched themselves. We'll have them run DNA, but that might not prove anything, either. It might not match anything in the system."

She sighed. "Well, it's a start."

This was their usual method of hashing out evidence, figuring out a case. She looked at the positives. Gary played devil's advocate, looking at the negatives.

"Detectives?"

Both officers turned as another uniformed officer approached. "We may have something else."

"What is it?"

He held up a tablet, flicked the screen a few times, then turned it around for them to see.

"Security footage from the main entrance. We've been checking the closest parking areas, where someone might have walked in, and we found something."

"What's the time stamp?" Candace asked, shoving her sunglasses on top of her head and leaning closer to peer at the tiny letters in the corner of the screen.

"Um, 10:25 P.M. Definitely after hours, and definitely not a time when anyone should've been out here."

"What about a couple sneaking in to get busy?"

Candace threw him a look of disgust. "Really, Gary? It was cold last night."

He shrugged. "Some people have their kinks. I'm just sayin'."

"Play it for us, Ed," Candace requested, and the officer pushed a button on the screen, allowing the grainy black-and-white images to flicker to life.

Some kind of fancy car pulled into the circle drive. A driver got out. The images weren't clear enough to tell much, but he was male. His hair was cut very close and he wore a beard. He went around to the passenger side and opened the door, and helped out a woman. Petite. Light hair. The man wasn't overly tall, but his upper body appeared big. The woman looked small next to him. Also, she was wearing only a t-shirt and pants; no jacket or sweater, despite the chilliness of the night. The man cupped the woman's elbow and led her away from the car, in the direction of the wall.

The video winked out.

"Wait, that's it?" Candace demanded, glancing up from the screen.

"That's it, Detective, except for a shot of them returning approximately an hour later. I can show you, but there's not much to see. Their heads are down and you can't see their faces any better."

"None of the security cameras picked up the license plate?"

"Nope. Wrong angles. But one of our techs recognized the car as an Aston Martin."

Candace turned to her partner.

"That's something," Gary acknowledged. "The number of Aston owners in Fort Worth can't be astronomical. We're not talking about a Ford or a Chevy here."

"Nope," Candace agreed. She addressed the officer. "Ed, have the video sent to Terrance. Have him clean up the images, and zoom in on the faces. Have him get as clear an image as possible. It's not much, but it's a start."

"Will do."

Ed left, taking the tablet with him.

Alone, Candace and Gary exchanged looks. "You think that's the suspects?" Candace asked.

Gary firmed his lips. Shook his head. "We have no bodies for the M.E. to determine time of death, but we know whatever went down happened during the night, because it sure wasn't here yesterday. Then we have this footage; they were out here, and headed into the Gardens. Clearly, they were up to something. But...could be a romantic tryst," Gary warned.

"Could be, but I doubt it."

"Why do you doubt it?"

"Gut feeling? Instinct? I'm pretty sure they were involved. The question is, how? Victims or killer?"

"We can't even prove if there was a victim. Or a killer."

"Well, we know something went down here last night, Gary!" Candace snapped. "Blood, a tooth, a burned space—something happened here, and, whatever it was, it wasn't pretty."

"All I'm saying is, unless more evidence turns up, you'll have a real hard time proving anything in court."

She sighed, jerking her sunglasses down, settling them on the end of her nose. "You're a pain in the neck, but you're right. Fine. We'll do our job, then. We'll look for more evidence."

## CHAPTER SIXTEEN

"Morning, sleepyhead. Time to rise and shine."

I was lying face down in the mattress with a pillow over my head. Carter's voice was muffled due to the pillow, but it was the second time he'd spoken, so I guessed that meant he wasn't giving up.

"Mmmm. Go away," I moaned.

"There's no going away, kid. Check out is at 11. It's 10:20 now. I'm not paying this dump another dime. You need to get up."

I didn't want to get up. I'd actually been drifting in and out of sleep ever since the sun broke the horizon and started filtering into our room. I'd flopped onto my stomach and put the pillow over my head to shut out the light and try to stay asleep. When I was asleep, unless I had nightmares, I didn't have to face a reality that included Carter and his ability to shift into a living bronze statue. I didn't have to face the fact that my parents were worried sick about me, or I was missing out on classes and clinicals that I didn't know how I'd ever make up. Asleep, dreaming, I could be home, safe and sound, where everything was normal...which I had been, until Carter started pestering me.

"You could've let me sleep until 10:45," I grumbled, finally finding the willpower to flip over and push myself up. "It's not like I have to change clothes and do my hair and makeup."

Carter half-chuckled.

"Wouldn't hurt you to. You're a mess."

I glared up at him, standing next to the bed.

"You are such a jerk."

"What, you want me to lie and tell you you're beautiful when you look like that?"

"I don't want you to say anything," I retorted, standing. "I don't care what you think I look like. I want you out of my life. That's what I really want."

"Ouch."

Without bothering to retrieve my glasses from the nightstand, I stormed past him standing there, still wearing only jeans, holding two foam cups, presumably of coffee, went into the little room with the toilet and slammed the door. It was the only place I could escape him. After locking it, I leaned my back against the door and shut my eyes.

Carter's remarks hadn't hurt my feelings. Not really. I was beginning to figure out he liked badgering me because it made me mad. With someone else, I might've been able to ignore it. Normally, I wasn't argumentative, and I wasn't confrontational. Normally, I was better at letting slights go, or else emotionally curling up in a ball and licking my wounds rather than responding.

Carter, though. Somehow he had this ability to get a rise out of me. He was such a smart mouth. Whether it was him, the situation we were in, or both, I didn't know. I wasn't truly mad about it. I was just…I didn't even know. Homesick. Heartsick. Uncertain. I'd survived the night, but what would today bring? Carter had made it clear I wouldn't be going home. So where would we go next? I didn't think I could stand being cooped up with him much longer.

"Hey."

A rap on the door. Carter's voice speaking to me through the door.

"Coffee's out here."

"I don't drink coffee."

"You don't— I thought all Americans drank coffee."

All Americans? That was a funny thing to say. Was he not American? He didn't have a heavy Texas accent, that was for sure. Then again, as an Army brat, neither did I.

"I don't," I responded now. "Would you leave me alone?"

"Okay, but don't take too long. We need to get moving."

"To where?" I shot back.

He hesitated. "Still trying to figure that out. I'll let you know after breakfast."

*What breakfast?* I wondered.

It wasn't like we had any food with us, except my leftover nachos from last night. This hotel was too cheap to offer even a free continental breakfast. I was surprised it'd had a tiny coffee pot in the room. I didn't ask Carter, though, because I didn't want to hear his snappish comeback.

Instead, I pulled my clothes off and stepped into the shower. I stared up at the shower head for several seconds without actually turning the water on, shivering in my bare skin and from memories of the last time I'd tried to shower.

*Nosizwe doesn't know where we are,* I reminded myself. *And Carter's right outside. He won't let me get hurt.*

Despite the pep talk, it took me a minute to work up the courage to switch on the water. Even with warm water pouring over me, I had a hard time relaxing. I kept squinting up at the shower head, making sure no smoky white film was starting to seep out. I had to talk myself into soaping up, knowing I'd be forced to close my eyes until the soap was gone. When I reached for the soap, I saw the package was already opened and the bar already used, which meant Carter must've showered last night while I slept.

It was a little thing, but it made me feel odd. I picked it up anyway and started circling it between my palms to work up a lather. Using the same bar of soap. That same weird feeling of showering in the space where he'd showered. It was too intimate for a man I barely knew. Too much, too soon. Stuck in a motel room together, which made me wonder where he'd slept last night. Had he been in bed with me? That really gave me an odd feeling, as I let the water wash the soap from my skin. Mental images flashed up of him, shirtless, in the same bed where I'd been sleeping, lying next to me and how he must've looked. How his body looked. How his body must've looked here in the shower.

*Stop it!*

As soon as I recognized the track of my thoughts, I severed them.

"Stop it, Ellie," I whispered aloud. "What is the *matter* with you?"

I didn't know. My head was so messed up right now. Last night, I'd been too drained emotionally to be embarrassed or discomfited by Carter with his shirt off. This morning, the images seared through my head, coupled with memories of clinging to him after he'd saved me from the Nakki, nothing between our upper bodies except his soaked t-shirt that I'd been wearing. Or last night in the Botanic Garden, how I'd hid my face in his chest after I shot someone to save him. I could still smell his scent, even though I tried to reject the memory, and could still feel the crisp black hairs on his chest against my skin.

*That's enough*, I told myself sternly, shutting the water off, applying more force than necessary to the knobs.

*A minute ago you were thinking about how he made you mad in ways nobody else did, and now you're sitting here thinking about how he looks half-naked. What is wrong with you?*

I didn't know, but I could only surmise, as I pushed back the plastic shower curtain and reached for a towel, that the one was a mental and emotional reaction, and the other purely physical. My body was reacting to him simply because I'd never been that physically intimate with another man, and sure not a man who had used his strength to fight for me, save my life, more than once.

As I toweled off, I gave myself a stern lecture, reminding myself that physical attraction didn't matter. My head had to rule. If I guarded my thoughts, I'd be fine. No more allowing my brain to drift into the danger zone.

I felt slightly better as I put my clothes back on—better, except for the fact that I had to wear yesterday's clothes, and in the bathroom light I could definitely see spots of dried blood and flecks of vomit. Putting them on made me feel dirty again, as if I'd just undone any cleanness the shower had given, but I had no choice.

I emerged from the shower room, my hair twisted up in a towel, to see Carter sitting on the edge of the bed where I'd slept last night. A foam coffee cup was in one hand and his phone was in the other. He was scrolling, but glanced up as I emerged. His dark eyes flicked up to the top of my head and he smirked.

I stopped, putting my hands on my hips.

"What?"

He shrugged one shoulder, went back to his phone.

"Nothing."

"Nothing," I mimicked under my breath.

There it was. Moment of physical attraction gone. Back to Carter being Carter.

I turned to the counter. I was hoping to find a mini hair dryer built into the wall, but this place didn't even offer that.

Carter must've noticed I was searching for something, because he looked away from his phone.

"Something wrong?"

I sighed. "No. Not really. I mean, yes, but it's pretty small in the grand scheme of things. Hey, do you know where my purse is?" Using the mirror, I checked the room behind me. I remembered putting it in Blake's truck last night when we'd switched vehicles, but I didn't remember bringing it in. That didn't mean I hadn't, though. I'd been pretty out of it by the time we got inside here.

"I saw it when I went to lock the truck, and brought it in. It's—" He stood up and walked over to far corner of the room where he'd already stacked everything that we'd brought with us. I also noticed he was fully dressed, and had gathered the trash from last night's meal and put in the garbage can. He bent to move aside a couple of things, and came up with my purse. "Over here," he said, finishing the sentence as he turned to bring it back to me. He made a detour on the way over, snatching my glasses off the nightstand and handing them to me, along with the purse.

"Thank you."

He stepped back.

"No problem."

*What, no snarky quips?*

I almost said it, but shut my mouth at the last second as he walked away. I put my purse on the counter and dug out a comb. Unwinding the towel, I shook my hair free, bent to fluff it, then stood, flipping my hair back over my shoulders with a quick motion. I put on my glasses with one hand as I finger combed my wet hair with the other, working out a few of the snarls before attempting to comb it. As I did, I happened to glance into the mirror and notice Carter still sitting on the edge of the bed with his coffee. He wasn't staring at his phone, though. He was staring at me. Our eyes met in the mirror, and I felt my throat tighten at the intensity in his deep brown eyes.

Why was he looking at me like that? Why was he looking at me at all?

My hands went still, and for an instant I was so uncomfortable I couldn't move.

The stalemate was broken when his phone suddenly rang. His

focus snapped away as he answered it, rising to walk off as he put it to his ear.

"Hello?"

My breath, breath I didn't realize I'd been holding, released in a rush. When I reached for the comb, my hands trembled slightly. I tried to focus on my hair, on gently working the comb through it and not eavesdropping on Carter's conversation, but I couldn't help observing after a few seconds of the one-sided talk he went very still, very stiff. Then,

"That's not good."

A few seconds of silence while the other person spoke.

"How clear was it? Could they see faces? Anything to actually identify us?"

*Us? Identify us?*

That had my attention. I turned from the bathroom mirror and stood there, clutching my comb, not even pretending I wasn't eavesdropping. Anxiety kicked in. Was this about last night? About the shifters killed in the Botanic Garden?

"DNA?" Carter said next, and my heart dropped into my stomach. This had to be about the killings in the park. Had something been found? Amy had been thorough. I knew there was nothing left of the bodies themselves. Had there been any other markers left behind?

"How concerned should I be?"

A few seconds of silence.

"What does Rodriguez say?"

The other person spoke.

"Wow. That seems to be taking it pretty far." Carter ran his hand over his hair, rubbing his head. "He sure that's a good idea? He really thinks that would work?"

*What's a good idea? What would work?*

I felt like I was about to burst. My wet hair was all but forgotten until Carter said, "She's, um, she's not going to like this," and half-turned, casting me a wry glance. My mouth was dry. Something bad was happening. Something really bad on top of all the other bad things. He looked away and this time walked over to the door, saying, "Give me all the details so I can explain it to her." Opening the door, he stepped outside, shutting it behind himself.

I sagged against the countertop for a second, gripping it with both hands.

*Please,* I prayed, *please don't let whatever's going on delay me going home. Please get me out of this. Please protect my family. Please let me go home.*

I stayed like that for several seconds, fighting back fears before I was able to calm down enough to realize I needed to finish so we could leave, as Carter had advised earlier. I forced myself to set back to work on my hair, and had barely finished when I heard the door open. Carter re-entered our room. I spun around, demanded,

"What's going on?"

He sighed. A heavy sigh, full of frustration.

"I'll explain on the drive. You ready?"

His quick, up-and-down glance took in my appearance, from my still wet hair to my bare feet.

"I need to put my shoes on."

"Do that, while I carry our stuff out. We need to go."

Obediently, I fetched my purse while he gathered up the small pile of belongings we'd carried in with us. I hurried around the end of the bed and stuck my feet into the too-small slippers he'd bought for me even as he went out the door, clearly expecting me to follow. I stopped for one final look at the motel room where we'd spent the past several hours together, then flicked off the light and stepped outside, headed to the next phase of this crazy adventure.

## CHAPTER SEVENTEEN

The November sunshine was bright after the dimness of the room. I surveyed the parking lot, squinting a little, my fingers on the door handle while I waited for Carter to unlock the truck. Across the parking lot, a couple of other patrons, nearly as seedy looking as me, were up and about, also prepping to leave. Glum, I wondered if they'd passed a horrible night full of blood and fire and feuding too.

I heard the click of the lock, opened the door and climbed inside. By the time I'd fastened my seatbelt, Carter had dumped everything into the bench seat between us and swung up inside. He turned the key, igniting the engine, and twisted to look over his shoulder as he backed us out the parking lot. Once we were on the road, I kept casting little glances at him, waiting for him to speak, to explain what his phone conversation had been about. The set of his profile was daunting. His face was as hard as the bronze he shifted into, and his eyes were so dark they seemed angry. I wasn't sure if I should push the matter.

Instead, as meekly as possible, I asked, "Where are we headed now?"

"Blake wants his truck back," he replied, voice distant as if his thoughts were anywhere except me and anything I had to say.

"So...what does that mean? Where are we going?"

"We're going to give him his truck back," he half-snapped, and I started a little.

Okay. That was the signal to cool it with the questions, apparently. I sunk into the seat and stared out the windshield, chewing my lower lip. We drove over a half an hour in silence, him looking angry and refusing to speak, me too nervous to ask what was going on. Finally, we exited 820 and took a side ramp that circled around, eventually leading us down onto the main street of Saginaw, a small town with huge grain elevators right by the railroad tracks—the only things that stuck up for miles in a sea of flat landscape and thousands of houses. I studied the train tracks, the flour mills, the grain elevators out my window as Carter cruised down the main thoroughfare for a mile or two, finally pulling off into the parking lot of a popular fast food restaurant. He parked as far from the main road as possible, beneath one of the few trees that livened the concrete landscape. He set the brake but left the engine running, leaning back in the seat as he pulled out his phone to check a text. After sending a reply, he slid the phone into his back pocket.

"Blake'll be here in a minute," he said, turning to me. I nearly jumped but caught myself. After such a long stretch of stony silence, his voice seemed abnormally loud. "I'm going to run in there and get something to eat. You hungry?"

I shook my head. "No, thanks."

At that, he raised his eyebrows in mock surprise, a little of his sardonic humor returning.

"You're not hungry? The girl who ate half the menu last night?"

I was casting about for some smart reply, when my stomach released a growl. Abruptly, it had sprung to life, reminding me—

and him—that I actually was hungry, even if I hadn't known it till he mentioned food.

Carter snorted and shook his head.

"Be right back. Keep an eye out. Plenty of people around, so you should be safe, but, just in case..."

He pulled out his gun, laying it on the floorboard between us.

"You know what to do."

He stepped down from the truck, halted, looked at me over his shoulder. "As a matter of curiosity, how did you know what to do last night? Your dad?"

I licked my lips, unable to tear my focus from his weapon, which I recognized from weapons training as a SIG Sauer P226. "Yeah." My voice was faint. Clearing my throat, I tried again. "Yeah. My dad and my mom, actually. My mom was a champion skeet shooter in her teens. They both made sure my brother Drew and I could handle guns. Tyler's too young right now."

"I see. They did a good job. In fact, they did such a good job it kind of begs the question why you weren't carrying when all this happened."

I stared at him quizzically. "Because before now I never felt like I was particularly in danger. Nobody wanted to kill me that I knew of. I never felt like I needed to carry. But you can bet I will after this."

Carter chuckled, but his humor faded into seriousness as he said, "Well, you did great last night. That wasn't an easy shot. And...thank you."

My gaze flicked up at this—possibly the first compliment he'd given me, not to mention the first time he'd thanked me for saving his life. The door slammed as he walked away. Moment gone. My stare dropped back to the gun.

*You know what to do.*
*You did great last night.*
*That wasn't an easy shot.*

The words chimed in my brain, but were overridden with the

fervent wish to take it back, to take it all back. To never have gone to the Costas home last night so I'd never have been forced to kill anyone, never been entangled in this mess, never known shapeshifters were real or—

A tap on the glass made me gasp aloud. I whirled, my hand diving for the gun, only to see Blake standing there next to my window, smiling at me. It took a second for my breath to resume and my racing heart to slow. Carefully, I withdrew my hand from the weapon and leaned over to roll the window down.

"Morning."

"Good morning."

I hadn't gotten a good look at him in the Garden last night, dark as it had been, but I still recognized his rough features. Last night, I'd seen them splashed with blood from the great boar he'd killed with his machetes. He had a grizzled, almost half-wild look about him, but this morning, he was clean—cleaner than me, actually. His long beard was sprinkled with grey, and the dark blonde of his ponytail had more of the same. There was a scar above and below one eye, and his skin looked baked from the sun. "Carter inside?" he asked, leaning his corded forearms on the windowsill, seemingly in no hurry to go anywhere.

"Yes," I replied, a little uneasy. "He's getting breakfast. Should be out in a minute."

A train rumbled by. Its clatters, creaks, and clangs temporarily forestalled conversation, leaving me to doubt the wisdom of rolling down my window and answering his questions.

I didn't know this guy. I'd seen what he was capable of doing. How did I know he wouldn't decide to hurt me or kidnap me? What if he was a double agent and working for Nosizwe? What if—

The train passed, and Blake picked up the subject.

"You guys haven't had breakfast yet? This late in the day?'

"I slept in this morning," I said. "Didn't get much sleep last night. Neither of us did."

"That so?" he asked, and winked. "Carter was pretty good, then?"

I felt my face get hot.

"That's—that's not what I meant," I sputtered, aghast that anyone would think that we—Carter and me, that he and I had...

"I know, I'm just messin' with you," Blake said, chuckling. "Damn, you're as much of an ingénue as he said."

"As who said?"

"Carter." He stepped back, slapping the windowsill. "Here he comes now. Nice talking to you, Ellie."

I sat there rigid, mortified but curious, as he walked around the front of the truck to speak with Carter. He held a couple of drinks and paper bags, which he placed on the hood while he and Blake conversed. I watched them, wondering what exactly Carter had told Blake about me, presumably in the few minutes before the boar-shifter had attacked. An ingénue? I wasn't one hundred percent sure what that meant, but I could hazard a guess. Sounded like Carter was making fun of me, again. This time to Blake, whoever he was. I was more than a little annoyed, not to mention embarrassed, but since there wasn't anything I could do about it at the moment I hunkered in the cab, glowering at the men through the windshield while they talked. I didn't have a watch or phone clock to gauge the time, but I reckoned several minutes had passed before the pair finished up their conversation, ending it with a handshake.

Blake opened the door while Carter carried the food around to the non-descript five passenger sedan parked beside us. That wasn't what we'd driven last night, but maybe Blake had returned the fancy sports car to the Costas mansion, exchanging it for this vehicle.

"Time to get out, Ellie. This is where we switch again."

I unfastened my seatbelt and hopped out, just as Carter approached my side of the vehicle to gather up his gun and the rest of our belongings. For an instant, I was trapped, hemmed in between the vehicle and the shapeshifter. I froze, staring at him, moving only when he said, "Get in the car, kid. I'll grab everything else," and half stepped aside so I could duck away.

I scurried around him and the trunk of the new car, opening the passenger side door and sliding into the seat. My heart was beating a little more rapidly, and my nerves didn't calm, even when I smelled the food on the console between us, or when Carter slipped inside the door Blake had left open. Blake's truck backed out of the parking lot as Carter shut his door, locked it.

He threw our belongings into the backseat, and offered me the food bags.

"Didn't know what to get you, but since you like crap Mexican fast food so much, I got you a couple of breakfast burritos and some hot sauce."

"Thanks," I said softly, my hands clutching the bag.

I was hungry, but I was also to the point that I was so nervous I felt sick. I wasn't sure my stomach could handle food. I couldn't take it anymore. I blurted out, "What's going on? Back at the hotel room—all that stuff you said on the phone. You said you'd tell me."

He was unwrapping a breakfast biscuit with sausage and cheese.

"Eat first, then I'll tell you."

"I don't want to eat first. I want to hear it now."

"I'm serious. You better eat first," he said, taking a bite of his own food.

"Why?"

I clutched the bag a little tighter, staring at him a little harder, willing him to give in and explain.

"Because, once you hear, you're not going to want to eat."

I think I physically felt the color drain from my face.

"Is it that bad?"

He lifted one shoulder, continuing to unwrap the breakfast sandwich and eat.

"Depends on how you look at it. Not to me, it isn't—not necessarily, but it might be to you."

My mind whirled, trying to figure out what could be so terrible to me that it would make me lose my appetite, but wasn't that big a deal to him.

"Is it—is it my family?"

They were only humans to him. He'd promised to make this right and get me back to them, but what if he'd only said that to calm me down? He'd made his distaste for humans in general abundantly clear. I had a hard time believing he really cared at all about my family's welfare. Or mine, either, for that matter, except that it was his job right now.

"No, it's not your family. I've got guards sitting on your house and your family at all times. Nobody's leaving the house without a tail. They're fine for now."

"Then—"

"C'mon, Ellie, would you cooperate for once? I'm waiting on a phone call to finalize everything, anyway. Should be any minute. Just eat. By the time you're done, the phone will probably ring."

I don't know why, but his remark, *Would you cooperate for once?* stung a little. How had I been uncooperative? I'd been dragged all over Fort Worth last night, attacked, nearly killed, terrified out of my mind, and even killed a woman to defend Carter. I hadn't resisted with kicking and screaming and arguing. Not much anyway. Considering the circumstances, I thought I'd been very cooperative, but apparently Carter didn't see it that way. Which made me wonder how exactly Carter did see me.

Human. The enemy. Worthless, except Mr. Costas had ordered him to keep me alive. And, apparently, uncooperative.

Rather than fight, I attempted to eat. The breakfast burrito tasted like sawdust, but I choked down half of it anyway. Carter had brought me a water instead of coffee, which I guess meant that he was paying some attention to my likes and dislikes. I sipped on the water through the plastic straw like most people would've sipped on their coffee, more for something to do in the tense silence of the car than because I was thirsty. Carter, meanwhile, plowed through two breakfast sandwiches and then asked if I wanted my other burrito.

"No, thanks." I shook my head, so he ate that too, balling up the wrappers and tossing them into the floorboard behind the seats.

I shot him a surprised frown. His apartment had been meticulous, but he was throwing trash in the car? He caught the look.

"What?"

I raised my eyebrows. "Throwing trash?"

He was nonchalant. "Not my car, not my problem. Mr. Costas has—"

"People to do everything, including detail his cars. I get it," I finished. I still couldn't imagine trashing someone else's car, though.

"How did you wind up working for Mr. Costas, anyway?" I asked, brushing crumbs from my lap.

The pants were so stained and dirty that I felt downright gross. I desperately wanted clean clothes, but I wasn't sure how or where I'd get them.

Carter took his time replying. To me, it had been a casual question, spur of the moment, meant to break the silence. I guess he didn't receive it that way.

"Long story," he finally said, and when he did his voice was sharp and short. The tones were final, in a, *Don't ask again* way.

Okay, man of mystery.

I decided to leave the topic alone, which worked because his phone rang. He pulled it out, already exiting the car, slamming the door and walking several feet away so I couldn't overhear what was being said. I admit I was curious. I tried to read his lips and guess, but he must've felt me watching him, because he turned his back.

In nervous silence I waited alone until he finished and got back inside. He looked over at me and chuckled grimly.

"It's not as bad as all that, Ellie. You don't have to look at me like I'm about to smash your face in."

Like he had the Mothman's last night? I winced. Poor choice of words. The memory was ugly, brutal.

"What's going on?" I asked, shoving the mental images away. I couldn't think about that now.

He leaned back in the seat, folded his arms, stared at me directly.

"Last night, the plan to throw Nosizwe off our tracks and take out her shifters worked. As far as James or anyone else can pick up, you're safe for now. Nosizwe has gone quiet. Unfortunately, we may have thrown her off your tail, but now we've got the cops on ours."

*The cops?*

Again, I felt my face blanch.

The cops? But I'd never been in trouble in my life, aside from one speeding ticket. I didn't break the law.

*Except for killing someone and trying to cover it up,* my conscience accused. *You knew better last night. You just let them talk you out of it.*

"My sources are telling me that groundskeepers at the Botanic Garden found the scene of our fight early this morning before the park opened. The cops were called. They even brought in homicide detectives, since it looked like someone might have been offed. They don't have much, apparently. How could they? The bodies are gone. They've got some blood. A tooth. Burned spots. Along with that, they have something else. Apparently, there's been recent vandalism at the park, and they had security cameras set up. I didn't know that. Seems you and I were caught on tape last night."

"We—we were... Do they know who we are?"

Carter pursed his lips. "Not yet. And they may not figure it out. Sources say they're still trying to clean the images up, but they were pretty blurry. Man with short hair and a beard. Small blonde woman. Car's license plates didn't show up, but they know it was an Aston, so that's something they can track if they don't decide to drop it."

"Then...then..." I was stammering. "Then...how bad is it?"

Again, Carter shrugged one shoulder. I didn't know whether to be frustrated or soothed by his almost lackadaisical attitude. Didn't he understand what was happening here? Bad enough to have monsters and shifters wanting to kill me. Now the cops, who I'd always thought I could count on to help me, might be after me too! Where could I turn after this?

I was starting to flip out. Carter must've seen it, because he straightened, leaning across the console to put a hand on my shoulder, squeeze.

"Breathe, Ellie. Breathe. It isn't that bad. Like I said, they don't have any bodies. You saw what Amy did. Even if they can extract DNA from the tooth or the blood, even if it's in the system, there's no corpses. They'll have a hard time proving anyone was actually killed. They can't prove it, and it's awfully hard to make a case with no bodies. Also, they're going to have a hard time tracing us just off the security footage. Even if they do, we're far from sunk. Mr. Costas has the best team of attorneys in the Metroplex. Believe me, money and power talk. He owns lawyers and judges, ADAs and plenty of other connections. You really think he'll let you go to jail for this?"

I was unconsciously shaking my head, trying to fight down the panic. Trying to think, to breathe, as Carter had demanded.

"I—I don't know. I don't know why he'd stick his neck out for me. I'm nothing to him. I—"

"He said you're family. You saved his son. You saved his wife. You're as much family as his own flesh and blood. He will not let you go down for this. There may be some hassle, but it'll all work out in the end, okay? Trust me. Our sources are watching the case closely. Lawyers are already on it. Which reminds me..."

He stopped. Drew a breath, released it through his nose.

"You ever heard of Miguel Rodriguez? Of Rodriguez, Stanton, and Vern?"

"Th-the lawyers?"

I had heard of them, in passing. Maybe at the hospital or on the news. They were high-powered attorneys.

"Yes, the lawyers. Most folks can't afford a consultation, much less have the senior partner on retainer. Rodriguez has passed along what we can start doing now to protect ourselves in case the heat turns up. An ounce of prevention is worth a pound of cure—you ever hear that saying? It's an American saying. Ben Franklin. Anyway, that's what he wants us to do. Start protecting ourselves now so he doesn't have to clean up the crap show later, in case things go south."

"What's he recommending?" I asked, licking my parched lips.

Carter's hand moved from my shoulder, sliding down my arm, gently, not quite caressingly, but gently, all the way down to my wrist where he covered my hand on the console with his.

"Rodriguez thinks we should get married," he said quietly.

## CHAPTER EIGHTEEN

It was like an explosion going off, or a volcano erupting. Starting off slow, building up in the tenseness of her body, in the mental processes behind her eyes. Mounting, building as the notion sunk in, and then—bam! The fireworks went off. She tugged her hand away, horror all over her face.

"*Married?*" she practically screeched, in the same decibel that had hurt his ears last night in his apartment. "*What?* Are you insane?"

"No, but I'm probably going to be deaf before this is all over," Carter muttered, rubbing his inner ear.

She overlooked the jibe.

"Why? Why? Why? Why would we get married?" she spluttered. "That doesn't make a bit of sense."

"Actually, it does. It makes a lot of sense. You ever hear of spousal immunity or marital communications privilege?"

"I—I don't know. Maybe, sometime. From a cop show or something. What is it, exactly?"

"In Texas, the first one is basically the right of one spouse not to have to testify against the other. Marital communications privilege is essentially the right of either spouse to keep certain communications that were only intended for each other private."

"Meaning..."

"Meaning, if we were married, even if the cops do decide something bad went down last night, and even if they do identify us through the security footage, they can bring us in for questioning but they can't force either of us to talk about what actually happened last night."

Her face was paler than normal, and her eyes were wide, but she was listening.

"What about Amy, Blake?" she stammered. "They were there also."

"True, but there's nothing tying Blake or Amy to the scene. Only us."

"What if something does turn up to tie them to the scene?"

"It won't, but even if it did, that's another problem for another day. I guess they can get married too."

She didn't respond to the joke.

Carter sighed. "This is a temporary fix, Ellie. Did you catch that? *Temporary*. Getting married now doesn't mean staying married forever. It's only a quick fix in case things go south; something to protect us until the lawyers can get us out. Something to possibly keep the lawyers from ever having to get us out. That's all it is."

"What's the point of having expensive lawyers if you have to resort to wild tricks like this to keep from getting in trouble?" she demanded, clearly unconvinced. "I don't like the idea. I don't like it one bit."

"The best lawyers in the world may not be able to keep the cops from taking you down to the station for questioning. You ever been questioned by the cops?"

"No, have you?" she retorted.

"No, and I don't intend to, either. But, if it happens—*if*—this covers both our butts for the time being. They get us in there, start turning the screws, asking questions...we claim spousal privilege. We don't have to say a word about why we were there or what went down because we're married, it was only for us, and that's legally protected. It keeps us from spending the night in lockup—or being arraigned, or anything like that—until the lawyers can handle it. Understand?"

"No." She turned away, shaking her head fervently, to stare out the windshield. "No, I don't understand. I don't understand any of this. I don't know why this is happening. I don't—"

She stopped to breathe, fighting for control. Her breath sounded shaky, but she didn't fall to pieces.

*Be kind to her. She's terrified.*

Again, Ciara's words rang in his ears. As if learning shifters existed and wanted to kill her, as if surviving multiple assaults in one night weren't plenty, now here he came with this news. That the cops might be after her, and she needed to marry him to protect herself.

Marry the monster. Beauty and the beast.

Carter almost laughed. He really did. Had they stumbled into some sort of twisted fairytale? It was beginning to feel like that. Only, this was no fairytale, and there would be no happily ever after for the two of them.

"C'mon, Ellie, calm down," he said. "I promise it's not as bad as it sounds. It's not that big a deal, really."

"Not that big a deal?" She whipped her head around to pin him with a glare. "Not that big a deal? You're sitting here telling me I may be at risk for going to jail, and I have to freaking marry you to stay out of it, and it's not that big a deal?"

"It doesn't have to be any bigger of a deal than you make it!" he responded harshly. "I don't know what's going on in your brain —if you've been reading too many historical romance novels or what, but I'm not going to marry you and suddenly demand my *husband's rights*." He wagged finger quotes sarcastically. "I'm not going to expect us to move in together to save face. Not going to expect you to stay at my apartment and bring me my pipe and slippers when I get home from work. None of that. It's nothing, Ellie. It's a piece of paper with our names and signatures on it. That's it. Just a legal document to offer us legal protection.

"When the danger's past, when Mr. Costas' people make everything go away, which they will, then the *marriage* goes away too. Like it never happened. Because it didn't. No real marriage took place, okay? It's just a precaution."

She stared back, her lower lip trembling, still looking like she was on the verge of crying.

"I can't—I can't feel about it that way," she whispered. "Marriage is real. It is to me, anyway."

"Oh my—"

He looked away, biting his tongue to keep from spouting something that would really offend her. Counted to ten. Breathed before turning back to her.

"That's what I meant when I said it doesn't have to be a bigger deal than you make it," he reiterated. "You can sit there and act all holy and spout religious values about marriage, or you can accept that this is absolutely nothing except a legal tactic to protect yourself. Don't your beliefs allow self-defense? Look at it that way. It's self-defense. Nothing more, nothing less."

She sighed shakily.

"I don't know. I just don't know," she mumbled. She removed her glasses so she could rub her forehead. "It seems like such a ridiculous, huge step to me."

"It's not. Annulments aren't hard to obtain. Especially if you've got good lawyers. Which we do."

"But what if something happens and the annulment falls through?"

"Then we get divorced. Done like it never happened."

"I don't believe in getting divorced."

Carter could feel his entire body tensing, but he restrained the frustration.

"I can respect that," he said, "in a real marriage. But this isn't a real marriage."

How many times did he have to explain? It was simple. Any other unmarried woman wouldn't have thought twice about it. Just his luck he wound up with the one girl who had to throw a shoe.

"Can I—can I have some time to think about it?" she finally asked, and Carter felt the tautness in his shoulders ease. It meant she was considering the idea.

"I can't give you much," he said. "An hour. Tops."

"Are you kidding me?" She lifted her chin. Her frustration was visible.

"Sorry, kid. There's another element to it. In Texas, spousal privilege only covers incidents occurring while the couple was married."

"We weren't married last night."

"Exactly. We have people who can fix the date, but it's got to be close so the discrepancy isn't obvious. The longer we wait, the harder it'll be to make it look right."

"You mean—you mean we lie about being married, and then we lie about the date we got married?"

"On paper, we got married yesterday morning instead of this morning. One number change—that's all it is, and we're legally protected from talking to the cops about what happened in the Botanic Garden last night."

"Why don't we just forge a marriage license then or whatever instead of actually getting married?"

"Too easy for cops to blow our cover if they need to. A marriage license but no actual wedding? No witnesses to a wedding? This way, if it turns out they're serious enough to trace it, we have both a license *and* witnesses who will attest we got married last night instead of today. They can't poke holes in that."

She rolled her eyes. "Because, let me guess: Mr. Costas has

court clerks and justices of the peace and whoever else in his back pocket to make sure the fake date isn't caught."

"Anything can be done if you've got money."

"Boy, he really is a mafia don," she mumbled.

"Pardon me?"

She shook her head, stared out the window. "Nothing."

The set of her face had gone from horrified to aggravated. She sat there, arms folded, saying nothing for several minutes. Carter couldn't gauge what was going on in her mind until she muttered, "I don't like being bullied into this."

That stung. Was that how she saw it?

"I'm not trying to bully you," he said. "I hate bullies. You don't have to do this if you're completely opposed to it. Not like I'm going to hold a gun on you and force you. We can take our chances with the cops, if you'd rather. However, it could kind of help you out with your family," he added, making another attempt to persuade her.

She refused to look at him. "How so?"

"Well, one of these days you'll go home. They'll ask about this. Getting married gives you a reason why you didn't come home last night; why you were acting so out of character."

"Huh." She laughed harshly. "They'd never believe that. They'd never believe I decided to run out and get married to *you* on the spur of the moment. Having a shotgun wedding isn't something I'd do at all, much less with *you*."

The way she'd said it...twice. *Married to* you. It was a flat-out insult. Carter felt his blood start to heat.

"It may be a bad story, but it's a better cover story than you were being chased by people who can shapeshift into monsters. You got another idea? Surely you're allowed to make the occasional bad decision or act rash and do something crazy—like run off and marry a freak. You can't possibly be perfect all the time. Or, wait. Maybe you can. Because you're Ellie. And you never do anything wrong."

Now she swung around to glare at him. Her freckles stood out in sharp contrast to the color of her skin. She was mad. Her mouth opened, then shut. Opened again, releasing one syllable, the start of something. Then shut. She clamped her lips together for a few seconds. Breathed. In and out, through her nose.

Finally, her gaze dropped to her lap. In a tight, strained voice she said, "I know I'm not perfect, Carter. I never pretended to be perfect. I never said I was. I'm just trying to convey that my family isn't going to believe that I ran off on the spur of the moment and married someone they didn't know. That isn't like me. It's not anything I would do."

"Well, you're going to have to come up with some explanation for last night. This seems like as good an explanation as any. You don't have to tell them anything about who I really am. Tell them you met me in school, or at the hospital. Tell them we went on a few secret dates. Tell them you got drunk and did something stupid. Then you thought better of it and came home. We're separated. It's not going to work out. That's plausible, isn't it?"

"Not really. But I guess it's more plausible than the truth."

"See? There you go. That's what I'm aiming at."

She sighed, staring down at the unfinished burrito in her lap.

"They aren't going to like this. Not at all. Mom and Dad will be so disappointed in me."

"They may be disappointed, but they'll forgive you, right? Isn't that what your religion is supposed to be all about? Forgiveness?"

"Yeah. Yeah, I guess so." She sighed again, but finally looked up. "Maybe you're right."

"Nice to hear you admit it."

He smirked. She glared.

"Alright, Mr. Right All the Time, so we get married. So the date is fixed to make it look like we were married yesterday. If the police figure out who we are and come around, what do we tell them? *I don't have to talk to you because of spousal privilege?* Doesn't that sound like we have something to hide?"

"You don't have to say it in so many words. Just say you don't want to talk to them because you were out there last night with your husband. Anything you saw or heard or witnessed is strictly between us."

"Why would it be strictly between us?"

"Well, the possible implication, Ellie, would be that we're crazy newlyweds who went to the Botanic Garden for a romantic encounter, if you know what I mean."

He expected her to flush beet red. Instead, she arched an eyebrow like he'd lost his mind.

"It was *cold* last night."

"Maybe you wanted me to warm you up."

"Maybe I—no, that's just stupid. Nobody would believe that."

"What, that you wanted me to warm you up, or that we would sneak into the Garden for a date?"

"Either. Neither."

"So you don't think sneaking into the Garden at night is romantic? I bet some people would."

"Not when it's cold. That's stupid," she said again.

Carter couldn't help it. He laughed.

"You don't have a kinky bone in your body, do you?"

"I just don't happen to think sneaking into a park late at night when it's chilly out is romantic. Give me a nice hotel suite with rose petals and wine any day."

"Really. You've thought about this a lot, then?"

Now she was embarrassed, realizing she'd blurted out something that she probably would rather he not know.

"Shut up." She turned to look out the windshield again. "Just because I don't sleep around doesn't mean I haven't thought about sex. I'm human, okay? I want to have sex. I want to know what it's like. I'm just waiting till the right person to find out."

"And the right person would be..."

"My husband. I'm waiting until I get married. I'm sure you

could've guessed that, since you know everything else about me," she said, rolling her eyes.

"Hmm. Waiting on your husband. And I'm about to be your husband."

He meant it as a wisecrack. He wasn't expecting to see true disgust crease her features.

"That's sick."

Carter was taken aback. Angered.

"Wait, that's sick? The idea of having sex with me is sick? Is it me personally you're not attracted to, or is it sick because I'm different from you? Because I get the one, but the other... Wow. So much for *love thy neighbor* and the Golden Rule and all that stuff, huh, Ellie? It doesn't apply to people like me, because we're shifters, right? We're freaks."

To her credit, she instantly looked contrite, but Carter wasn't having it. She'd slipped up and said what she thought. What she really thought. And it reinforced everything he'd ever thought about her and people like her.

"I didn't mean that, Carter. I—"

He didn't want to hear her fake apologies.

"Yes, yes you did, Ellie. You meant it because you're human and I'm a shifter. You're the good girl and I'm the unfeeling brute who's keeping you alive right now. You're the saint and I'm the sinner. You're the beauty and I'm the beast.

"Are you sitting there with all these wild ideas running through your mind of me making love in my altered form? If you are, let me clue you in. It doesn't work that way. Shifters' sex lives are pretty much like anyone else's. If anything, you're the abnormal one here, because you're the one refusing to act on basic human instinct. So who's the freak now?"

She didn't argue. She didn't try to deny it. Instead, she plucked fretfully at a loose string in her lap, unable to bring herself to look him in the eye.

"I'm sorry," she whispered again. "I shouldn't have said that. It was wrong of me, and I'm sorry. But I didn't know."

"No, you didn't know. You made assumptions. You did what humans always do—make assumptions about us. Let me tell you something, kid. Humans aren't any nicer or better than shifters, no matter how normal their bodies may be."

"I know. I'm sorry, Carter. I shouldn't have said it, and I'm sorry. But you have to admit—" She steeled herself and looked up. –"You've said some pretty nasty stuff about me and people like me too. You don't understand me any more than I understand you. We're no good together, but we're stuck together anyway. And I guess we're really about to be stuck together if we get married. That's why—this whole thing. It's so crazy. It's futile. It doesn't make any sense."

He'd been mad enough to erupt mere moments ago, but what she said calmed him, knocking the wind out of his sails. She was right. Yes, she'd made assumptions about him. In all fairness, he had about her, too. She'd mocked the idea of sex with him. He'd mocked her sex life—or lack thereof—too. He wasn't any better than she was. She wasn't any better than him. Truth was, they were from two different worlds, worlds that never should have brushed. But they had brushed. No, they hadn't brushed—they'd collided. And, like it or not, whether they were any good together or not, they were definitely stuck together. And about to get married.

He blew out a gust of air, ran a hand over his head.

"Yeah. It's crazy, alright. And it doesn't make any sense. But I guess we're going to have to get along for a while, because this thing probably isn't ending quickly." Into the heavy silence, he said, "I'm sorry, Ellie."

She waited a beat. Two. Then, "I'm sorry too, Carter."

Like he'd done before, last night in his apartment, he held out his hand for her to shake. "Truce? Again?"

A wobbly smile turned up her lips, but she accepted the handshake.

"Truce."

"Good. Now that that's settled, you ready to go get married?"

"No. But do I have a choice?"

"There's always a choice. You're just running a bigger risk if you don't. I kind of doubt you want your parents visiting you in jail."

She considered that. "That's true. I do have a favor to ask, though."

"What's that?"

"Can we please get me some clean clothes before we ge— before we do this?" Carter noticed she couldn't even bring herself to say, *Get married*. "I'm so disgusting right now I can't stand it. This is worse than coming off a twelve hour shift at the hospital dealing with patients and bodily fluids all day."

The description of her job made him chuckle. Maybe he also felt bad about their prior argument, because he gave in immediately.

"Sure, we can get you something clean to wear."

## CHAPTER NINETEEN

He took me to the nearest big-box store, which was a few blocks away down Main Street. As we drove along, I studied the world outside the car windows, a world that felt entirely removed from Carter and myself. I saw more fast food restaurants, a liquor store, a grocery store, a coffee shop, and a billboard announcing an upcoming concert for Elia, an entertainment superstar from right next door in Dallas.

How, I wondered, did everything outside the car appear normal on the surface, while inside the car, inside myself, was a seething turmoil of mystery and fear and confusion? How many of the folks here in this small Texas city, going about their daily business, were privy to the fact that an entire race of people existed who could alter themselves into different creatures? How many of these folks *were* such people?

It was a sobering idea.

We arrived and parked. Before heading inside, he opened his wallet, pulled out a debit card, and handed it to me.

"Here. I don't want you using your card in case your parents decide to call the cops and they try to trace you. Use mine. Pin number is 1358. Get whatever you need."

I accepted it, feeling uncertain.

"Is there a budget?"

He didn't appear to understand the question. "Why would there be a budget?"

I tried to brush the moment off. "Never mind. I'll be responsible and only get what I need."

He genuinely didn't seem to care. "Do whatever you want."

I stuck the debit card in my wallet, repeating the pin number in my head as we headed inside, separating at the main entrance. I spent the next half hour seeking clothes and shoes that fit, buying a new jacket, pajamas, socks, and even bras and underwear, since I had no idea how long I was supposed to be living on the run. I also bought toiletries and a small suitcase to hold everything. While I was trying on clothes, I kept debating, wondering what I should wear. After all, I was about to go get married. Married! The concept was so farfetched that it didn't seem real, and yet, there it was. I was about to go marry a man I'd known less than twenty-four hours, a man who wasn't even fully human, a man with supernatural abilities, a man who seemed as unbothered by the killing and disposing of his enemies as deciding what to eat for dinner.

A man I'd killed to protect.

I was standing by a rack of slacks in the tiny business-casual section when that thought struck. I clutched the clothing rack, closing my eyes to keep it together.

"What am I doing? What am I *doing*?" I whispered aloud. "I must be insane. I can't do this."

My mouth was dry. Marry Carter? What if he was lying to me? What if he decided not to have the marriage annulled afterward? Could I fight it? I didn't know anything about the legalities of an annulment. What if he wouldn't sign the papers? What if—

*Okay, now you are being insane,* my better judgment warned. *A., it's not like you're such a prize some guy you barely know is going to force you to stay married to him. That's ridiculous. B., he can't keep you married* to him if you don't want to be. Nobody can do that. People divorce their spouses all the time. C., this is only about legal protection. Carter isn't interested in you. He's made that abundantly clear. He doesn't even like you. You're nothing but a job to him.

A job.

"Think of it like that," I told myself. "It's a job. Getting married is a job. All part of the process until this nightmare is cleared up and you can go home."

People dressed for their respective jobs. How was I supposed to dress to get married, even if it was part of the job? Obviously, I wasn't going to go buy a white gown, and I didn't know what kind of ceremony we going to have, but I couldn't stand the thought of getting married, fake or not, in jeans and a hoodie, either. Finally, I picked something nice that I could wear again to church or dinner. A simple black dress with a wrap waist off the clearance rack, and a floral cardigan to go over it. Matching earrings. Ballet flats.

After I paid for everything, I went to the women's restrooms, waited for the biggest stall, and then changed out of my disgusting clothes from last night into my new purchases. I put what I'd been wearing into an empty plastic store sack and tossed it in the trash. Those clothes were a visible reminder of the most horrible night of my life, and I never wanted to see them again. Besides, I didn't know if those clothes could be used as evidence against me, should the cops continue to pursue this case. I doubted they'd be able to track them down here. Anyway, the garbage would undoubtedly go out before they could.

Before leaving the women's restroom to meet Carter, I took a few minutes to use the new hairbrush I'd bought, weave my hair into a braid, apply some mascara and a neutral lip stick, and fix the new earrings in my ears. Finished, I took a moment to study my reflection in the mirror. I looked apprehensive. I looked as apprehensive as I'd looked yesterday evening, getting ready to visit the Costas home for dinner.

*Stop.*

I had to shut down my brain. I had to quit thinking or I'd either collapse, go crazy, or run. For a split second, running seemed like a good idea, until I remembered I had nowhere to go. Instead, I gathered up my purchases and went to meet Carter. He was sitting inside the tiny fast-food sandwich shop at the front of the store, waiting on me. As usual, he was on his phone—although, unlike most people, I suspected he was always on his phone because he was conducting business, not scrolling social media apps. It was hard to picture a man like him being on social media. I doubted he'd have the time for it. As I approached, I saw him glance up, down, then back up—obviously doing a double take. I stopped, uneasy.

"What's wrong?"

Had I made the wrong choice with this outfit? Should I have worn jeans? Should I have gotten something nicer—although, to be fair, this was about as nice as this type of store offered.

He shook his head, and rose, shoving his phone into his back pocket. I noticed he'd gotten new clothes too. New jeans, a t-shirt underneath, and an unbuttoned flannel long-sleeve over that, probably to hide his gun.

"Nothing," he said, walking around the barrier wall between restaurant and store and approaching me. He took a couple of bags and the suitcase from my hands. "You look great. Let's go."

"I look great?" I was genuinely surprised to hear him say that. "I can't believe I heard that from you."

"I meant you look great compared to how you looked last night and this morning. Let me put it this way—you couldn't look worse than you did then."

"Gee, thanks for the compliment. Nice to know, in spite of everything, that you still find me attractive."

"Who says I don't?"

I didn't believe for one second that he found me attractive, but I didn't care and I didn't have the energy to keep the repartee going. We passed out of the dim entrance of the store and back into the bright autumn day. I spotted our car halfway down the row. Nerves hit me like a ton of bricks, and I stopped. Stared.

Next to me, Carter stopped as well.

"You okay?" he asked quietly. "You ready to do this?"

"No."

"No, you're not okay or no you're not ready to do this?"

"No, I'm not okay, and, no, I'm not ready to do this." I released a breath. "But I guess I'm going to anyway."

## CHAPTER TWENTY

Ellie was silent for most of the drive back to the Costas compound. Carter took back roads and detours as much as possible, constantly checking vehicles behind and beside them for any signs that they were being followed. In the meantime, between glancing in mirrors, he glanced over at her more than once. She was stiff as a board in the seat next to him, her hands clenched in her lap. She looked like she was going to her execution. Which, if Nosizwe had had her way, she would have been executed, taken out, last night. He'd prevented that. He was doing what he could now to prevent her from getting into any legal trouble. She didn't want to marry him. He didn't want to marry her, either. But he was. Because it was his job.

Out of the blue, she finally asked, "How old are you, Carter?"

He blinked, threw her a look.

"Thirty. Why?"

She shrugged one shoulder. Stiff.

"I guess I'm trying to figure out why you've never been married."

"Is that any of your business?"

"No," she admitted. Then, "Yes." Her voice firmed a little. "Yes, actually, it is, if we're about to get married. I was just wondering if you had a wife you hadn't mentioned. If this whole thing—this cover up—is even valid. If Mr. Costas has the kind of power and people who could make it look like we're married, even if we're not because you're married to someone else. If you are married, you need to let me know now. I'm not going to marry you, even fake marry you, if you're already married. I—"

"Okay, stop." Clearly, her mind was chasing rabbit trails. "I'm not married, Ellie. I can promise you that," he told her, trying to reassure her. "I've never been married. This marriage is legal, but it's also only a device to protect ourselves. Remember that."

He figured he'd better remind her of that. No telling what other batty ideas were flitting through her brain.

"Why?"

"Why what? Why are we protecting ourselves?"

"No. Why haven't you ever gotten married?"

"What kind of a question is that?" he snorted. "Why haven't you ever gotten married?"

"I'm only twenty-one. You're thirty."

"So? In your world, I'm supposed to be married by this age?"

"A lot of people are, or have been. I was just curious."

In spite of himself, he picked up on the tiny thread of hurt in her voice.

*Stop being so caustic to her*, he chided himself, checking the mirrors again. But it was hard not to. Being caustic made her mad and kept her at bay. Until she got hurt. Then he felt bad for hurting her. Like now. To make up for his tones, he said, "I don't spend much time with women. I do, for my job, but not dating them. I guess I haven't had the time to find anyone I wanted to marry."

That wasn't the real reason, but he hoped it was enough of an explanation for her to back off from the line of questioning.

"Why don't you date much? You're not unattractive or anything."

Again, he looked at her, surprised. This time she caught it, and seemed embarrassed.

"What? I'm just saying I don't see any reason for you not to have romance in your life."

"You know what I can turn into, and you don't see any reason for me not to have romance in my life?"

He couldn't help his tone that time. She'd literally called him a freak and a monster, but now she was flipping, saying she didn't understand why he didn't have ladies all over him. Crazy woman.

"Well...well...I mean, what about other...shifters? Female shifters? There are women shifters, right? I saw some last night."

"Of course there are, Ellie. Where do you think little shifter babies come from? Or do you even know where babies come from?"

"Ha ha. I'm in school to be a nurse, Carter. I know the science on reproduction better than you do."

"Science," he scoffed. "Nothing like firsthand experience."

"I've witnessed several births firsthand, thank you very much."

"That's not what I meant."

"I know what you meant."

He let a few moments pass in tense silence before opening up, surprising himself by admitting, "I occasionally date. Some. I could date more if I wanted to. I could date human women or shifters, but dating involves sex and sex risks getting someone pregnant."

She turned to face him, and there was genuine surprise on her features, either at what he'd said or by what he was admitting to her.

"Why wouldn't you want that?" she asked. "Do you have morals against it?"

"Morals?" he almost laughed. "Morals, yes, but not in the way you're meaning. I don't have anything against sleeping with a woman I'm dating. I do have something against bringing another child like me into the world."

He could almost see the questions spinning behind her hazel eyes. "What's wrong with a child like you?" she said, very softly.

Now he did laugh. Short. Sharp. Frustrated.

"That's funny, coming from you, Ellie. How many names have you called me now?"

She didn't wilt this time.

"I've had less than twenty-four hours to wrap my brain around the fact that shifters exist. You're going to have to cut me some slack. You've been a shifter your entire life. It's nothing new to you. I guess I don't understand why you're afraid of bringing another child like you into the world."

"Actually, I haven't been a shifter my entire life. Shifting usually starts to manifest during puberty. Until that time, kids can grow up thinking they're normal, only to find out one day they're not."

She caught the bitterness in his tones. Not that he was trying to hide it.

"Is that what happened to you, Carter?"

He gripped the steering wheel a little tighter, wondering why he was telling her this.

"Yeah. Yeah, that's what happened to me. I didn't know. My parents didn't know. Apparently, some shifter genes are rarer than others. The results of shifters interbreeding with humans. It weakens the bloodlines. But the gene can still be passed along. It can pop up years later, when you're least expecting it. When nobody thinks to look for it. When nobody suspects it."

She kept quiet, waiting for him to continue. He didn't want to delve into the ugly story about the day he'd first shifted; the day his life had splintered and his self-conceptions shattered. But he did tell her, "My mother is English. I got my first name from her dad. My father is Greek and that's where I lived, originally. Greece. When I first started to change, Uh…" He stopped, cleared his throat, clearing his mind of memories of a young boy's terror.

"My parents…they were the good kind of parents. There are stories of parents blindsided by their kids changing. Some so scared of the monster their kid became that they killed them. Some took them to the church, for exorcisms. To have the demons cast out of their offspring. Only, it wasn't a demon, of course. It was the natural outcome of something their kids had inherited. They put their kids through hell for nothing. Some allowed their kids to be medically experimented on. Some had them locked away in asylums. Some…" He stopped. "You get the picture. My parents, well, my mother especially was blindsided, but my father talked to my ya-ya—my grandma—and she retained memories of family history. Real hush-hush stuff. She knew what was going on. When my parents found out, they started researching who could help me. They found Sean Costas, and sent me to the States to live with him. I've been here ever since."

"That's why you haven't seen your family in twenty years," she summarized.

"Yep. That's why."

He didn't want to go on explaining, but he'd opened this can of worms. And for once she was listening to him without judgment, without arguing. Maybe even a little sympathy. He didn't like her feeling sorry for him, but he wanted her to understand. Humans never had and never did understand, in his experience, but possibly Ellie could.

"That's why I don't date much," he said, going back to the original topic. "Every time I've slept with a woman in the back of my mind I'm thinking, What if protection fails? Because it does. I knock this chick up, and maybe I don't ever know. Maybe she wouldn't even know who the father is. Maybe she does know it's mine, but she won't let me see my kid or be in its life. And maybe that kid's a shifter, like me, carrying the Talos gene. Maybe it won't be that kid, but it could be a grandkid. Or great-grandkid. But I'm not around, I'm not in its life to help when the Talos takes over. Not even there to make sure family history gets passed down so my descendants would know what's going on. Maybe it'll be lucky, like me, and wind up with a Sean Costas to help. Maybe it wouldn't. But the risk—it's always there. Kind of spoils the fun, you know?"

She didn't know, because she was a virgin. But she looked empathetic, as if she did.

"What about other shifters, then?"

"What about them?"

"What happens if two shifters, um, you know—sleep together?"

Carter shrugged. "Same as humans and the genes they carry. The stronger shifter gene usually prevails, meaning whichever shifter bloodline is stronger, that's what the kid will be. Or, if both bloodlines are equally strong, or weak, the two strains sometimes cancel each other out. They may not have shifter offspring at all. Or not for several generations, like with humans. Then you run into the same problem. Occasionally, the two bloodlines will mingle, meaning the baby is born very, very wrong. Deformed. The odds of it happening are about the same as winning the lottery, but when it happens, it shows up right away. Babies like that...they don't make it."

"Oh my gosh. That's so sad," she said with genuine pity. "Mr. and Mrs. Costas," she added. "They have a son. Jackson turned out okay."

"They took the chance and it worked out for them," he agreed. "Like I said, the bad cases are rare, but they're enough that while some shifters carry on chasing tail like humans do, others are a little more restrained. Most of us are, actually. It's sort of an unwritten rule within our community."

"Restrained?" Her empathy suddenly disappeared, replaced by

a teasing grin. "So, what you're trying to tell me, in a very roundabout way, is that you're a virgin too?"

"What? No, I'm not trying to say that."

She sat there, grinning evilly.

"Knock it off, Ellie. I'm not. I just don't live to get laid like a lot of men do, okay? And this whole thing is why I'm not married. Not even at thirty."

The truth was, most of his encounters were short, non-personal flings, fueled by desperation when the lust or the loneliness got to be too much. He always regretted them afterward, wondering what if? What if? What if he'd potentially brought a kid into the world and ruined its life before that life had even begun?

She didn't need to know that, though. She didn't need to know how strongly he felt about it, or why. And she didn't, because she chuckled and changed the subject.

"I'm just bugging you, Carter. Your personal life is your personal life. I only wanted to make sure you weren't actually married before we did...this."

He shook his head, staring out the windshield. "No. I'm not."

Out of the corner of his vision, he saw her nod. Her demeanor sobered. She remained silent for several minutes, absorbing what he'd told her. The Costas home came into view. As it did, she cleared her throat, and said quietly, "You like to make jokes about my religious beliefs, and poke fun at me for them. But, you know, at the heart of all I believe is the idea of self-sacrifice for others. And you—everything you just said, what you're doing for your potential offspring...that's pretty self-sacrificial. And even what you're doing for me, too."

He snorted a laugh. "Don't try to proselytize me, Ellie. And don't make me into a better man than I am. You're a job. Nothing more. Mr. Costas says to keep you alive, so I keep you alive."

He'd expected her to look hurt. She didn't look hurt. She

looked thoughtful, as if she could somehow sense he was putting on a front.

It wasn't a front. Not much of one, anyway.

She was a job. That was it.

Carter continued to tell himself that the rest of the short drive through the gates and up the long driveway to the mansion itself.

## CHAPTER TWENTY-ONE

Office of the Medical Examiner, Fort Worth, Texas

"C'mon, Mavis, give me something."

Detective Ewing tried not to sound as impatient as she felt, but the case was eating at her. True, it was only hours old, but it was weird and she wanted answers.

For her part, Stella Mavis, chief M.E. for the city of Fort Worth, just looked aggravated.

"It's too soon for much, Detective. These were dumped in my lap only a few hours ago. You can't expect miracles."

"When it's a possible multiple homicide? Actually, I can and I do."

Mavis sighed, looked up from her microscope and shoved her glasses to the top of her greying head.

"I'm giving this top priority as a favor for you and Detective Tozzi," she said, nodding towards Gary. "But I am not—I repeat, *not*—a miracle worker. All of the testing and running DNA for potential matches will take a while."

"Can't you give us anything?" Candace nearly begged.

Next to her, Gary stayed silent. She was better at this than he was—better at hounding folks at the lab to get what she wanted. And she usually succeeded, too. Her mother had always told her she had the tenacity of a bulldog. Bite down and not let go. Her mother attributed it to her grandpa, who had put in the work and overcome the hardships to become a police detective in Dallas back in an era when black men weren't necessarily welcomed with open arms to such positions. Her grandpa's example had been one she'd determined from an early age to follow. That same tenacity kept her at the top of her field, resolved to give each case that came her way her absolute all. Like now. Even if it meant harassing Mavis for a favor.

The M.E. sighed again, putting her hand on her hip.

"This will never hold up in a court of law, because it hasn't been thoroughly tested. But preliminary evidence indicates at least three separate blood types, and it's looking like DNA from the tooth matches one of them."

Candace felt excitement build, but she tamped it down so she could think.

"So we might have three victims?"

"Possibly. Maybe four. I haven't run the fourth sample yet."

Candace tossed Gary a look over her shoulder, as if to say, *See there? I was right.*

"Too early to call them victims yet," he reminded her. "No bodies, no victims. Could've been four or more folks out there having a bonfire. They got in a brawl. Flying fists brought blood. Doesn't mean anyone died."

"That's pretty farfetched," Candace grumped, leading the way out of the lab. "Thanks, Mavis," she called back to the M.E., who'd already returned to work. "Give me a ring as soon as you hear anything else, please."

"Will do," Mavis muttered.

The door closed behind them.

"Farfetched?" her partner repeated, picking up the conversation as they headed down the corridor. "What's going to be harder to sell to a jury? My bonfire-brawl theory, or your theory of multiple murders with no bodies left behind? Like you said earlier, burning bodies typically takes way too long and leaves evidence. There was no evidence. We didn't even have ashes to sift through! The defense can call any number of experts, including the fire chief, to attest to that. It's impossible for someone to have burned up three or four bodies in that short an amount of time and left nothing. You know this, Candace."

"I know something isn't right," she retorted, stopping in the hall and turning to face Gary. "And so do you. Something went down in the Garden last night. And I have a feeling it was a heckuvalot more than just a good party gone bad."

Gary tilted his head. "I'm not arguing with you. I'm reminding you the defense could poke holes a mile wide in this story. That's if we can even find anyone to bring to trial."

"Nothing on the couple in the parking lot, yet?"

"I haven't heard anything," her partner responded. "Let's check with CSU."

Inside the Fort Worth Crime Lab, they cornered John Evans, a lead tech, who actually had more to spill than Mavis.

"Hey, you two, I was about to call," he said, leaving a group of three subordinates and walking over.

"Really? What do you have?" Gary asked.

"Bad news on the bullet casing. Nothing in the system. Good news on the security footage. I heard from Digital Forensics. They've been crunching numbers on Aston Martin owners in the Dallas-Fort Worth area. They've been narrowing that down based on the model of your car. This is going sheerly off looks, since they can't run the plates, but they think they're within a two to three year radius. When they cleaned up the video, they could see a slight dent in the left rear fender, so they've narrowed that down by the number of Astons in reported accidents within the past year."

"And?"

"And, as you might guess, the number isn't high. They've got their top five suspects. Guess who number two on the list is registered to?"

"Who?"

"Ridge Lawson."

Candace and Gary exchanged glances.

"Who?" Candace asked. "Are we supposed to recognize the name?"

Evans grinned. "Not necessarily, but I can tell you who he works for and I can promise you'll recognize *that* name."

"Tell us," Candace urged.

"Costas. Sean Costas. Lawson manages the guy's fleet of automobiles. Costas has very good, and very expensive tastes. Apparently, this particular Aston was in a minor scrape last week, and the new fender was ordered but not yet replaced."

"Wow." Candace felt as if a bomb had gone off. "Wow," she said again.

Gary narrowed his eyes, shook his head. "Don't," he warned. "Don't get too excited. You heard Evans. There are four others on the list. This is far from conclusive or from building a case."

"True," Evans acknowledged. "Also, we pulled Lawson's driving record. Judging by the video and his driver's license, that was definitely not him driving, even if it was his car. Which stands to reason. A man like Sean Costas has to have drivers. Probably more than one."

"See?" Gary's tone was warning, telling her not to jump too far too fast. To slow down and think it over. "In other words, we've basically got nothing," he said to Evans.

Evans shrugged. "We'll keep looking. It's early yet. Could be a very interesting coincidence and nothing more."

"*Very* interesting," Candace murmured, turning away. "Thanks, John."

He waved a hand. "Anytime."

Outside the lab, Detectives Tozzi and Ewing faced each other again.

"You heard that, right? The car might be linked to Sean Costas? This could be huge, Gary. Huge."

"You're right," he agreed. "Way too huge for us to go prying around when that's all you've got to go on."

"What do you mean all?" she challenged. "Blood types from three different victims. Possibly four. A tooth. A car linked back to an employee of Sean Costas. Something went down there, and you know as well as I do that Sean Costas is probably linked to any number of unsolved homicides and disappearances and physical assaults and money laundering and who knows what all in the Metroplex. He's a mob boss, Gary. A mafia don. His gang runs the city. You know it. I know it. The entire police force knows it."

Unconsciously or not, her tone had lowered until she was nearly hissing. This was the type of stuff all cops were aware of, but nobody dared talk about. Not out loud. Sean Costas had been on the Fort Worth PD's radar long before she'd ever joined the force. There were countless crimes linked or attributed to him and his alleged gang, but nothing proved, ever.

"The entire police force also knows a man like Costas has the best lawyers in the state on retainer. They know he's probably got rats and moles everywhere, in the police department, the judicial system, the DA's office…"

"Then maybe he needs to be brought down," she interjected.

"It's going to take a lot more than this to bring Costas down. His lawyers will laugh us out of court. Actually, they wouldn't, because you couldn't even get him in court over something this flimsy."

Candace sighed, thinking hard. "Don't suppose we could get a judge to sign a warrant or issue a subpoena?"

"For what?"

"To search the car? To canvas anyone who had access to it? Any drivers or other personnel who were cleared to drive it?"

Gary snorted a laugh. "Are you kidding? Evans himself said they had five top suspects. *Top* suspects. That means there's more. No judge in his or her right mind would ever sign anything affecting one of Costas's employees based on such shaky evidence. Face it, Candace. This isn't your smoking gun to bring down the Costas Empire. Not unless a lot more evidence turns up."

Detective Ewing thrust away from the wall, headed towards the exit door. "You're right," she agreed, "which means we keep looking. And I have an idea."

"What's that?"

"Trust me."

Gary didn't argue, but stayed silent until they were back on their home turf. He trailed her through long, bland hallways and back into the bustling open area portioned off by desks and chairs, filing cabinets and coffee stands.

"Have a seat," she invited, motioning Gary to sit next to her as she dropped into the chair in front of her computer desk. A couple clicks of the mouse brought up an internet search engine. She typed in "Sean Costas, Fort Worth/Dallas Texas," hit enter, and then clicked "images."

"What are you doing?" Gary leaned closer to view the images as she started scrolling.

"Call it a hunch," she mumbled, distracted by the moving line of photos.

"What kind of hunch?"

"Remember the couple in the car?"

"Of course. Digital Forensics is still working on clearing up the images so we can get a better look—"

"Well, I was just thinking, if it's somebody working for Sean Costas that's high enough up the chain of command that he's allowed to drive one his prized cars, he might be in some pictures with him, right?

"Maybe…" Gary sounded skeptical, but the syllables had barely died away when,

"Whoa! Hold the line!" Candace exclaimed, bolting upright in the chair. She double clicked on an image to enlarge it. "See that? Who does he look like?"

Hovering in the background of one image of Sean Costas with his wife Ciara, in her wheelchair, at some fancy black tie event, was a man. Very short hair. Wearing a suit. Built, clearly seen through the suit. Goatee.

"I can't deny it," Gary agreed. "It's a stretch, but he does kind of resemble the guy in the security footage."

"Let's see if we can find him in any other pictures," Candace murmured, already back to scrolling. In fact, it wasn't hard. Within minutes she'd found and bookmarked several shots containing the unknown man, always hovering in the background.

"Looks like he's a bodyguard or something," she observed.

"Would Sean Costas really give a mere bodyguard access to one of his personal vehicles?"

Again, Gary was playing devil's advocate.

"Maybe. Maybe not. Depends on what it was being used for. Maybe he's more than a bodyguard. He might run things for Costas."

"Things? What sort of things, Candace?"

"I don't know. Whatever legal or illegal hijinks a man like Costas is into. All I'm saying is, this is our best lead. This guy, right here…" She tapped the screen with a manicured fingernail… "Looks an awful lot like the guy in the security footage from the Botanic Garden. There's a chance the vehicle in the footage is registered to someone who works for Sean Costas. What are the odds it's a mere coincidence?"

"Still not enough for a warrant," Gary reminded her.

"Maybe not. But enough for us to go talk to somebody?"

"Who? We don't even know who that is. You think you can call up the Costas mansion and say, 'Hey, we're the police, mind if we have a chat?'"

"I will if I have to," she snapped, growing defensive. "Why are you fighting me on this?"

"Because you're being unrealistic!" Gary snapped back, causing nearby officers to swivel and look. "You're not going to get anywhere. You might as well drop it!"

Normally, they were the partners who got along and worked well together, when other partners might be combative, petty, competitive, or fraying at the scenes. Whatever chemistry their chief had seen when he put them together, it was real and it worked. Had worked for the past two and a half years.

Reminding herself of that, Candace took a deep breath.

"I will not drop a potential connection between Sean Costas and what could be a multiple homicide," she said, keeping her voice down. "I'd love it if you would back me up on this when I take it to the captain."

"You're involving Hollands? Already?"

Candace refused to be intimidated by the disbelief in her partner's voice. "Yes. Already. I'm bringing it to him. He might put in a call for us. Find us somebody we can talk to within the Costas circle. Just talk. No subpoenas. No warrants. Just talk. You with me?"

She pushed back her chair with a scrape, rose.

Sighing, Gary rose too.

"I think you're crazy and Hollands is going to laugh us out of his office," he said. "But you've been right before when I was wrong. I'm with you. We'll see how far this gets."

"Thanks, Gary." She slapped him on the shoulder as she stepped past, headed for the enclosed office at the end of the open room. "You're the best."

"Yeah..." he countered doubtfully.

Candace wasn't sure what reaction to expect when she

brought the evidence she was following before Hollands, but it wasn't for Hollands to sit back in his chair, chin framed by his fingers, listening thoughtfully as she explained what she'd discovered and what she'd like to do. She really wasn't prepared for him, at the end of her recital, to lean forward, clasping his hands on the desk in front of him.

"Tell you what," he said. "When Digital Forensics get the cleaned-up images back to you, if it really does look like the same guy as the one in the pictures you found, bring it back to me. I can call in a few favors. I'm betting we can find somebody in Costas's ranks to talk to. I'm sure his thousand-dollar-an-hour attorneys will circle the wagons as soon as we pick up the phone, but I'm willing to try if you are."

Candace did her best to shield her excitement, offering a, "Thanks, Captain," even as Gary, behind her, parried, "Are you sure about this, Captain?"

"I am," Hollands replied, dead-eyeing Gary. "Sean Costas has been a pain in my backside for years. I wouldn't mind seeing him squirm for a while. I know he'll get out of the fire, but I'd like his feet held to it first."

He waved a hand. "You're both dismissed. Get back to me if and when you have more to go on."

Candace couldn't help flashing a triumphant grin at her fellow detective as they exited the office.

"That went better than I could've expected," she said. "And, speaking of fire, I'm about to go light one under Digital Forensics' tail."

## **CHAPTER TWENTY-TWO**

I thought I'd calmed some on the drive here, but as soon as we parked in front of the Costas mansion everything came back. Suddenly, I was transported to the nightmare that had begun on this exact same spot. Had it only been last night? I felt like years had passed. Had it really only been a matter of hours ago that Carter had virtually thrown me into a car, here in this place, and driven off with me, refusing to tell me where we were going? Was it really less than a day ago that I'd first seen him shift, first seen shapeshifters at all, first seen someone killed in front of me, first killed someone myself?

I sat frozen on the front seat as Carter turned off the engine, opened the door, and stepped out. A couple of people walked up to greet him. Tracy. The sight of her brought back memories of her shotgun blasting, lighting up the night, dropping the shifter who was about to rip my spine out. Next to her was a young man with floppy black hair, pale skin, intricate tattoos on his neck and right hand, and black plugs in his ear lobes. In his grey t-shirt under a black leather jacket, he looked like the Goth or Emo kid from when that was popular several years ago, but he was clearly older than me, so too old to be a teen going through a phase.

First Tracy, then he, greeted Carter. I heard Carter call him "James," and recognized the name. This was the guy who apparently ran the tech side of everything for Sean Costas, for Carter. Carter had referred to him and been in contact with him more than once since last night. It was interesting to put a face with the name. He wasn't exactly what I would've pictured. Absently, I wondered if he was a shifter too. Of course, he had to be, since he was so intimately involved with everything around here. What did he shift into? How about Tracy?

From my seat in the car, through Carter's open door I could hear Carter speaking with his colleagues. Heard him inquire,

"Everything ready?"

"We're good to go," James replied. His hands were in his jeans pockets, and he sort of slumped forward in a careless, lazy way. However, his dark eyes were very bright, letting you know he was paying a lot more attention than his lackadaisical posture indicated. "We've got the date fixed. Got the right JOP. Everything's set. All you have to do is get her in there and get on with it."

*They're talking about our wedding*, I realized, and felt knots twist in the pit of my stomach.

"Where is she, anyway?" Tracy now asked, leaning around Carter to peer into the car. "Did you change your mind and dump her somewhere?"

Carter shifted his stance to check behind him, even as Tracy leaned in. He hadn't realized I was still in the vehicle.

"Hello, Ellie," Tracy said. Her voice was gentle. Her face empathetic. "I see you survived last night."

My throat clutched up at finally, finally seeing some sympathy out of someone.

"Barely," I whispered.

She winced, smiled. "I heard. That's rough. Hopefully things will calm down for a few days."

I wanted to say, "I hope so," but there I was, parked right next to where Sean Costas had beaten a wounded man to death, about to go inside and marry a man I'd known mere hours. A man who was as unbothered by blood and death as most people were by squishing a spider.

Carter leaned down to catch my eye, even as Tracy withdrew to give him space.

"You getting out of there, or what?"

His tone was a lot less sympathetic than Tracy's. He didn't care. To him, this was all about doing his job. That's what he'd said, anyway. But what type of man was willing to risk his life to protect a woman and even marry her because that was part of his job? What did that say about him? His loyalty to me, as the job, or a blind devotion to Sean Costas? He'd said Sean had helped him, and seemed to attribute a lot to that help, but he hadn't explained how. I was confused, confused by the various sides I'd seen of Carter. Confused by why I was about to go marry him.

Confused. Nervous. Scared.

But I walked around the end of the car and over to him, just the same.

He nodded towards James, whose bright eyes flashed as they scanned me from head to toe. Assessing.

"Ellie St. James, meet James. James—Ellie St. James," offered Carter.

"Nice name," James said, reaching out to shake my hand.

"You—you too." I swallowed to hide the stammer in my voice, worked up a smile, and shook his hand.

"All right, niceties done. We're going inside."

Carter's hand went to the small of my back and I practically jumped out of my skin. He felt it and shot me a look.

"What?"

"Nothing." I shook my head.

He frowned but let it go as he started ushering me inside. Clearly, he was in a mood, and I wasn't the only one who noticed.

"Gee, Carter, such a romantic," James laughed, as he and Tracy fell into step behind us.

"Don't make me tell you what you are," Carter growled.

James chuckled, unbothered, but my stomach was roiling too much to take part in the conversation. I tried not to look at the spot where the shifter's body had lain last night, but I couldn't stop my eyes from swerving there as we walked past and into the house. Nothing. No blood, no marks remained to tell of where that young man, whoever he'd been, had breathed his last.

*Mr. Costas has people for everything*, Carter had told me. Apparently, that extended to cleaning up dead bodies on his doorstep. Which made me wonder, how many other bodies had his people disposed of through the years? How many deaths had Carter been involved with? How many by his hand?

And what was I thinking, marrying him, even fake marrying him?

The panic started in my toes and spiraled up my legs, through my stomach, and into my neck. My throat closed off. I couldn't breathe. Carter's hand on my back felt heavy, hot, despite the layers of clothing.

*I can't do this,* I thought. *I can't do this.*

I started to pull away. I needed to get outside for a few minutes. Had to get some fresh air. Clear my head. Calm down. Before I could free myself I heard a familiar voice booming across the house's marble entryway.

"Carter. Ellie. Good to see you back. Glad you survived the night. I knew you would. If anybody could get Nosizwe's shifters off your tail, it would be Carter. Are you two ready?"

Sean Costas. I blinked rapidly to dispel the mental images of his flesh and skin transforming into a Minotaur. A human, morphing into a creature from Greek mythology. He stood there smiling sympathetically, his grey eyes twinkling. Like he felt sorry for me, but this was all somehow a joke. Or humorous.

It wasn't a joke and it wasn't humorous. For a split-second, I felt a wash of anger. At Sean Costas. At Carter. At everyone in the house. At the entire situation. All I'd wanted to do was save a child's life. I hadn't wanted to be brought into the Costas fold. If they'd merely told me thank you and left me alone, none of this would've happened.

"We're ready," Carter answered, speaking for us both. "After this is done, we need to a have a sit-down and figure out what we're going to do from here on out. Come up with a workable plan. She can't stay on the run forever. Neither can I."

"Agreed." Mr. Costas closed the last few steps between us. His hand outstretched, he indicated a short corridor to the left. "This way, everyone."

Carter kept an arm around my back. My feet felt wooden but they moved because he moved, ushering me along. James and Tracy fell into step behind us.

"Why are they coming?" I whispered to the man escorting me.

He tilted his chin, giving me a sideways look as if I was ignorant.

"Witnesses," he responded quietly, "like we discussed earlier. Enough to make sure it's legal. Enough to cover our butts if anyone tries to poke holes in our story. But not so many the truth will leak."

I got it now. Tracy had been there last night and seen everything. She was in the know. James seemed to be Carter's go-to, so obviously he was too.

My irritation extended to them, as well as the Costases and Carter. Better judgment intervened.

*It's not their fault,* a voice whispered in my head. *It's not any of their fault. Nobody planned for Nosizwe's shifters to attack last night while you were here. Who could've foreseen that? It was a crazy series of events. They're doing what they can to take care of you. Even Carter. Especially Carter. I mean, who marries a woman to keep her out of jail?*

*Except that he's marrying you to keep himself out of jail too,* argued the other side of my brain. *Spousal immunity also protects him.*

Nevertheless, this was an awfully big step, for him as well as me. There was no denying it, and there was also no denying that, for whatever reason, I didn't break free and run as we walked into a sitting room or living room or den—whatever you'd call a room like this in a rich person's mansion. There were couches and chairs, end tables, a fireplace with a mantle, fresh flowers in vases, and soft, thick plush carpet. Floor to ceiling windows faced the winterized lawn behind this part of the house, allowing daylight to stream in. I didn't know why I wasn't pulling away. Was it because I was scared to, or because I was relying on Carter, just like I'd relied on him last night to keep me safe, no matter how much he intimidated me?

I had no immediate answer to that question, nor did I have time to figure it out. Ciara Costas was inside the room already, having coffee with some unremarkable little short, bald man in a suit. She smiled a greeting as we entered.

"Ah, here they are," she said. "Carter, Ellie, I'm so glad you're both alright. Ellie, don't you look lovely?"

She was being sweet. The soft sweater she wore had undoubtedly cost more than my entire outfit, especially since my dress had come off the clearance rack.

Her guest set down his coffee cup as well, turning to look at us.

"Is this the happy couple?"

Carter's scowl could've melted ice. I had a feeling if I could've seen my face I was pale as a ghost. Nervous. Downright terrified.

We were anything but a happy couple.

"Let's get this over with," Carter growled.

The justice of the peace—I assumed that's who he was, anyway, and briefly questioned what on earth Mr. Costas had on him to get him to go along with this—raised his brows in surprise, but didn't respond.

"Of course, of course," he agreed. "Well..."

He reached for a small black book lying on the coffee table next to the fancy silver coffee service. Again, a sense of unreality washed over me.

*Give me Mom's Mr. Coffee coffee maker and the chipped mug collection she's packed all over the United States,* I thought sadly as the justice of the peace stood up, clutching his book.

"How do you want to do this?" he asked.

Carter said nothing, but continued to scowl. I stood next to him, knees shaking beneath my dress, too nervous and too nauseous to say anything.

Thankfully, Mrs. Costas took over.

"Why not in front of the fireplace?" she said. "That would look nice. James, Carter, would you move the coffee table and chairs? Honey? Will you get the tray?"

Carter released me so he could help James fulfill her request. Mr. Costas picked up the tray, setting it on a nearby end table as, working together, the other men moved furniture aside, clearing a space in front of the mantle. The justice of the peace took a stand with his back to the fireplace, the fire, clutching his book in both hands. Mr. Costas stood behind his wife's wheelchair as Carter returned and took my hand, drawing me forward a few steps until we were standing before the officiant. At Ciara Costas's bidding, James edged around behind Carter and Tracy behind me. Almost like a maid of honor, a best man. Almost as if this were a real wedding that actually meant something, instead of a big sham.

The justice of the peace cleared his throat. "Are we ready?"

"Do it," Carter snapped.

I glanced up at him.

*He doesn't like this any better than I do,* I realized.

The official started to speak, but I didn't hear a word he was saying. I'd been to weddings. My father had officiated several. I knew the familiar words. I didn't have to pay attention to know what was being said. Instead, I stared at Carter, trying to figure out what he was thinking. More than once, he'd made his distrust, his dislike of humans obvious. Yet here he was, about to marry one. Me. We had nothing in common except the Costases, as his employers and my benefactors of sorts. We had no shared history or memories, except of defying death several times in one night. No shared affection. No attraction.

Well, maybe that wasn't entirely true.

There'd been moments where I'd reacted to him. Where he might have reacted to me. I couldn't really tell. He shifted moods as easily as he shifted forms. All I knew was he was completely unhappy about what was taking place, even though earlier he'd acted like it was no big deal. His unhappiness gave me a brand-new perspective. I almost felt sorry for him. He was almost as much a victim of circumstances as I was.

*He's just as trapped as you,* I told myself, staring up into his grim face. *He's not doing this because he wants to, or out of any loyalty to you. He's doing his job. And right now, that job must suck. It must really, really suck.*

Carter wasn't looking at my face. He was staring darkly at the justice of the peace. The poor officiant kept glancing up from his book, seeing that unflinching stare, stumbling over a word or two, then glancing back down at his book like he was trying not to notice. He couldn't not notice a death stare like that, though. Boy, if looks could kill, that officiant's head would've been outside on a pike somewhere.

Poor guy. Poor Carter.

The entire thing struck me so crazy after the second or third time it happened that a quiet snicker escaped. Now the officiant glanced up at me with a furrow between his eyebrows, as if he was trying to figure out why the bride had giggled. Carter's gaze swung around to me, and then he was giving me the same look he'd been giving the justice of the peace. For the first time, it didn't scare me. In fact, it only made me feel sorry for him. His anger had to be a direct result of his being so uncomfortable with the situation. I should've been the one who was a distressed—and I was—but in some ways he was handling this worse than I was.

As for the officiant? I pitied him. This had to be the weirdest wedding he'd ever performed, with a furiously glaring groom and a nervous, snickering bride. There he was yammering on about love and trust and commitment, while Carter's hand clutched mine tighter and tighter—probably because my palms were so cold he thought I was about to faint or freak out. Thankfully, the justice of the peace kept it short and sweet, maybe because he knew, or deduced from the obvious, that this wasn't a love match and there was no need for all the fancy love talk.

He came to the vows, starting with Carter, asking if he wanted to take me as his wedded wife, if he'd love me and cherish me, etc. And as I stared up at him, I remembered him telling me about the risks of fathering a child who might inherit his specific genetics, and him saying, *And this whole thing is why I'm not married. Not even at thirty.*

"I will," Carter spoke up, answering the officiant's questions. Under his breath he muttered, "Hurry up and finish this damn thing."

He caught my raised eyebrows, and shot me an apologetic look.

"Sorry," he whispered.

The justice of the peace paused. He'd already begun addressing me, but stopped mid-sentence to ask, "I beg your pardon?"

"It's nothing," I smiled, edging a little closer to my fake groom. "He was saying how happy he was to be marrying me."

Behind us, I heard James snort a laugh, which he covered by turning away and coughing. Carter was *not* amused. My grin broadened. It wasn't fair, but for the first time since this whole insane business had begun I could see the discomfort reeking from him, and even though I sympathized I almost...enjoyed it. For once, he was every bit as miserable as me.

"Yes, he—he certainly looks like it," the justice of the peace mumbled, which made me giggle again.

"I swear, Ellie, I'm going to—" Carter warned in a whisper, but I never heard his actual threat because just then it was my turn to speak up and say, "I will." Which overrode whatever Carter had been about to say.

Then came the next part, where we had to speak and make actual promises to each other. That was more than a little awkward, with an angry Carter staring down at me, promising to love and keep me for richer or for poorer, in sickness and in health, for better or for worse...while not meaning a dang word of it. It felt even stranger for me to murmur, "I, Ellie, take you Carter, to be my wedded husband..." all the while knowing I had no intention of ever taking him to be my wedded husband or of me being his wedded wife. But I made the promises, all the same, and I guess I did it satisfactorily, because the officiant went right on to the ring ceremony.

When he started to speak about rings, their importance and symbolism, I felt a tiny surge of panic. I hadn't thought anything about rings. Hadn't planned for them. Did we have to have rings? Not all couples wore rings, I reminded myself. When the justice of the peace asked Carter the traditional, "Have you a ring?" I fully expected Carter to wave the man off, tell him we weren't bothering with that. I was not expecting him to let go of my hand and dig in his jean's pocket. I think my mouth fell open when he removed his hand from his pocket, and clutched in his fingers I could see a wedding band. Not just a band, a set. Two rings. White gold. A band, and then a band with diamonds set in the shape of a flower.

*He bought me a ring?*

Confusion boiled my brain as I watched Carter pick up my hand and slide the set onto the appropriate finger. It was a little large but it stayed in place, catching the light, sparkling.

*Why did he buy me a ring? It's got to be fake. Probably one of those cubic zirconia things. It's still pretty, though. But why would he buy it for me? This is all for legalities, so why would he bother with putting on a show?*

I was staring so intently at the ring on my hand that I hadn't heard a word the officiant said. It took him repeating my name a couple of times before he broke through the mental fog and I realized he was speaking to me, asking if I had a ring.

"I'm sorry, I—I don't have a ring. For him," I stammered, embarrassed. "My gaze swung up to Carter's, and I said again, "I'm sorry. I didn't think about it."

His answer was blasé. "It's nothing."

The officiant took that as his cue to conclude the ceremony, but I kept gazing, fixated, at my hand in Carter's and the wedding set encircling my third finger.

*It's nothing?*

It wasn't nothing. At the very least, it meant he'd put some thought into this, into what we were doing. Whether he'd done it for show, or because he felt sorry for me, knowing how I felt about the idea of even fake marrying him, or as some sort of sympathetic nod to the importance I placed on marriage, he'd purchased a ring for me, without saying a word about it, kept it in his pocket, pulled it out at the appropriate time. All of the sudden, my earlier humor was gone. Maybe to him the gesture did mean nothing, but I didn't feel like laughing any more. And I sure didn't feel like laughing when the officiant finished his brief concluding remarks with,

"By the power invested in me by the state of Texas, I now pronounce you husband and wife. Carter, you may kiss your bride."

Again, my brain reeled with, *Uh oh. I didn't plan for this either.*

When I'd agreed to fake-marry him, I clearly hadn't considered the implications. A wedding ring. Having to kiss him.

Do *I have to kiss him? The justice of the peace is in on this, right? At least to a certain extent with the date change. We can skip the kiss.*

I actually opened my mouth to say, "We can skip the kiss," but even as I did Carter was bending down towards me. He was already so close that it was either shut my mouth or invite a

French kiss—which I wasn't about to do. I sealed my lips just in time for his mouth to land on mine.

A quick, simple brush of his mouth would've sufficed, especially since this was all pretense anyway. But there was no pretense about how firmly his lips pressed against mine, no pretense about the way his hand stole around to cup the back of my head, as if to either caress me or hold me in place so I couldn't duck away. There was no pretense about the feel of his lips, or how, all of the sudden, my eyes closed as my heartrate sped up, my breathing faltered, and my entire body flushed.

I didn't know if that was from anger or mortification.

I didn't know why Carter chose to kiss me like that, if it was to make things look good for the officiant, or as some sort of payback—making me uncomfortable because he was so uncomfortable. As his hand dropped and he drew away, breaking the physical contact, my eyes opened and I'm sure he could see the confusion written across my face. He didn't look confused, but he didn't look angry, either, like he had a few minutes ago. He looked...solemn. Almost as if he realized he'd invited something down on us by kissing me the way he had.

## CHAPTER TWENTY-THREE

Behind us, I heard Mr. Costas clear his throat softly, reminding everyone the moment was past. There was dead silence. Carter dropped my hand like it had been on fire and was burning him. Now the justice of the peace cleared his throat in the awkward silence of the room.

"If you'll give me a minute, I'll get the paperwork together for both of you to sign," he said. He put his book aside and Carter and I stepped apart so he could pass. Carter looked at me and nodded, as if to say, "Okay, hard part's through," then walked away, leaving me standing alone in front of the fireplace. The bride, left at the altar, married but alone. In a daze, I turned in place, staring at him, still feeling the pressure of his mouth on mine. The impact of his kiss reverberated through my body. My knees literally felt weak. Maybe I'd been through too much lately, and his kiss topped it all off. I didn't know what to do, what to say, where to look. I'd never felt so abandoned in my life.

Tracy must've seen how awkward I felt, because I heard her say quietly, sympathy in her voice, "You want to sit down, Ellie?"

I responded with a shaky nod. She put her hand on my shoulder and sort of guided me over to a seat on the couch, next to Mrs. Costas's wheelchair. Mrs. Costas smiled, leaned over to pat my hand.

"You did beautifully, Ellie. I'm sorry you had to go through all this, but our lawyers think it will be very temporary. We'll get this mess cleaned up and then you and Carter can be legally separated, like nothing ever happened."

"Yes, ma'am," I replied, forcing the words out of a throat that felt like it was closing up on me.

That was just it, though. Something had happened. I'd gotten married, for heaven's sake. And he'd put a ring on my finger. And he'd kissed me like...like he really meant it. Like he *wanted* to kiss me. Like everything else had been for show, but that kiss had conveyed something else entirely.

I kept looking down at my hands in my lap, gazing at them and that sparkling ring like they were the hands of a stranger, attached to my body. Until Tracy appeared in my line of vision, offering me a cup of steaming coffee.

"Here. You look like you could use this," she said. "Actually, you look like you could use a stiff drink. You're as pale as death right now. Relax, Ellie. Hard part's over. Carter can be uptight and obnoxious sometimes, but he's not a bad guy. And this isn't forever."

"I—I know," I said, and reached out to accept the cup. I didn't bother telling her that I didn't drink coffee. She was being nice, and holding the mug gave me something to do while I waited on the justice of the peace and the paperwork.

Speaking of which, I said, "The marriage license...are we sure they can fix the date to cover for us?"

"*They?*" James quipped.

Apparently not having anything else to do, he'd drifted closer to Mrs. Costas, Tracy, and myself. He stood next to the couch, slumping, hands in pockets, which I was beginning to think must be his typical posture.

"Not *they*. You mean *me*. Yes, the date's fixed."

"I don't know how this works," I admitted. "I guess I just want to be sure this wasn't for nothing."

Tracy chuckled.

"James once hacked the CIA database for fun. Calling in favors from a couple folks and then fixing computer records on a little thing like a marriage license are not big deals, Ellie. I promise you. It's done. Stop worrying."

I felt my eyes bug. "Is that true?"

James shrugged one shoulder. "I was bored."

Next to me, Mrs. Costas sighed. "Oh, James..." She sounded like an exasperated mother dealing with her teenager. I'd heard the exact tone from my mom towards my brothers more than once.

Our conversation was broken up by the justice of the peace re-entering the room with the marriage license in hand. He walked over to where Mr. Costas and Carter stood, spreading out the paperwork on a table, pulling a pen from his breast pocket. I couldn't hear everything he was saying, but he pointed at a couple of places on the documents, probably telling him where to sign. I felt sickness in the pit of my stomach. I knew I should go join them and get it done, but this felt like the final step that cemented me in.

Tracy glanced at me quizzically. "Shouldn't you be going over there too?"

"I'll wait my turn," I replied.

My voice sounded strained in my own ears. I would wait until I didn't have a choice not to wait.

Tracy and James exchanged looks. They thought I didn't see, because I was staring at Carter dashing off his signature with quick, bold strokes of the pen, but I caught it out of the corner of my vision. I wasn't sure what the exchange meant. Maybe, "Why is she making such a big deal out of this?" Again, James shrugged one shoulder, and they let it drop.

Everybody was acting like it wasn't a big deal, but it was to me.

In less than twenty-four hours my entire life had been ripped apart and thrown into a whirlpool that kept spinning more and more furiously, sucking me under, and this felt like the final drop out of the bottom of the maelstrom?

I guess Carter finished, because he looked up and caught my attention.

"Ellie?"

Knowing I couldn't stall any longer, I set down my coffee cup and rose. It only took a few steps to navigate my way over, and then I was standing between Carter and the justice of the peace, whose name I didn't know, staring down at the blank lines awaiting my signature. The justice of the peace indicated the first place I needed to sign, which was directly across from Carter's name.

*Carter Ballis* it read.

Grasping the pen tightly to hide the slight trembling in my fingers, I wrote *Eleanor St. James* opposite that.

I skipped down to the next place I needed to sign, even as I heard the officiant say, "...and if you decide to change your name, Ellie, you'll need this marriage license to apply for a new social security card and to change your name on your driver's license. You'll need your birth certificate also, of course, and..."

My hand froze mid-signature.

Change my name?

How far did this deception go? Was I going to have to change my name too? Lots of women didn't anymore. Surely I wouldn't have to if I didn't want to.

I felt Carter poke me gently. My gaze shot up to his, and I saw him shake his head slightly, reassuring me.

*It won't have to go that far.*

A sigh escaped at the guarantee that this one thing wouldn't be torn from my grasp. I said, "Okay," to the justice of the peace at the end of his instructions, and finished signing the documents.

"And we're all done," he said, gathering up the paperwork he needed to take with him. I heard him give Carter a few extra instructions about the license, but I didn't really hear or care. My part was done. The pressure in my chest that had been building this whole time released in a quiet sigh.

It was done. It hadn't been so bad, had it? I'd survived.

*Look at me, I survived.*

The officiant shook hands with Carter, then with me.

"Congratulations, folks," he said.

"Thank you. I'll walk you out," Carter responded. James brought the officiant his little book. He took it and then Carter escorted him to the foyer. I sort of trailed along behind, because I wasn't quite sure what was expected or what I should be doing now. Carter had said something about sitting down and coming up with a workable plan. What would that involve?

My train of thought was cut off by the door opening, the officiant telling us goodbye, and leaving. Not one second later Carter's phone rang. I saw the expression that came over his face after he answered and the person on the other end started talking. His dark brows lifted slightly in surprise.

"What? She's here?" he asked.

The other person kept talking. Carter's gaze shifted to me, then away.

"That's fine," he said. "Tell her to wait five minutes, then let her come. Send Jack, Amy, Britt, and Paul. Get them here now, before she arrives. I want them inside. Send team two to cover the house—entrances and exits. I want back up in place in case things go south. I doubt she's planning anything crazy if she's willingly walking into the lion's den, but you can't be sure with her. Make sure team three is on the lookout for stragglers. Put a rush on it."

He punched the button to end the call and slid his phone into his pocket. I think he'd temporarily forgotten I was standing there, because when I said, "Carter, what's going on?" he stared at me like his mind was a million miles away. He returned to reality, and the look he gave me was sober and intense, with something else mixed in. A dash of worry? Protectiveness?

"What is it?" I repeated, starting to feel nervous.

"Nosizwe is at the gates, asking for a truce. Asking to see Mr. Costas," he said.

## CHAPTER TWENTY-FOUR

The name hit me like a punch in the gut. Nosizwe? The woman whose shifters had been trying to kill me since last night?

"What? Why? Why would she be coming here?"

"She wants to talk about the Stones," Carter replied. "That's all she said to the guard at the gate."

"What Stones?"

"The Stones of Fire." Even though he answered me, his focus was already turning elsewhere. He stared down the corridor towards the room we'd just come from. The room where we'd gotten married.

"The ancient magical artifacts you mentioned last night?" I asked.

"What?" He threw me a look. "Oh, yeah, I did mention them. Yes, that's what she wants to discuss, which means I have to talk to Mr. Costas, get this set up. She'll be here in a few minutes. In fact, I want you to go upstairs. Stay out of sight."

"What? Why?"

"Because there's no need for Nosizwe to get a look at you or be reminded further that you exist. Go upstairs and stay out of sight until this is over."

"But I—"

I didn't even know what I was going to protest. I wasn't particularly eager to see Nosizwe, except out of curiosity to catch a glimpse of the woman who opposed Sean Costas. I simply didn't like Carter's domineering attitude and him telling me what to do.

"Ellie, I don't have time to argue with you," Carter interrupted. He faced me full on, looking down at me, unconsciously or consciously using his superior height and bulk to intimidate me into obedience. "Now, you're going to get upstairs, find an empty room, and you're going to stay there until I come to get you, okay? Just cooperate. It's for your own safety. Don't make me carry you up there."

He'd threatened me with that before. I didn't think he'd actually do it.

"Carter—"

He took a menacing step towards me. Instantly, I retreated, backing away.

*Maybe he would.*

"*Go*, Ellie." He said it quietly, but his tone brooked no refusals. "Get out of here."

I stared at him a second longer then obeyed, turning around and heading for the stairs. Even as I started up I heard the sound of his boots on the floor as he walked away, his footsteps brisk. Determined. He was head of security for this entire place. For Mr. Costas. For all these people, these shifters. It was his job to run things like this, make sure everyone stayed safe. Including me.

I acknowledged all of this as I went upstairs, uncertain where to go.

*Find an empty room*, he'd said.

Okay, but what if I went in a wrong room while searching for an empty one? I went down the first hallway I encountered, bypassing the closed doors, assuming they were bedrooms, looking for an open one. Didn't take long before I found a spacious family room, another den of sorts, or game room. It had comfy couches, bookcases, a gigantic television, a ping-pong table, air hockey...all sorts of stuff. There were massive windows that looked out over the lawns, the swimming pool. Even a private lazy river. I'd never seen one before, except on TV. I went and gazed out at the scene below for a while, but in light of what was taking place downstairs it didn't hold my interest.

I was unsure what to do with myself. I walked around the room, looking at things, stopped to study the books in the bookcases, read a few spines. My mind couldn't seem to settle on any one thing. It flitted helplessly from the events of last night, to wondering how my family was and when I could contact them again. What Nosizwe was doing here, and how long the meeting downstairs would take. What were the Stones of Fire? Would Carter be at the meeting? Probably, since he was an integral part of the household and its many operations.

Speaking of Carter, our wedding, fake though it was, kept playing through my mind. Every moment of it. The vows. The ring. The kiss.

*The kiss.*

I slumped on the couch and closed my eyes.

*This situation just keeps getting more and more messed up,* I thought. *I need to go home. I need to see my family.*

My family...

Nosizwe was here, presumably downstairs at this very minute.

*What if—what if I could talk to her?*

The idea implanted itself into my brain. Took root.

*That may not be such a good idea.*

*But it's not a bad one, either. She's already tried to kill me, thinking I'm involved with the Costas family. What if I tell her I'm not? What if I explain the whole situation, about Jackson and everything? How it's all a big misunderstanding? She might be reasonable. She might listen. She might understand.*

Or she might decide I really did need to die. However, she already seemed bent on that, so what did I have to lose?

I got up, feeling nervous and queasy, but also resolved. Maybe I was being stupid, but I didn't see any other way to end this. My family and I couldn't live the rest of our lives in the shadow of Carter's protection. I didn't see any way to finish this except to meet Nosizwe face to face and let her know I didn't have a dog in this fight. I wasn't involved. All I wanted was to be out of it. To get away from the Costas mafia, Carter, her, and their world of shifters. I wanted my life back, and this seemed the best way to get it. If she was a halfway reasonable person, surely she'd understand.

I started downstairs, glancing around uneasily. I'd made the first landing and turned the corner for the second before I spotted Carter's guard. Or Carter's guard spotted me. He was some sort of thing I couldn't label. He crouched on the balcony railing, down at the bottom, as if his feet were glued to it. He was winged. His eyes were a brilliant sapphire blue. His teeth were pointed. I could see that when he said,

"You're Carter's girl, right? You better get back upstairs."

I stopped short. "I'm not his girl," I said, feigning more bravery than I felt. "And Carter's not my boss."

The winged man didn't have eyebrows, but his eyes got momentarily bigger, like he would have raised his brows, if he'd had them.

"He's not, huh? Well, he is my boss. And I got my orders. Nobody comes down here from up there. Nobody from down here goes up there."

"Fine," I said, sinking to a seat on the landing. "I'll just wait, then."

"Wait for what?"

I didn't want to divulge any more of my business to this stranger.

"I'll just wait."

He gave me a sideways look, and turned away, muttering, "Carter's not gonna like this."

*I don't care what Carter likes.*

I kept my mouth closed to keep the words from spilling out, knowing they weren't entirely true. The truth was, I didn't *want* to care what Carter liked, and on a personal level I didn't. Not necessarily. But the side of me that remembered everything he'd done to keep me safe actually did care, because I knew, no matter his personal feelings towards me, the Carter who had snapped into coordinating safety measures for Nosizwe's visit was the same Carter who had personally coordinated to kill the shifters on my tail last night. He'd kept me safe so far. Apparently, he'd even ordered this...whatever it was...to keep an eye out for me.

Carter was determined to follow his boss's orders and safeguard me. Unfortunately for him, I was determined to keep my family safe and even free us from this jam. And if that meant confronting Nosizwe head on, against Carter's wishes, so be it.

Like I'd said, Carter wasn't my boss. My fake husband, maybe...but not my boss.

I settled in to wait, and it felt like it was killing me. I pulled my dress down over my knees, clasped my hands, and tried to look cool and calm. Inside, my stomach was churning. The breakfast burrito I'd eaten earlier this morning was not sitting well. I was squeezing my hands so tight that the wedding ring Carter had put on my finger pressed against the pinky of my right hand, leaving a temporary mark in my flesh. Nevertheless, I wasn't about to go anywhere. The guard kept scanning the area, and every time he'd make one of his slow scans his eyes would pass over me. I ignored him. He was doing his job. I was doing what I had to do, too. I wasn't planning on making any problems for him. At least not until Nosizwe came into view.

That happened about a half-hour after I took my seat on the stairs. There was an enormous ornamental clock on the wall above the entrance to the formal dining room. I kept checking it, watching the minutes tick by, wondering about the Stones that had been mentioned several times and how long it would take Mr. Costas and Nosizwe to discuss them. I briefly considered quizzing the guard about them, but he didn't seem inclined to conversation, and I wasn't sure if I could get anything out of him anyway. I needed Carter to slow down for five seconds and explain some things, but he was either in a talking mood or he wasn't. So far, he hadn't seemed willing to give up any information about the Stones.

Stones of Fire, I think he'd called them. What could that mean?

Like I said, about a half-hour after I'd first seated myself on the steps, I heard a door open. I heard voices, several voices, mingling. I couldn't tell if they were angry, but they sounded taut. I picked up on the tension. Footsteps approached from down the hall, and several men and women filed into view, Carter among them. He was on the outskirts, looking watchful. But my gaze skipped right across him and stopped on the woman in the middle of the pack.

"Elia?"

I whispered it aloud as I got to my feet.

I knew her! I'd seen her billboard only this morning in downtown Saginaw. She was a singer, an entertainer, a celebrity. An A-lister, and a Texas darling, since her main home was nearby in Dallas. She was taller than most of the men present, including Carter. Her ebony skin gleamed in the mansion's soft lighting, and her hair was divided into multiple braids, then woven into a beautiful, elaborate coif. She had the carriage and bearing of a queen. Regal, but with a funky, hip-hop vibe to her clothing and jewelry. In contrast, the people surrounding her were dressed in black. Not quite in uniforms, but their clothing gave them a uniform appearance, making them stand out. There were at least six of them—she hadn't walked into the lion's den unguarded.

I'd wondered, as I was sitting there, how I would know who

Nosizwe was when I saw her, but it all made sense. Elia had made a name for herself outside of her music and glitzy performances as an outspoken activist for the marginalized. She donated massive sums of money, mentioned her causes in acceptance speeches at awards ceremonies, and didn't shy away from throwing her hat into the ring of politics, encouraging her vast fan base to vote for those politicians she saw as most likely to defend minority groups. A number of her viewpoints bordered on extreme, even to some of her fellow celebrities, but as I gaped at her I suddenly understood.

She was Mr. Costas' chief rival. She was a shapeshifter, leading her own shifter clan. Doubtless, all of her bodyguards were shifters, as well. She advocated for minorities because, as a shifter, she was a unique one. She considered her people marginalized—or knew they would be, if humans were aware of their existence. In upholding these specific groups she was trying to pave the way for acceptance for a whole different group of people—humans who could shift into animals, monsters, creatures from myth and legend. She was using her platform to help herself and others like her. I couldn't blame her at all, but I didn't understand why that put her at odds with Mr. Costas. Shouldn't they be on the same side?

*She might be reasonable if I talk to her,* I thought as I stared down at her. She and her group had stopped in the foyer so she could exchange final words with Mr. Costas. *She's always advocating for human rights. That means she has to have some compassion. Maybe she'll understand when I tell her this is all a mistake.*

Gathering my courage, I started down the steps. The shifter guarding the stairs was observing the group on the floor. He'd forgotten about me until I was right up on him, trying to sneak around him. He must've caught sight of me out of the corner of his eye. His head twisted around and he hissed at me. I jumped back, startled, at the venom in his bright blue eyes.

"No one goes down," he reminded me.

Panicking, I glanced towards the doorway. Nosizwe was about to leave. She'd turned from Mr. Costas, looking angry. Her head was high, her bearing that of a monarch refusing to deal with the rabble. I couldn't let her go without at least trying. I took my chances and called her name.

"Elia!"

# CHAPTER TWENTY-FIVE

The guard on the railing hopped down and jumped in front of me even as Elia/ Nosizwe paused, turned.

"Who called me that?" she demanded.

Maybe in the Costas household she was known by her shifter name, not her stage name. I had gotten her attention, anyway.

"I did," I said, trying to maneuver around the guard who kept hopping in front of me. He was adamant about not letting me down, and I was adamant about getting down.

Carter's head had snapped up when he heard my voice. There was absolute murder in his eyes when he saw what I was trying to do. I couldn't hear him hiss, "Ellie, get back," but I read his lips when he said it. Ignoring him, I focused on Elia. She was facing me now, puzzled, trying to figure out why this crazy girl was obviously attempting to get around the creature on the stairs and why the guard wouldn't let her.

"Who is she? What does she want?" I heard her ask.

I didn't know who she was asking. Her bodyguards? Mr. Costas? Carter? James? James was there, and he looked pretty surprised to see me attempting to breach Carter's security measures.

"She's nobody," I heard Carter growl. "A fan. She just wants a picture with you."

He was trying to cover for me. I wasn't having it.

"That's not true. My name's Ellie and I want to talk to you," I huffed. The guard still wasn't giving in, so I finally stopped, hands on my hips, and snapped, "Look, she's already seen me. Would you *move?*"

Silence. The guard stared at me. Twisted his head around to look at Carter. Carter was glaring at me as angrily as he'd glared at the officiant during our wedding ceremony. Nosizwe was smirking as if the whole situation was amusing.

"Oh, let her through," the shifter leader said. "If she wants a selfie that badly..."

Her accent was as exotic as her appearance. I didn't know much about her history, prior to her catapult to fame, but I knew she'd been born and raised in southern Africa before she'd migrated to the States as a teen. Her lyrical voice still held heavy traces of her upbringing.

Even after Nosizwe's demand, the guard hesitated, staring at Carter who stubbornly refused to give in. I took advantage of his attention switch and dodged around him, headed down the last few stairs. He made a grab at me, but I evaded it, dashing down the final few steps into the foyer. More cautiously now I approached Elia and her group, who were all watching me. Some with humor, like they were used to people acting crazy around her, trying to get close enough for an autograph or a selfie. Some with bewilderment, like they might have been used to it but they were surprised to see it happening here in their enemy's home base. Others looked suspicious. Most of Mr. Costas' people looked surprised or downright angry. Carter's scorching glare literally could have killed. I could feel its burn but refused to acknowledge him.

I stopped close to her, feeling dwarfed by the tall singer and her fit, impressive bodyguards. There were still a couple between her and me, but we were as face to face as I'd ever thought to be with the shifter leader and entertainment queen.

"What do you want, girl?" she asked me. "An autograph? A picture? I've never had anyone from Sean's side request that. All any of them want from me is to see me dead."

"I'm not from Sean—Mr. Costas—I'm not from Mr. Costas's side," I corrected myself. It didn't feel right to call him by his first name. "I'm not from anyone's side. I'm—I'm Ellie."

I thought she might recognize the name. She didn't seem to.

"Ellie?"

"Ellie," I repeated. My hands were twisting nervously in front of me. I had to consciously make them stop. "You...actually sent someone to kill me last night. First a water shifter. Then—then several others. One of your lieutenants, included. Carter and Blake took them out."

I saw it the instant recognition took hold. Her face darkened.

"Turner died because of you?"

"Well, no. Well, yes. Well, it was all a big misunderstanding."

"How was Turner's death a misunderstanding? Or my other shifters' deaths, either?"

"It was a misunderstanding because I'm not a part of this. Any of this," I replied, drawing a circle, pointing out the Costases, Carter, and the rest. "I saved Jackson Costas' life, but I didn't know who his father was. I just saw a kid about to get hurt and I reacted. I wasn't expecting to be invited here. I sure wasn't expecting to see your—your shifters attack that night. I didn't even know shifters existed. I didn't know you existed. I did try to save Mrs. Costas, but that was me trying to keep someone from getting killed. I—"

Nosizwe had folded her arms across her chest. She didn't look like she believed a word I was saying.

"It's true," I protested, rubbing my forehead, trying desperately to think of a way to convince her. "I'm not a shapeshifter. I got brought into this by accident. I was hoping you would understand that and just...let me go. Let me go back to my life. I don't have a dog in this fight. I don't have anything to do with whatever's going on between Mr. Costas and you. I just want out, and I want my family out. Please..."

Her onyx eyes had narrowed to pin pricks. Her bodyguards' expressions ranged from bewildered to affronted. I don't think any of them quite knew what to do with this bumbling explanation. I wasn't sure it sounded plausible even to me, and I'd lived it!

Finally, Nosizwe said, "I don't know what game you are playing, here, but it's a reckless one. Why would you be here, at the Costas mansion, then running with Carter—" She swept out a hand to include him. "—If you weren't involved with the Costas family?"

"I told you, I—"

"Why were you at Carter's place last night, in his shower, if you weren't involved with him? Are you his girl?"

I felt my cheeks flush as I glanced guiltily at Carter. Okay, the entire world didn't need to know I'd been at his apartment last night. This sounded way different than it actually was.

"If you'd listen..." I tried to say.

She didn't want to listen.

"It doesn't matter to me who you are. What your involvement is with the Costas family. Whatever you're doing here—that's not my concern. My concern is that you *are* here. You were here last night when Sean killed one of my shifters. That means you're with them. You *are* involved. And unless Sean and I can come to some sort of agreement about the Stones, we will be at war." She bent, nearly putting her face in mine. "And that makes you my enemy."

I couldn't help it. I reeled back from the sheer hatred in her expression. It was unbelievable to me that I'd gotten so twisted up in such a mess so fast. Unbelievable that someone could hate me so badly because of somebody else.

"Please," I tried again. "You don't understand. I'm not even a shifter! Tell her, Carter," I begged, turning to him, imploring. "Tell her the truth. Tell her I'm not a shifter, and that I'm not involved."

Carter's death stare hadn't softened a bit, but he did grind out, "She's not involved, Nosizwe. It is a misunderstanding. She doesn't have anything to do with the Stones or the Costas family, beyond saving his son's life."

I noticed he didn't admit that I wasn't a shifter. I don't know if Nosizwe/Elia caught that or not, but she didn't seem to care.

"Perhaps she wasn't involved at first," the mob boss said, "but she's as deep in it now as anyone."

"No." I almost sobbed when she said that. "No, that's not true."

"As long as you are here, or anywhere near Sean Costas or any of his people, you are no friend of mine." She said it with finality. The implication was clear. Not only was I not a friend, I was an enemy too. "I lost good people because of you. One day, I'll return the favor."

"We're done." Jerking her head at her bodyguards, she said, "Let's go."

"Wait!"

I called her back. She halted, turned slowly.

"Why? What else can you possibly have to say?"

"I just—" I crept forward a couple of steps. Immediately, a bodyguard inserted himself between the shifter leader and me. Nosizwe laughed humorously and shoved him back.

"She's no threat," the entertainer said.

I halted where I was, gazing up pleadingly.

"No, I'm not a threat," I agreed. "But even if you think I am—even if you don't believe I'm not involved with the Costas family... please. Please take it out on me. Leave my family alone. I don't care what happens to me as long as they're safe."

I did care what happened to me. I knew she had shifters who could rip me limb from limb. That was more than a little terrifying. But I'd willingly take the brunt of her wrath if it meant my father and mother, my brothers, would be protected.

Nosizwe considered me for a long moment. "I can't tell if you are brave or stupid or both," she said. "Either way, I'm finished with this conversation."

She beckoned to her entourage and they swarmed around her, falling into step, ushering her to the front doors, both of which were open, in a sea of black clothing and hard faces. At the threshold, she stopped, turned back to Sean Costas and said, "Think over my offer, Sean. I'll give you a three day truce from the time I leave your home for you to consider. After that, the gloves come off."

"I will consider it," Sean answered. "But I warn you, Nosizwe, if you're planning to take the gloves off, I can assure you I'll hit harder and faster than you."

"Huh." She laughed. "I will burn you and your city to the ground, if I have to, in order to get control of those Stones. Make peace with me, or be prepared for war."

"Better get ready yourself, then," Sean replied.

Nosizwe matched him stare for stare a few tense moments longer, then tossed her head and left, stride long, looking every inch a monarch. She strode out to her car, her gate perfect despite towering stiletto heels, which was some sort of fancy, six-figure sports car I couldn't put a name to. She slid behind the wheel as a bodyguard got in next to her. The other guards piled into inconspicuous sedans in front and behind. Engines roared to life, tires spit up bits of debris, exhaust poured from the pipes, and in mere seconds all three vehicles were gone, vanishing down the tree lined driveway.

Silence.

I thought I'd been forgotten during Elia's and Mr. Costas' final exchange. I was mistaken. The sound of the cars roaring down the drive hadn't faded before Carter pushed through the circle of people between us to stand right in front of me, glaring.

"What was that? What the hell do you think you're doing?"

My lips parted at the venom in his voice.

"I was only trying to help."

It sounded lame even to my ears. Weak.

"Trying to help?" He was practically shouting. He was as good as shouting. I'd seen him angry before, but not this angry. "Trying to help?" he repeated. "Helping would've been doing what I told you to do and staying upstairs and out of sight. But, no, you couldn't do that, could you, Ellie? You had to step in. You had to interfere."

"I wasn't trying to interfere," I retorted, my voice rising to match his. I drew a shaky breath, tried to calm down. I didn't like being yelled at. I sure didn't like being yelled at in front of all these people. "I was trying to help my family. I was trying to protect them."

"You help your family by letting me do my job! Not by disobeying the orders I gave you for your safety and theirs!"

He made a sharp, slashing motion with both fists. I knew it was a gesture born out of sheer frustration, but I jumped backwards anyway. I'd seen those fists beat another shifter to death when he was in his bronze state. If they could do that to him, what could they do to me?

He caught my reaction and froze, staring at me angrily, breathing heavy. Tracy spoke up into the stunned silence that had draped over the crowd.

"Carter," was all she said. Quietly. Calling him back to earth. Back to his senses.

In response, he threw a glare over his shoulder.

"Shut it. I'm not going to hit her. I wouldn't do that."

"I know you wouldn't." Tracy was unfazed. "But you need to calm down. This isn't helping anything. She's scared to death."

Carter's burning gaze swung back to me. I must've looked pretty bad for Tracy to interfere. I felt nauseous. I'd made a mistake. I should have listened to Carter. I should have. But I'd been desperate to help. To reason with Nosizwe and get my family off the hook. Unfortunately, whatever battle raged between these two mob bosses was so deep that I was caught in the crosshairs no matter what I did.

"You were already in a hole," he finally said. "But you've managed to dig it even deeper. You made my job that much harder. Thanks, Ellie."

"I just wanted to protect my family," I whispered.

"You can't protect your family," he growled. "*I* can protect your family. *We* can protect your family. We were working on it. Then you had to go and throw them right in Nosizwe's face. If she was ignoring them before, you can bet she won't now, thanks to you."

"That wasn't what I meant to have happen!"

"Then you should've listened to me."

"I don't even know you!" Finally, I lost it. I yelled at him. Really yelled. I could physically feel the blood rush to my head, the heat to my face. "How am I supposed to trust you? I don't know any of you! I didn't ask to get involved in this. I'm not on your side. I'm not on their side. I just want out!"

"Well, good luck," Carter responded. His volume had lowered, and the old clipped, sardonic tones were back. "You're well and truly marked. You're on the Costas side now. Welcome to the war."

I was so mad I wanted to hit him. My fists balled up before reason inserted itself, saying that would not only be wrong, it would be foolhardy. Slowly I forced my fingers to unwind, to flex. I took a strong breath to get control of myself.

"No." I shook my head. "No. I'm done. I'm not getting involved any further in this insanity. You all want to slaughter each other over some stupid Stones or whatever? Fine. Go ahead. But I'm out."

I tried to shove around Carter. He stepped in front of me. Laughed.

"Where do you think you're going?"

"Home," I said. "Would you get out of my way?"

"Home?" He laughed again, dubiously, like I'd gone insane. "You're not going anywhere."

"Why not?" I lifted my chin, challenging him. "You said it's over. We're all involved now, anyway. So what's the harm? We're done no matter what. If I'm going to face my death, I'd rather face it there with them than here with you. I'm going home."

"No," he said shortly, "you're not. Stop acting crazy, Ellie. You're not thinking clearly, and you're not going home right now."

"Stop me," I sneered.

That was probably not a wise thing to say to a man like Carter Ballis.

His face hardened a fraction, but otherwise he offered no warning before he ducked and grabbed me, one arm around my waist and the other behind my knees. He knocked me off my feet and had thrown me over his shoulder faster than I could think or react. My glasses slid down my nose, but I caught them with my left hand.

"Hey!" I yelled. I slammed my fist into his back, between his shoulder blades. It didn't faze him, but it actually hurt my hand. "Hey, put me down. Hey!"

He shoved his way through the group, ignoring their gasps and exclamations. I heard Tracy and Mrs. Costas both say, "Carter!" in a way that was equally shocked and reproving. My head was swimming from my upside-down perch, but I saw Mr. Costas, arms crossed, watching the scene, expressionless. Like he wasn't planning on interfering.

"Put me down, you jerk!" I shouted, trying to wriggle against his grasp, but the arm around my legs, pinning me to his shoulder was like a band of iron.

"Not until you can think clearly enough to listen to me. Until then, I'm putting you somewhere safe. For your own good."

"Carter, is this really necessary?" Mrs. Costas called after us, wheeling her chair out of the circle of bystanders.

I was hoping his boss's wife might have some effect on him, but he just jogged up the stairs like my weight meant nothing, ignoring her. My stomach bumped against his shoulder with every step and I had to clench my jaws to keep my teeth from rattling together. I felt tears burning my eyes. Tears of frustration, humiliation, and outright rage. I couldn't do anything about it. I couldn't hurt him. I couldn't get away from him. All I could do was hang there, over his shoulder, like a seething, furious, half-blind rag doll as he carried me into a bedroom and dumped me unceremoniously on the bed. Instantly, I rebounded, getting up on my knees and scooting backwards away from him.

"I'm not staying here," I warned, shoving my glasses back on my face.

"Yes, you are."

He didn't even look back as he strode for the door. "I'm going to see what I can do to clean up this mess. Until then, this is where you'll be. Hang tight, kid."

Then he went out, shutting the door after himself. I heard fumbling at the door handle. A click. As soon as the echo of his footsteps had faded I jumped up and dashed over to try the handle.

It was locked from the outside.

I'd gone from guest to prisoner in the Costas mansion.

## CHAPTER TWENTY-SIX

Livid, Carter stormed back down the stairs, so full of rage and aggression that he would have almost welcomed an attack by Nosizwe's shifters for the chance of having somewhere legitimate to direct his anger. He couldn't believe what Ellie had done. After all his work to hide her away, keep her safe. After the risks he'd taken, including personal, bodily ones to himself. After coddling and caring for her, trying to shield her from Mr. Costas' rival, she had to go and do something idiotic like try to persuade Nosizwe that she wasn't involved with the Costas mob and didn't deserve to be a target.

How ignorant, how naive could anybody possibly be? Nosizwe didn't play harmless games. Ellie should have known that from the past twenty-four hours, when her shifters had tried multiple times to kill her. And that last bit—practically begging the shifter queen to take out her anger on her, Ellie, as if that would appease Nosizwe and make her leave her family alone. Like Nosizwe had said, Carter couldn't tell if Ellie was brave or stupid. But it was obvious, no matter how foolishly she'd acted, that she loved her family. She was willing to bear the brunt of the shifter leader's wrath if it meant sparing them.

Words she'd said to him earlier this morning on the drive to the Costas estate pushed into his mind now.

*You like to make jokes about my religious beliefs, and poke fun at me for them. But, you know, at the heart of all I believe is the idea of self-sacrifice for others.*

Self-sacrifice. She'd basically offered to sacrifice herself in order to save her family, and Carter was sure she would've gone through with it, too. It would never have worked, but at the very least she certainly practiced what she preached.

Even if Carter couldn't appreciate what she'd done, was enraged by her idealism and recklessness, the hidden, inner Talos could understand and respect the idea of safeguarding someone else, no matter the cost.

Carter shoved the Talos back down. He didn't want to hear from it. Not today. He was too angry. Too angry that all of his hard work had been jeopardized like that.

He reached the landing and jogged lightly the rest of the way down. Some of the crowd at the bottom of the staircase had disappeared. Several of them were standing around, looking awkward, like they didn't know what to do without him there to direct them. Some of them, like his employers, Tracy, and James, were waiting on either an explanation or a discussion about what to do next with the information Nosizwe had brought and the offer she'd made, as well as what was to be done with Ellie.

That was the problem, Carter thought, reaching the marble floor and heading towards them. He wasn't even sure what to do about the girl. Not now. Not after this. How was he supposed to get her out of this one? Locking her in the room upstairs was a temporary measure: fine for now, but she couldn't stay there indefinitely. Although, truth be told, he was mad enough that he didn't mind the idea of keeping her locked away for a while until she absorbed a little sense into her head.

"Everything well?" Sean asked.

Carter stopped, thrusting his hands into his jeans pockets.

"I put her in the holding room," he said, "where she's going to stay for now." He glanced around the foyer with a dark look, warning everyone to pay attention. "Nobody even thinks about letting her out. I don't care how sorry you feel for her. The kitchen can send three meals a day up to her. There's a bathroom in the suite. I've got her bag and will send it up so she has extra clothes. She'll be fine for a day or two until we can figure out what to do."

Nobody argued.

The only people with the authority to circumvent his orders were the Costases themselves. Sean trusted him to make his own decisions in the matter. Ciara clearly disapproved, but had probably decided this wasn't the best time to start an argument. She wouldn't like his method of protecting Ellie, but what else was he supposed to do with her? If Ciara had any better ideas, he would listen.

Anyway, it wasn't like she was in a prison or locked away in a dungeon. The holding room was on the third floor of the mansion, so there was no going out the windows with their unbreakable glass panes, even if the windows unlocked, which they didn't. The door locked from the outside. It certainly wasn't the kind of place to keep dangerous shifters, but on the rare occasions they'd had to host an emissary of Nosizwe or had captured a less dangerous shifter from whom they needed information, it worked fine. Ellie wouldn't suffer there.

"Unless you've got level four access, get back to your jobs," Carter went on. "Show's over for now. But keep an eye out for any ghosts—any loiterers or fliers or anything out of place. I think Nosizwe will keep her word to lay low for the next three days, but be watching. That's it for now. You're dismissed."

Since *level four access* only included people who might actually have a say in Sean's decision whether or not to accept his rival's offer, everyone trailed off except the Costases, Carter, James, and Rory. Rory handled all of the miscellaneous and odd jobs that didn't quite fit into his or James' job descriptions. She was a fixer and a go-getter for the family. A great deal of her work involved managing paperwork and phone calls, as well as acting as a liaison between the various parts of the Costas enterprises. As soon as the others had gone, she said,

"Carter, I got a phone call from our contact at the Fort Worth police department. They're pushing. Seems they've identified you from security footage at the Botanic Garden last night. Or they're close to making a positive identification, anyway. They noticed the ding on the car's fender, cross-referenced it with any reported accidents involving Martins from the past few weeks, and came up with a list of potential vehicles. Ours was on the list."

Carter felt his gut tighten. He wasn't truly surprised, but the news was obviously far from welcome.

"One of the lead detectives on the case is a real bulldog when it comes to solving a crime," Rory went on. "In her research, she saw pictures of you shadowing Sean and Ciara at various events. She could tell you looked like the man in the security footage, although it is doubtful whether they can make the ID stick. Still, they're pushing their captain to be able to talk to you."

Carter swore. Just what he needed on top of everything else.

"You call Rodriguez yet?"

"He says they have nothing. They can't make a case without a body, and Amy made sure there's no body, correct?"

"Absolutely correct."

Of that he was positive.

"Rodriguez says the best course of action might be to agree to talk to them, with him present. Well, you wouldn't actually say anything. You would let him do all of the talking. You're newly married. You were there with your wife, but in a different part of the Garden. You didn't see anything. They can't make you or Ellie talk about what either of you may have seen, because of spousal privilege. Unless they can physically tie you to the scene, you should be in the clear. Rodriguez thinks, if push comes to shove and their captain does give them the green light to interview you, it might be time to give them your cover story and let them know this is the last time they'll be saying anything to either of you. You're not some rinky-dink drug pusher on a street corner. You work for the Costases, and they won't be railroaded. He said it may be time to let the Fort Worth PD know that, so next time they decide to get nosy they'll think twice.

"What do you think?" Rory finished. She stood there dressed in a professional dark suit, holding a clipboard, a Bluetooth ear piece in her right ear, nearly hidden by her chin-length blonde hair.

Carter shrugged. "Whatever Miguel thinks. He's the expert. This is what he gets paid for."

Rory nodded crisply. "I'll give him a call," she said, jotting down a note on her clipboard.

She wheeled to walk away, but Carter called her back.

"Wait, Rory?"

"Yes?"

She turned, one finger already on the Bluetooth device, prepared to make that call.

"Tell Miguel if he thinks we should talk, they talk to me only. They do not talk to Ellie. Not a word. She will not be there. Make sure he knows that. I don't trust her not to get flustered and spill more than she should."

Plus, if anyone was going to get thrown under the bus, it wouldn't be Ellie. If worse came to worst, he'd take his chances with the legal system, rather than risk her. If blame wound up being assigned, he would take it. Never mind the fact that Ellie had also killed someone out there. They'd never be able to prove it was her. If they even proved a killing had taken place—not likely—and Rodriguez couldn't get him off right away, Carter would take the fall. He knew he could take care of himself in lock up. The idea of Ellie locked away...well, Carter was surprised by how distasteful it was. By how quickly the Talos rose up with the need to protect her. Protect her from the cops and the legal system, as well as Nosizwe.

After all, he'd promised Ellie that he'd figure out this puzzle and reunite her with her family. At the time, he'd been mainly trying to calm her down, not wanting to deal with a hysterical woman. But a promise was a promise, right?

## CHAPTER TWENTY-SEVEN

The morning dragged on with no one to see and no one to talk to. There was a shelf with a few books on it. I perused those briefly and found a mixture of romance novels, classic literature, westerns, and detective stories. Nothing held my interest, so I walked back to the bed, picked up the remote off the nightstand, and flicked the TV on. I flipped channels mindlessly, but nothing on television was as interesting or eventful as my life for the past few days. Nothing caught my attention at all except an entertainment channel doing a piece on Elia. Normally not something I'd have watched, but I sat there observing until it was over, still trying to mentally match the entertainer on the screen with my newfound knowledge that she was a shapeshifter and the leader of her own shifter army.

When the segment ended, I clicked it off the TV and stood up, walking back to the large windows to look out for the hundredth time.

I put my hand on the glass as I peered down below. My left hand. As I did, the diamond on my finger caught my eye. I drew back to study it again. Part of me was still so aggravated at Carter for his rough handling that I felt like taking the ring off and flushing it down the toilet. The other part of me said it was sensible to keep it on as part of the marriage sham. I was so full of conflicting emotions that I didn't know what to think. I didn't want to think about anything, but my kind kept insisting on replaying every minute of my time since my arrival yesterday evening at the Costas mansion, right up to my confrontation with Nosizwe/Elias and Carter throwing me over his shoulder and hauling me upstairs, locking me in.

*I still can't believe he did that.*

Moving to the bed, I flopped back onto the mattress with a sigh.

*Carter Ballis.*

I couldn't figure him out. He alternated between surly silence and outright provoking me. Cynicism and outrageous teasing. But he'd willingly put himself between danger and me, married me, defended me, kissed me.

My entire body flushed. I laid two fingers on my mouth, feeling the pressure of his lips and the way his hand had cupped the back of my head, his fingers briefly tangling in my hair.

Or was it willingly?

*He said you were just a job,* my brain reminded me.

The woman inside responded, *You don't kiss someone like that merely for a job.*

Why did you kiss someone like that? For show? It was a pretty stinkin' good show, if that was the case. He hadn't needed to kiss me the way he had. Crazy as it seemed, could he really be attracted to me?

That seemed unlikely.

Maybe he was simply being a guy and taking advantage of the moment to get a kiss in.

Ultimately, I might never know the real reason for it. I tried to put it out of my mind by rolling over and closing my eyes to take a nap. I breathed deeply a few times in an effort to settle down when someone knocked at the door.

"Ellie?"

Quickly, I sat up, swiping loose hairs out of my eyes.

"Mrs. Costas?"

"May I come in?"

"I...uuuh...the door's locked," I answered.

"I can unlock it," she responded. "I'd like to speak with you, if you don't mind."

"Of course not," I said, already jumping up and heading for the door as I heard the lock click and saw the handle turning. I reached it in time to pull it open, holding it for her to wheel her chair inside. For a fleeting second, the idea of rushing past her and trying to make it to the stairs, make it outside, tempted me. Then I saw the man and woman behind her. They may have been bodyguards, or they may have been meant to keep me from bolting. Either way, it worked.

I was about to close the door after Mrs. Costas had wheeled herself in, but I stopped when the man presented something to me.

"Carter sent this for you," he said.

It was my suitcase from the car.

I accepted it, feeling a sting of dismay. Had Carter sent it to be thoughtful, or to get it out of the car, or because I was going to be here for a while?

I thanked the man and shut the door. Placing the suitcase against the wall, I walked over to where Mrs. Costas had parked her wheelchair beside a fancy arm chair with plush brocade upholstery. She gestured for me to sit down, which I did.

"How are you?" she asked. "Is there anything you'd like? You've been up here for a couple of hours. Are you hungry?"

"A little," I responded. "I guess I didn't eat much this morning."

"I don't blame you. After last night, and then being told about the big step this morning..." She smiled sympathetically. "Give me a moment, and I'll have some lunch sent up. What would you like?"

"Ummmm..." That caught me off guard. How did eating work in a place like this? Did they cook whatever you wanted on demand, like a restaurant? Or did they send out for it?

"Just—just whatever they're making," I answered, hoping that was the correct response.

"I believe tomato-basil soup and smoked turkey and arugula sandwiches are on the menu for this afternoon," Mrs. Costas said. "Although you may have something else, if you'd prefer."

"Oh no, that sounds great. It sounds great," I repeated. Much better than what I usually took with me for lunch. Peanut butter and jelly. Lunch meat with plastic-y American "cheese." I was pretty sure there wouldn't be anything cheap or fake about what came up from the kitchens here.

I waited while Mrs. Costas put in a call downstairs from the cell phone she pulled from her pocket. The phone made me think of the burner phone Carter had procured for me last night. I wondered if I could have another one to call my family. I wanted desperately to talk to them, hear their voices. I was worried sick about them, especially after what had transpired a little bit ago between Nosizwe and me. Then I thought contacting them might not be such a great idea. I was terrified of doing anything else that could put them in danger.

*I guess I could ask Carter what he thinks.*

Then I recalled how angry he was at me, specifically for going against his advice.

*No way will he help you out now*, I told myself glumly.

Mrs. Costas must've noticed my expression. She'd ended her call but left the phone in her lap.

"You look so sad, Ellie," she remarked. "I'm sorry you've become involved in our problems. Sean and I both feel terrible that you saved our Jackson only to be caught up in our affairs.

Please know we never intended for any of this to turn out the way it did."

I worked up a smile. "I'm sure you didn't. It was just really bad timing. For everyone."

Me, them, Carter…

To distract myself from grim musings, I inquired, "How is Jackson?"

A warm glow lit up her face at the mention of her son. "He's well," she replied. "His father and I try to shield him as much as possible from the irregularities of our lives. With Nosizwe's new ultimatum, we're seriously considering sending him away to stay with my family over the upcoming holidays. We think it might be best that he's absent for a while.

"How are you holding up?" she inquired, switching the conversation back to me.

"How?" I almost gave the pat, "I'm fine," but decided to be honest. "I'm a mess. I've never been this big a mess in my life. I haven't seen my family in a couple of days. I know they're worried about me and I'm worried sick about them. I can't go to them or contact them. I married a man I barely know, and then he locked me in this room, and I'm guessing, from the people standing outside, that you're not here to let me out."

She winced and shook her head.

"I'm sorry. I wish I could. But Carter would not be happy."

"Aren't you his boss?" I asked bluntly.

"Boss? I suppose, technically, as his employer I am his boss. However, the truth is, Carter has a lot of free reign. He knows more about the ins and outs of protecting the family and our business endeavors, not to mention our people, than either Sean or I do. That's his job. It's his entire life. He is very good at what he does. We place great faith in him and his abilities. If he makes a decision, it's usually our decision, as well. We don't circumvent him lightly."

"I've noticed everyone listens to him," I observed.

"That is because Carter is...unique. Of course, all shifters are unique compared to humans, but Carter is unique even in the world of shifters."

"How's that?"

She tilted her head. "How much do you know about Greek mythology?"

"Ummm..." I considered the question. "I know some. Of course, elements of it are everywhere in our society. Plus, well, you know my dad's career background: you have to have some understanding of Greek and Roman culture and mythology to understand the world of the New Testament. So there's that. I know about Zeus, the main god. His wife, Hera. Uh...Aphrodite, the goddess of love. Poseidon, the guy with the trident, who was the god of the sea. Oh, and of course the story of the Trojan War. Helen of Troy, whose face launched a thousand ships..."

I trailed off, realizing I was rambling. She'd been sitting there patiently, but I sensed she wasn't really quizzing me on my knowledge of Greek mythology. She was going somewhere with this

"You're definitely acquainted with it, then," she approved. "But, let me ask you, have you ever heard of the Talos?"

"No," I answered. "Not except for hearing Carter mention it. I assumed it was simply a name for what he...uh, turns into."

"It's a much lesser known Greek myth," Ciara Costas explained. "Most people have never heard of it. It isn't as famous as Hercules or Achilles or some of those. Its origins and meaning are disputed among scholars, and many of them think the myth was something of a mystery to the Greeks themselves."

"What does that have to do with Carter?"

"Carter is the Talos. Like you said, that is what he shifts into."

I shivered, picturing him in my mind. One moment, a normal human being. The next, a ripple passed over his body. His skin and flesh altered to bronze. His facial features smoothed out into those of a bronze statue.

"The rarer the myth usually indicates the fewer shifters there have been for the myth to gain traction. Usually, but not always," she explained. "However, Carter is just such a case. There was only one Talos in Greek mythology. He was a living bronze statue. The predominant legend says Talos was a gift from Zeus to his lover, Europa, and was built by Hephaestus, the god of armor and weaponry, fire and forges. Talos' job was to circle the island of Crete, where Europa lived, three times a day. He kept pirates and invaders from its shore. He was a bodyguard, a protector. That's what he was fashioned and created to be. That's all he can be. It's his very nature."

A light glimmered in my brain.

"That's why Carter is your head of security and is so good at his job, is what you're saying."

"Yes, exactly. Carter is extraordinary. There was only one Talos, according to mythology. So far as we know, there has only ever been one family line that carried the Talos gene."

"Carter told me he came from Greece but that his mother was English," I said. "He didn't tell me a lot, but he said his parents are still there and he came to live with Mr. Costas when he was a kid."

"He did. His parents sent him here. They knew my husband could give Carter what he needed. Things they never could."

"What was that?"

"Training. A home. A place in this world. Most of all, safety," she replied, looking me dead in the eye. "You think shifters are dangerous and scary, don't you? Well, the world can be every bit as dangerous and scary for shifters. Carter, unfortunately, found that out at a young age."

"He was hurt? It wasn't his parents, was it? He told me they were the good kind of parents. That they didn't take him to doctors or psychiatrists or to the church for an exorcism, but sent him here."

"No, it wasn't his parents who hurt him," she answered soberly. A little sadly. "Mind you, I wasn't married to Sean when

Carter arrived. That was several years before my time here. But I've known him since he was a teen. And I know his history."

"Which was?"

She looked up at me from beneath long, jet black lashes, considering.

"Carter probably wouldn't like me telling you this."

I half-opened my mouth to protest. To say something about how I'd been dragged all over Fort Worth by him the past couple of days and he apparently knew every bit about my personal life. Instead, I clicked my jaws shut. This was Mrs. Costas' decision. Maybe I had earned the right to know Carter's life history. Maybe I hadn't. I wanted to know, but it was up to her whether to share it or not.

"Then again," she said with a funny little smile, "you are married to him now. Which is, I'll admit, something I never dreamed I'd say. Carter has never been much of a lady's man. Too devoted to his work."

I glanced down at the ring on my hand.

"I am his work," I said softly.

"That's right, you are. You two have certainly been through a lot together. Which is why I'm going to tell you this. But you mustn't let him know that I told you. He hates talk of his past. I think he would erase it, if he could. He can't, though. His past shaped him into the man he is today."

"What happened?" I asked, resting my elbow on the arm of the chair and leaning towards her.

She rolled her thumbs thoughtfully across the top of her chair's wheels.

"Usually, a shifter's abilities begin to manifest around puberty. Most of us are aware of this. Usually, our parents, grandparents, and other relatives have prepared us for it. Carter lacked that advantage, though. His genes are so rare they hadn't manifested in generations. He was about eleven years old when he began to change. From what I've heard, prior to this incident, he was a perfectly normal little boy. Sweet. Amiable. Well-liked."

I didn't want to interrupt her story. I managed to choke down my snicker with a fake cough.

Carter sweet and amiable? Well-liked? That didn't sound a bit like the sarcastic, surly, caustic man I'd come to know. Maybe he was well-liked around here, in his own world with his own people. Except he didn't necessarily seem liked so much as respected. Except by the Costases. They seemed to like him.

Ciara raised an eyebrow at my cough, like she knew it wasn't real, but she went on with her story.

"From what I'm told, he had a heart for the children who were picked on or bullied. One friend, in particular, was a grade or two below him and autistic. Brilliant in some areas, but had a difficult time fitting in with the other kids. Communicating with them. Carter went out of his way to befriend this boy. Sat with him at lunch. Walked him to and from school. He didn't have to, but even then the Talos with its protector's instincts was probably stirring, without Carter or his parents having any idea.

"Well, one day the school bullies—a group of three—got Carter's friend alone between classes. They broke his glasses. Threw his books in the mud. They were taunting him. Teasing him. Carter saw it and intervened."

She stopped.

"And?" I prompted.

"And—it was then the Talos manifested itself for the first time." She let that sink in. "I'm sure you can imagine how traumatic that must have been. He thought he was protecting his friend, and then his entire body shifts, changes into a living, walking, breathing bronze statue. He had no idea. He didn't know it could happen. It would be the same as if you, Ellie, changed right now from yourself into—into—I don't know. A harpy. A mermaid. A panther. Can you imagine how shocked you'd be? How terrified? And he was a child. He had no idea of his family history or his genes. Not as it related to being a shifter."

Soberness fell over me, trying to imagine such a thing.

"The other kids were terrified too," Ciara Costas went on. "From what I understand, the change was fast—it only happened for a second. That's not uncommon. Shifting is very erratic until one learns to control it. It can appear and reappear at odd times and for no apparent reason, set off by changes in emotion, hormone fluctuations, that sort of thing. The Talos appeared long enough to scare the other children, but, rather than run, they went on the offensive. They attacked."

"Attacked Carter?"

"Yes." She nodded gravely. "His friend stood nearby, upset, unable to help. The other kids, the bullies, took out their cruelty on Carter. By the time someone fetched the teachers, he had a broken arm. Cracked rib. He was in hospital for several days."

"That's horrible," I said softly. As I did, I remembered Carter's statement about hating bullies. In light of his story, it made sense.

"It gets even worse," Ciara replied. "Carter, poor kid, was struggling to cope not only with what had happened, but the trauma of having shifted for the first time without any idea of what had happened to him. Meanwhile, the other children ran before the teachers actually saw who had attacked him. His autistic friend couldn't give any names. The bullies were suspected, but without actual proof the school couldn't do anything. It was Carter's word against theirs. I can only suppose his parents felt like they didn't have a choice in the matter. Carter wound up going back to school after he was released from the hospital..."

"Oh no." I felt sickness squirm in the pit of my stomach. I wasn't sure I wanted to hear the rest.

"Oh, yes. He was cornered at some point in the boys' locker room by the same group. They called him a monster and a freak and all sorts of horrible names."

*Horrible names like I called him. No wonder he's acted like a jerk to me. No wonder he dislikes and distrusts regular humans. Here I am, proving everything right he's ever believed about us,* I thought, feeling ashamed. *I owe him an apology. For that, anyway.*

"They kept demanding he change," Ciara said. "But he didn't have the control, at that point, to change on his own. All he could do was try to defend himself from them. Which, with a broken arm, wasn't going well. The bullies were determined. They'd brought a camera, as I understand. None of the other kids had believed their story about Carter shifting into a bronze person. In a final attempt to get him to shift, they dragged up Carter's friend, the autistic boy, and started attacking him..."

I closed my eyes for a second. Carter's first introduction into the world of shifters versus humans had been raw and full of violence, the kind of violence no child should have to see, much less endure. As if puberty itself wasn't plenty difficult for most kids, throw being a shifter with no idea of your capabilities on top of it. Then these horrific events. Now, I understood Mrs. Costas' assertion that this had made Carter into the man he was today. Bitter and angry against normal humans, carrying a grudge against the world itself. And I couldn't blame him, not after hearing this.

"...they might have killed him," Mrs. Costas was saying, and I blinked, forcing myself to return to her voice and the rest of the story. "But the Talos took over. Carter shifted. His protector's instincts kicked in, and he fought back to defend his friend. He was still weak and had a broken arm, though. And no control whatsoever over the Talos. He fought them off once, even managed to destroy their camera, but then he shifted back to his human side. And, well..."

"It happened all over again," I surmised.

"Yes. It was ugly. They could have killed him. I was told teachers arrived and pulled the other boys off Carter. By the time they did, he was severely injured, but he was also on top of his friend, taking the beating for him. The other boy was mostly unharmed. Carter, though—he spent weeks in hospital. The bullies were expelled and Carter never returned to school. During his recovery, he told his parents the entire tale, including about his shifting. I don't know how much convincing it took, but they believed him and started seeking answers."

"Carter mentioned his grandma had some idea of what was going on," I interjected.

"Yes, that's what I understand too. Only whispers of whispers had been retained in the family memory. It was one of those things people didn't talk about, but she remembered the rumors from her childhood. With enough research, Carter's family was able to piece together not only what was happening to their son, but also to find out about my husband. Eventually, they made the decision to send Carter here, to Sean, for safety and training."

"Why didn't they come with him?"

"It can be very difficult to migrate legally to another country," Ciara explained. "There was no marriage, no refugee status, nothing to ease their transition here, and they were far from wealthy. Besides that, they had other obligations in their homeland, dealing with their aging parents. Their jobs. Between Sean and them, they were able to get Carter here, and through the years Sean's people oversaw the necessary paperwork for him to stay and eventually gain U.S. citizenship.

"Carter told me he hasn't seen his family in twenty years," I said. "Did he never want to go back?"

"Sean offered," Ciara answered. "After he'd been here a few years, Sean offered to send him home for a visit. Of course, since becoming an adult and working for Sean he could have gone whenever he wished."

"But he didn't."

"No, he didn't. I would imagine, even though he is grateful to his parents for getting him the help he needed, there has to be some sting still there. Some sting that he was merely a child and they sent him away. Maybe it isn't fair to his parents, considering the spot they were in. Perhaps it is. I'm sure he has very mixed feelings about it. However, I do know he phones them sometimes. They stay in contact. It isn't as if Carter hates them and has nothing to do with them. I believe he supports them financially, as well, although he says little about it. I only know because he mentioned it once to Sean."

"I see," I said, even though my mind was whirling. I really didn't see. I thought I'd faced challenges in my life. Clearly, I couldn't even begin to understand the challenges Carter had tackled, growing up into a legacy he hadn't known he had, being separated from his parents, raised an ocean away.

"May I ask," I said, since she seemed to be open to talking and this was my first chance of gaining solid information about the strange world into which I'd fallen, "why did Carter's parents send him here? Why to your husband? Does he normally take in refugees?"

Mrs. Costas smiled with one corner of her mouth. "Shifter refugees, yes, or they find their way here. Seek him out."

"Why him? Why here?"

"Well," she said, "to answer that you'd have to know the history of the struggle between Nosizwe and himself, of the Stones of Fire, and how they pertain to shifters in general. There is a lot of background to that question."

"Right now, I don't have anything but time," I chuckled ruefully. "Carter's mentioned the Stones a few times, but he didn't go into much detail. I would love to have some answers," I said, daring to her look her straight in the eye.

She opened her mouth to reply, but a knock at the door prevented her. A man with blonde hair and big shoulders cracked my door, sticking his head in to say, "Mrs. Costas, lunch is here."

She wheeled her chair around to face him. "Thank you, Paul. Please let them in."

She tilted her chin back towards me. "We'll talk further in a minute."

# CHAPTER TWENTY-EIGHT

A couple of people dressed in simple clothes with muted colors wheeled a cart into my room, a cart with a silver soup tureen, a covered platter, an elegant silver coffee carafe, little fancy cups with spouts, and gracefully curved spoons for cream and sugar. I admit my eyes widened when they brought it in. The plates were china and the napkins were cloth. At home, lunch was in the middle of the school day and usually meant paper plates and whatever was fast and easy to gobble down. This was an entirely new world for me. All of it, from the wealthy home with its lavish amenities to a world of feuding shifter gangs.

Thankfully, the servers or servants or whoever they were that brought in the food wheeled the cart in front of Mrs. Costas, as the hostess. She asked if I wanted coffee. I shook my head.

"No, thank you. I don't drink it."

"You don't?" She seemed as surprised as Carter had been by that revelation. "When I first arrived from Ireland, I was surprised by the number of coffee houses and how everyone here seemed to drink it. The popularity of coffee is rising back home, but nothing like it is here. I couldn't find anyone who preferred hot tea, although I later learned they are out there. Would you prefer hot tea, instead?"

I chuckled. "No, thank you. Iced tea would be great, though."

"In November?" She rolled her eyes. "This is what I mean. You Americans—you Texans, especially—have some very odd habits."

Nevertheless, she asked one of the servers to send up some sweet iced tea for me. When they left the room, she gestured towards the serving cart, saying, "Please, serve yourself, Ellie."

Someone rapped on the door. We both turned. Mr. Costas stood there, filling the doorframe with his height and broad shoulders.

"Florence told me she'd sent lunch up here for you two. Alright if I join you?"

"Of course, dear," Mrs. Costas agreed, smiling warmly at her husband.

I felt my nerves growing as he crossed the carpet, grabbing a nearby side chair and drawing it up even with ours. I couldn't stop my eyes from flicking over the man, from his neatly combed salt-and-pepper hair to the tattoos on his arms, once again displayed since his shirt sleeves were rolled up to his elbows. I couldn't quit picturing him in my mind, changing last night in the blink of an eye to a huge Minotaur, with thick black hide, a bull's powerful head, including wicked horns, and a man's lower half. Most of all, I couldn't quit seeing him beating the brains out of the griffin-shifter who'd threatened his wife and nearly killed me.

I swallowed hard and stared down at my lap. Suddenly, I wasn't very hungry anymore.

"Ellie? Are you all right?"

I glanced up. Faked a smile.

"I'm fine. I—"

I didn't know what to say. What excuse to make.

"I'm fine," I said again, lamely.

Mrs. Costas looked at me a little strangely, like she could tell something was off. Thankfully, she let it go. Her husband said, "May I serve you, love?"

"Of course, thank you, my dear."

She smiled at him as he leaned over to pull a tray from a second level of the serving cart. He put the necessary dishes on it, then started filling her soup bowl, chose a sandwich off the platter for her plate, tapped precise amounts of salt and pepper into her soup, and poured exact amounts of cream and sugar in her coffee. Like he'd been with her long enough, had been married to her long enough, and knew her well enough to know exactly how she liked everything.

I marveled a little at this, at their almost old-fashioned good manners—maybe due to their wealth and status in society, or else their European heritage. Equally remarkable was the respectful, loving way he treated his wife. He'd beat a man's face in with the butt of a gun last night, but the way he looked at his wife and the way he treated her spoke of nothing except love and gentleness. And I would say one thing for Sean Costas. In all the research I'd done on him prior to the unfortunate dinner last night, I hadn't seen a whiff of scandal about him running around on her. It seemed most multi-billionaires kept mistresses and changed wives often. Sean Costas had been married once, to Ciara, and no rumors of mistresses existed. He genuinely seemed to love her, which made me wonder if even a mob boss, the leader of a gang of shifters, a controversial figure in the business world, and a shapeshifter himself could have a solid, human side. At least towards his family.

He took the tray and hooked it over the arms of her wheelchair, so it was easily accessible to her, then sat down and gestured to me.

"Go ahead, Ellie. I'll wait. Unless you'd allow me to serve you, too?"

I'd been so deep in my thoughts that I almost jumped when he spoke.

"Oh, no, thank you," I said. "It's fine. I can get it myself. I'm not used to people waiting on me."

Then I realized how rude that might have sounded—that I was implying Mrs. Costas needed to be waited on hand and foot because she was in a wheelchair. Embarrassed, I rushed to say, "I mean, we don't have servants or anything. I mean, I'm used to helping out with the cooking and cleaning, not having someone do it for me. Not that there's anything wrong with having someone do it for you. I mean..."

I was digging the hole deeper. The more I tried to explain myself, the more awkward I sounded.

Mrs. Costas laughed, raising the china coffee cup to her lips.

"It's fine, Ellie. We know what you meant. You don't have to feel as though you're walking on tiptoe around us. We're not that easily offended."

"I'm really sorry," I mumbled, sure by now that my cheeks were flaming red. I wasn't meant for this world. Actually either of the worlds represented here, wealth or shapeshifter. I was meant for the world from which I'd come, and where I wanted desperately to return.

"You don't have to be," Mr. Costas assured me. He bent, fetched another tray, and handed it to me. "Here you are. Go ahead."

"Thank you." I accepted it and started filling it with soup and a sandwich, a spoon, a napkin.

A glass of sweet tea arrived and was placed on the coaster on the table next to me. I thanked the girl who brought it. She was leaving as Mrs. Costas said to her husband, "I was telling Ellie a little of Carter's background. Explaining about his gifts and how he came to work for us."

"Were you now?" he asked, sitting back with a cup of coffee. He crossed his ankle over his knee, and I couldn't help noticing how perfectly his shoes were shined.

"Carter is one of my most valuable assets," he said, turning his iron-grey stare on me. "There's nobody I trust more to defend my family. That's why I gave you to him."

My surprise must have shown on my face. Mr. Costas saw it and chuckled. "Gave you to him to keep alive, I mean," he clarified. "He did a good job of it, too. Here you are. Not every shifter could have protected you from Nosizwe and her people. From what I hear, it was a bloody night."

I looked down at the sandwich on my china plate. The one bite I'd taken had been delicious but it soured in my stomach as memories of that bloody night washed over me.

"Yes, it was."

"We're very sorry, Ellie," Mrs. Costas said softly. "Sorry that you were caught up in this due to your saving our son. However, we're grateful Carter kept you alive. Please know we will find a way to end this madness. Eventually."

"Carter said I ruined my chances of getting out of it when I talked to Nosizwe," I said, fighting down the sting of disappointment. "He's really mad at me for that."

"Carter doesn't like it when people circumvent the limits he's set for their safety. Believe me—he's been unhappy with me a time or two when I skirted the security he put in place," Mr. Costas chuckled. "He also has a hot temper. But he would never harm the people he's defending. You don't have to be afraid of him, Ellie. He'll do his best to extract you and your family from this situation. It may take some time, but I have absolute faith in him."

I blew out a puff of air.

"I'm not afraid of him. Not really," I said, toying with the handle of my spoon. It wasn't much of a lie.

"Not only would Carter never hurt you, anyway, but he can't," Mrs. Costas assured me. "He's the Talos, and he's been charged with your care. He will not let you go until he's sure you're safe. He literally can't do less."

I wasn't sure I understood her meaning. Did that mean there

was, like, some magical imperative on him due to Mr. Costas' orders that would keep him defending me until he was sure I was safe? That was so crazy it was almost unbelievable, and made me so uncomfortable I didn't want to think about it. I didn't want to think about Carter Ballis being under a supernatural restraint to keep me alive, keep me safe, because of the bronze creature that he could shift into. Especially not now, with the ring on my finger.

I deliberately moved my hand to make it catch the sunlight.

*How many men would willingly marry a stranger to protect her from the law? Or was it himself he was trying to protect? Or both?*

I felt tired, confused, and was extremely grateful when Mrs. Costas picked up the flagging conversation, redirecting it by saying to her husband, "I told Ellie about the incident in Carter's childhood that caused him to be sent here. She asked why here, why to you. I was going to answer when lunch, and then you, arrived."

Mr. Costas took a sip of his coffee, eyeing me over the delicate glass rim.

"That's not something I generally explain to outsiders," he said. His voice was stern.

I started to say, "Okay, you don't have to." Of all people on Earth, I didn't want to get on his bad side at this moment.

Instead, he went on to say, "But you're part of my family now. And I can't imagine you're going to go around telling anyone. Even if you did," he half-chuckled, "who would believe you?"

"Nobody," I answered quietly. "I don't even know how I'm going to explain any of this to my family...except for a quickie wedding to Carter. They're going to have a hard enough time believing that, much less the truth about—um, shifters and all."

Ciara Costas giggled a little. "I wonder which one would surprise them more?"

Her green eyes sparkled at the joke, and that drew out one of my own. "I don't know. Either story is pretty shocking."

She giggled again and I felt myself smile in spite of the many layers and under-layers of danger and mystery swirling around me.

Mr. Costas hadn't said anything, but underneath his trim mustache his mouth seemed to quirk with humor.

"Anyway," he said, drawing our attention back to himself, "this is not something I want spread everywhere if or when you return home. Am I understood?"

I nodded, instantly sober. *Keep it quiet.*

He cut his eyes to his wife, who was also serious again. She dipped her chin, encouraging him, and his steely gaze came back to me.

"Carter came to me, as has everyone you see here on my estate, for a very specific reason. They are all shapeshifters. So am I. You saw that last night. So is my wife."

I glanced over at Mrs. Costas in her wheelchair. She gave me a tiny smile.

"It's true," she said. "Perhaps I can show you later."

"Ciara and I are shifters from a long line of shifters, shifters from both sides of our families. Ciara is Irish," he said, gesturing towards her. "I am Irish and Greek. My father's family immigrated to the States from Greece around one hundred fifty years ago, and they brought something with them when they came—a Stone. They wanted to settle somewhere where they could easily guard it, where no one would think to look for them. So, they settled in Texas, shortly after the close of the American Civil War. The city's population had been decimated by the war, and my ancestors saw an opportunity to not only go somewhere where they would be safe, but where they could prosper. Grow. They opened general stores, took part in the cattle trade, and helped revive this town, helped grow it into the city it is today.

"That's where my family's fortunes were made. That's where they began to build an empire in this new world—new to them. An empire where no one knew our family legacy."

"Your family legacy...of being shifters?" I asked.

Mr. Costas took a sip of coffee, nodded. "Yes. Being shifters. We hid here for generations, growing our family businesses and family fortunes as Fort Worth grew, as the country rebuilt after the war. The magic of our Stone helped. But it also began, through the years, to draw other shifters to us."

"Wait—the magic of *your* Stone. You are talking about the Stones of Fire? The Stones I keep hearing mentioned?"

The Costases exchanged glances. Then Mr. Costas said, "Again, yes. That is what my family brought with us. We had one of the Stones. Too many people in our former homeland knew. So we came to a wild and rugged new land where we could protect our family legacy, protect our Stone."

"What are the Stones?" I inquired. My voice was soft. I had a growing sense that this was the biggest piece of the puzzle. The key to unlocking the mystery. Something I would have to understand in order to understand any of this.

"You've heard of Atlantis?"

It took me a second to switch gears mentally. "The lost City of Atlantis, you mean? Yes, I've heard of it."

"How much do you know about it?"

His question reminded me of his wife's earlier, inquiring how much I knew about Greek mythology.

"Uh, not much," I replied. "I've heard the line about in a single day and night the island disappeared in the depths of the sea. Something like that."

"Mmmm. And what do you think about the story? Do you believe it?"

"I...um." I pursed my lips. "I don't know." I was uncertain what he wanted me to say. "I can't say I've ever given it much thought. I guess I always assumed it was just a myth, like all the other Greek myths."

"Except, having seen Carter and myself, you know that those so-called *myths* were based on fact."

That was true. Shapeshifters—a Talos. A Minotaur.

"Then, you're saying Atlantis *wasn't* just a myth?"

"Atlantis was a very real place. A very real island with a large and populous city. Atlantis derived its power from the Stones of Fire, tablets with magical inscriptions that, when decoded, could open the doorway to another realm, the realm of the supernatural. It's believed this realm is where the magic that fuels our ability to shapeshift originated, and that Atlantis was largely populated by shapeshifters."

I stared at him. This was so farfetched I would've thought he was pulling my leg. Except there he sat, and unless I was crazy, tripping, or dreaming, I'd seen him change into a Minotaur with my own eyes.

"How did Atlantis get ahold of these...these Stones of Fire?" I faltered.

"Nobody knows that," answered Mr. Costas, settling into his chair with a small sigh. "Atlantis, at the time Plato wrote of it, supposedly existed over nine thousand years before his day. That is a long time. So long that much of the facts have become shrouded in mystery. However, this is what we know now.

"The legend of the Stones is that leaders of other continents, jealous of Atlantis' power and fearful of its magic, made war against it. Plato describes the destruction of the Island as being due to a great earthquake, but we believe other world leaders came in force against the island and its military forces. After a terrible war, largely shifters against humans, Atlantis was overcome. Its conquerors used the power of the Stones to abolish Atlantis, causing it, like Plato said, to sink into the depths of the sea, never to be seen again.

The Stones were taken, but their magic prevented them from being destroyed. The human rulers wound up each taking one Stone to their home world; spreading them across the continents, so no one person could ever have them all and potentially rebuild an empire like Atlantis.

"That was thousands of years ago," he went on. "During that

time, civilizations rose and fell. The Stones were lost and found, lost and re-found, lost or stolen again. My family has guarded one particular Stone for over three hundred years. It was found by a shepherd boy in a cave—much like the story of the famous Dead Sea Scrolls. I'm sure you've heard that one."

I nodded.

"Ciara's family..." He gestured towards his wife. "They possessed a Stone, as well. Even longer than my family has guarded mine. Irish stories of fairies and the wee folk, leprechauns and banshees, magic and witchcraft are pretty famous. Where do you suppose many of those stories likely originated?"

"The Stones," I whispered, my mouth dry. "The Stones and their magic. Shifters."

"Exactly." My host nodded approvingly. "Many of our tales of the supernatural are actually based in reality. And that reality is the Stones and their power."

"Then, I take it shifters come to you because your family has one...a Stone?" I ventured, my mind racing to fit the pieces of the puzzle together.

"I have two, now. Ciara and I do. She came here a decade ago to marry me, bringing her family's Stone for safekeeping."

I glanced back and forth between the two of them. "That almost sounds like an arranged marriage."

Thank goodness Ciara wasn't easily offended. She laughed. "Don't sound so surprised, Ellie. They may not technically be called that, but they still happen, especially between families with wealth and connections. Never mind what fairytales tell you: most people marry within their own ranks. It's simply a fact. Families with money like to add to their money. Families with connections like to add to those connections. And families with Stones, who have a similar ideology..."

"What ideology?" I prompted, when she trailed off. "What ideology do both of you have about the Stones that Elia doesn't?

What makes her hate you so much she'd feud with you, and you with her?"

"Therein lies the rub, doesn't it?" Mr. Costas balanced his coffee cup on the arm of his chair and leaned towards me. "I believe the Stones must be hidden away at all costs. It's the only way to protect my people—shifters—from the outside world. Historically, humanity has never been kind to us. I don't believe, even with the power of the Stones, that we can possibly hope to overcome humanity or put ourselves on equal footing with humans at large. There are simply not enough of us. We're the minority. We always have been; always will be.

"Nosizwe is the exact—and, I might even add—extreme opposite. She wants to unify the Stones and, thus, all shifters. She wants to use the magic of the Stones to not only protect our kind but to elevate us. She believes with the power of the Stones and a united front, we can become equal with humans. Create our own empire within empires. Have a representative at the United Nations. Maybe be recognized by the world governments as our own sovereign nation."

"In other words, my husband and I believe if all the Stones were located and their power unlocked, and even if all shifters were united, it would only cause the nations to rise up against us and destroy us, like they did Atlantis, thousands of years ago. On the other hand, Nosizwe sees herself as resurrecting Atlantis. Not the physical island, but she does see herself as reinventing our people into a new Atlantis. She comes from a historically powerful family in southern Africa, powerful due to their longstanding ownership of one of the Stones. Her name means *mother of the nation* in Xhosa, and I sometimes think she's determined to make that meaning literal, at least so far as our people are concerned. She believes that, with the more mainstream acceptance of other historically marginalized groups, shifters have the chance to become accepted and their rights validated. She truly believes we have the potential to become equals in society.

Respected. Feared, insofar that nobody would dare stand against us."

I studied the two of them.

"So, basically, you want to keep your world hidden away as much as possible, but Nosizwe, Elia, wants to reveal it?"

"Basically, yes," Mr. Costas said. "Shifters come to her, they come to me, from all over the world. My family has been here longer and our territory is already well-established, so my army has historically outnumbered hers. However, recent years have shown that people are much more willing to defend minorities than ever before, and Nosizwe has been using her public platform to push for that."

"She's wanting to push for acceptance for herself and other shifters someday."

"Exactly. And she's attracting a growing number of shifters to her cause, particularly younger ones. Her forces are growing. She's shoving me harder and harder. You saw that yourself, only last night."

I grimaced remembering.

"Today she called a truce so we could speak," Mr. Costas continued soberly. "According to legend, there are at least six Stones in existence. Recently, she got her hands on a second Stone —which is why she was here today. Before, nobody besides Ciara and I had more than one. The Stones contain an inscription, but the inscription is scattered across all six Stones. It can't be completely deciphered unless all of the Stones are put together. However, she thinks if we combined our four Stones we could possibly decode most of their inscription, which may help locate the other two Stones. If we managed to find them and discover what they say?" He shook his head. "There is no telling what powers we might unlock or unleash."

"But you aren't willing to take that chance."

He glanced at me from underneath thick brows. "Would you be, given our history, if it was you and your people? Look at

Atlantis. That is what I keep saying to Nosizwe. Look at Atlantis. It had the Stones. It had power, but even that couldn't save it from the outside world."

I drew a deep breath and sat back in my chair, lunch entirely forgotten. My mind was spinning. Information overload. The Stones of Fire. Atlantis. Shifters gangs warring over magical Stones and the future of their community. Worldwide stakes.

Maybe this did mean Nosizwe wasn't a terrible person, any more than Sean Costas was. Or perhaps they were both terrible people. Maybe they were both leaders put in the ugly position of having to do any and every thing to protect their kind. I didn't know. And it really wasn't my business to take sides. I wasn't a shifter.

Both of my hosts had fallen silent, sipping their respective tea and coffee, giving me space to think. As Mr. Costas' arm moved, raising his coffee cup, my eyes were caught by the tattoos on his skin.

"I get it now," I said.

He was in the act of putting the cup to his lips, and paused.

"I beg your pardon?"

"I get it now," I said, gesturing towards him. "Your tattoos. Even your family crest. I couldn't figure out why you had all of those different symbols on there that didn't seem to go together. Didn't seem to make sense. I get it now. Symbols of your heritage, both of you. Of your shifting abilities and of the Stones themselves."

"Sometimes it's good to be reminded what you're fighting for," Mr. Costas said simply.

"I guess. I mean, it's hard for me to wrap my mind around any of this. Hard for me to believe...

"Not that it matters what I believe," I added quickly, "but I guess—well, if I hadn't seen it with my own eyes..."

Mr. Costas' expression was solemn, but there was a slight twinkle in his eye.

"Your father was a Chaplain's Assistant, correct? And is now an ordained minister?"

I nodded. "Yes."

"Then you must be familiar with the stories from your religion: angels and demons. Animals that spoke. Trees with fruit that cursed mankind. Miracles of healing and resurrection. Ravens feeding a prophet in the desert. Do you believe them?"

I hesitated, trying to gauge his point. "Well, well, yes. Of course I do."

"Then, if you believe those things, is it too big a stretch to believe the things I've been telling you? Clearly, the supernatural exists. What if this is simply another layer of it?"

Mentally, I bounced back to Carter's apartment, to the handwritten verse framed and hanging on his wall. It now made sense in the context of the life he lived, making me wonder where he had gotten it. His grandma, perhaps, the one who had put in him touch with his shifter heritage?

"Um."

I didn't know how to respond to Mr. Costas. I'd never considered myself superstitious; had never believed in ghosts or anything like that. On the other hand, maybe the world was much bigger than I knew. Clearly, it was.

"You got me there," I finally said, shrugging helplessly. "Before meeting all of you, I wouldn't have listened to any of this, but now..." I shrugged again. "I guess I can say my horizons have definitely been expanded."

Not necessarily in a good way, but definitely expanded.

## CHAPTER TWENTY-NINE

Mr. and Mrs. Costas left after we finally finished lunch, and I took a nap. There wasn't much else to do, and I discovered my body was still tired from last night's events, even if my brain was buzzing. Physical needs outweighed mental. My systems shut down, at least for a while. By the time I woke up it was late afternoon. I watched TV. I paced. I tried to read. I was feeling more and more desperate, more and more like a caged animal. I needed to get out of this room. I needed to call my family again. I needed to do anything except what I was doing, which was nothing.

I hadn't heard from Carter since I'd freaking married him and then he'd locked me in here. From what I'd gathered during my conversation with the Costases, they were planning to leave my fate and me in his hands. Briefly, I considered picking up the phone and calling downstairs, see if somebody would get him on the line and let me talk to him. I already knew, since I'd already tried, that the phone had no buttons with which to punch in a phone number, meaning I couldn't call outside for help. When I'd picked it up apparently it went to a line directly inside the house, and they didn't allow outside calls unless cleared by Carter, Rory, James, or the Costases themselves. I didn't even know who Rory was. I didn't bother trying to lie to the operator and say I had permission, since I was pretty sure that would get me nowhere.

Now, as I sat there and stared at the phone, considering trying to get in touch with Carter, my stomach curled. He'd been so furious with me downstairs. So angry it was truly frightening. I hadn't really worried he would hit me; he didn't seem like the type to hit a woman. Shifter battles to the death aside, of course. But I'd seen his lethal side, a side every bit as callous and uncaring for the enemies he killed as Nosizwe was in sending her shifters after me. Not to mention the way he'd manhandled me, throwing me over his shoulder and locking me up here. I still couldn't believe he'd done that. Not only done it, but nobody had tried to stop him.

I couldn't simply sit and do nothing, though.

Bracing myself, I picked up the phone. When the operator answered, I asked to speak with Carter.

"I'll try to track him down for you," she replied. "Please wait."

I noticed she hadn't asked who I was. Either it didn't matter, or else she already knew what room I was calling from and, thus, who I was. I assumed the latter, because within a couple of minutes I heard a sound and then Carter's voice came on the line.

"What do you want, Ellie?"

No greeting. No pleasantries. Direct. To the point.

I swallowed down my apprehension, reminding myself that he wasn't going to hurt me and, aside from that, already had me locked up, so there wasn't a whole lot more he could do to me, was there?

"I was wondering if you had any updates on my situation," I said.

"You don't have to call to ask me that. When I have things figured out, you'll know. I'm busy. I need to—"

"Hold on a minute," I demanded, feeling irritation surge. "You're always brushing me off, and I'm getting tired of it. You don't get to lock me up as a prisoner, ignore me, and then refuse to tell me anything."

"What do you want me to tell you?"

I could hear a rhythmic tapping sound in the background, like he was impatient or irritated and was tapping something to keep himself in check. Also, his tone was clipped, but for once I didn't care if I was bugging him.

"I want you to tell me when you're going to let me out of here. I want you to tell me if my family's okay."

"They're fine. After you decided to *save the day* by confronting Nosizwe, I doubled the guard on them."

I gritted my teeth. Breathed.

"Can I talk to them?"

"I don't think that's such a good idea right now."

"Why?"

"Because you don't want to draw any unnecessary attention to them."

"Attention's already been drawn," I pointed out.

"Yeah, it has. Do you want to make it worse?"

"No, I want to let them know I'm alright."

"You already did that."

"For heaven's sake, Carter, just because you haven't seen your family in twenty years doesn't mean some of us don't care about seeing ours!" I lashed out, fed up with his callous attitude. "Would you bend—just once—and send someone up here with a burner phone or whatever secret crap you have to do and let me call my family?"

Silence on the other end, except for the tapping, which was a bit louder.

*Maybe I shouldn't have mentioned his family. Maybe I should have been sweet instead of demanding. Catch more flies with honey and all that. Maybe...*

"Ellie, I'll think about it," he said finally, and when he spoke his voice was gentler than I would have expected. "The truth is, I'm working on something that's taking every bit of my time and attention. Something for you and your family. Something that could end your involvement with us permanently. The less you bother me, the faster it will go. Can you trust me a little while longer?"

"That depends. What are you planning?"

"I'll let you know as soon as I know it will work. Trust me on this, Ellie. Okay?"

I didn't want to agree. Not that easily. Instead, I said, grudgingly, "Okay, I'll give you a little more time, but you better let me in on it soon or else let me out of here. I'm about to start banging on the door and screaming."

Carter chuckled. "Go ahead. Nobody will let you out."

"I can be pretty loud."

"Doesn't matter. Nobody will let you out. I told them not to."

"Fine. Then I'm going to use the lamp to break the window."

"And do what? Tie your sheets together and climb out? Sneak off the grounds? Climb over the wall? I have patrols all over the place, kid. Not to mention, you can't break that glass anyway. Even if you did, alarms would go off. Do you really think I'd have put you there if I couldn't keep you there? Nice try threatening me, though. I needed a laugh."

He was so aggravating. I wanted to smack him. I wished I had some sort of magic ability to reach through the phone and actually do it. Since I didn't, I said, "Well, at the very least I can keep calling and harassing you."

"Until I tell Chelsey not to put you through anymore. I've got to go. Be patient, Ellie."

"Carter—"

Too late. I heard a click. He'd already hung up.

Fuming, I slammed the receiver back onto its cradle.

*Shouldn't even have bothered to call,* I griped to myself, except I didn't really regret it. At least I'd wrung an assurance from him that he did have a plan he was working on. Something to end my association here permanently.

## CHAPTER THIRTY

Fort Worth Police Department, Investigative and Support Command

"Hey, guess who I just spoke with?"

"Who did you just speak with?"

A re-warmed mug of coffee in hand, Gary took a seat on the edge of Candace's desk. She noted the dried drips of liquid on the sides of the mug and idly wondered how many cups he'd consumed today. The man needed to cut back on his caffeine. Probably, every officer in the Fort Worth PD did.

"A woman named Elaina Ramirez. Miguel Rodriguez' personal secretary."

"*Really.*" Her partner's grey eyebrows rose.

"Really."

Detective Ewing leaned back in her chair, crossing her arms over her chest. She couldn't help feeling the slightest bit smug, even though she tried not to show it.

Tried a little bit, anyway.

"While you were out getting lunch, the captain called me into his office. Said the man in the pictures I found had been positively ID'd. His name is Carter Ballis and he works directly for Sean Costas. Head of security, or something."

"If he's head of security, then he's pretty far up the food chain in the Costas Empire," Gary remarked. The words were casual, but Candace detected a slight edge to them. A warning?

"Exactly. The techs say there's a strong possibility he could be the man in the footage from the Botanic Garden last night. He's certainly high enough that he might be allowed to use one of Mr. Costas' expensive European cars."

"Is any of this enough for a warrant?"

"For someone working for Sean Costas? Heck, no," Candace scoffed, sitting upright. Her chair squeaked as she leaned forward, dropping her voice. "But it is enough that the Captain gave me the go ahead to contact the Costases. I tried. I kept going through assistant after assistant, and finally wound up being transferred directly to Miguel Rodriguez' office."

"Where you spoke to his assistant."

"Yep."

"Did you tell her any of the details of the case?"

"No, of course not. Do I look like a rookie to you?" Candace picked up a pen, began tapping it on the edge of her desk. "I did, however, tell her we were looking at a personal employee of Sean Costas as a possible witness to a crime and I gave her his name. She said Mr. Rodriguez was in a meeting right now, but to expect a return call soon."

"A crime we don't even know was committed..." her partner interrupted, rolling his eyes.

In spite of herself, in spite of knowing this was Gary's standard cautious approach, Candace heard annoyance creeping into her voice.

"So you think all of our evidence magically appeared out there without a crime being committed?"

"Still could have been teenagers sneaking out for beer and a bonfire and a brawl erupted."

"That's the theory you're sticking with?"

"I'm not saying that's my theory. I'm saying any hack of a defense attorney could bring it up and blow holes a mile wide through our case. Bam. Reasonable doubt, right there."

"What about the casing?"

Gary gave her a look. "It's Texas, Candace. How many people are walking around with a gun on their hip? People get drunk and excited and shoot them off. We still don't have bodies. We don't know—"

"Okay, okay," she finally snapped, slapping her pen against the desk with more force than necessary. "I get what you're saying. I do. This may go nowhere. But can you at least celebrate with me that I pushed it this far? I just talked to the personal secretary of the most powerful lawyer in freaking Fort Worth, Texas. And I cut through all the layers, all the crap, simply by saying we were looking at somebody personally connected with Sean Costas. They immediately patched me through to her. She said he's going to call me back. That indicates they're either scared or have something to hide."

"Orrrr...they're letting you know they're throwing up a wall. You're not going to get to Sean Costas or anyone personally connected with him with such a flimsy case, Candace. I admire your hard work and your grit. But I'm telling you—this isn't my first run-in with the Costas Empire. I know what I'm talking about. We had a drug dealer dead to rights that was tied to his operations. Before we could convene a grand jury, all of the witnesses went missing or suddenly got real quiet. They changed their minds. They hadn't seen anything. They couldn't testify. And that was just for a petty drug dealer who wasn't even personally connected to him or his household.

"I'm telling you—that lawyer will never let you near Sean Costas. If this guy—this head of security, Carter Ballis—means anything to Mr. Costas, he won't let you near him, either."

Candace glowered at her partner. "You're a real killjoy, Gary."

"I'm a realist."

"No, you're a pessimist and a killjoy, like I said."

"I'm only trying to—"

"I know. You don't want me to get my hopes up. They're not. At the same time, I'm going to take my victories where I can get them. Until I talk to Miguel Rodriguez and hear what he has to say, I'm still going to consider this a win.

"Is this going to be the smoking gun that will bring down the Costas Empire? I doubt it. Not very likely. But will it give them a scare, make them think twice about their underground activities? Who knows? Maybe. Even that's worth something."

"Or it'll make them more diligent to cover things up."

Now it was Candace's turn to roll her eyes, shake her head. She turned away from Gary and back to her computer.

"You're a real ray of sunshine. Glad you appreciate my efforts. Instead of all the naysaying, why don't you get online and see what else you can dig up about this Carter Ballis? Help me out instead of spreading doom and gloom."

Gary didn't argue. In fact, he rose, walked around the corner of the desk and seated himself at his own. He set down his coffee cup and put his hand on his mouse. Candace heard clicking and the clacking of computer keys. Something about his silence was not only not reassuring, it was actually ominous, provoking little worms of doubt that crawled into her soul and gnawed away at her earlier self-confidence.

What if Gary was right, and this was a big waste of time? Was Sean Costas really going to let them get close to one of his personal employees, especially somebody as important as his very own head of security?

*No way to know that until I talk to the lawyer,* she told herself.

Until then, she'd keep looking. With any luck, something else would turn up.

## CHAPTER THIRTY-ONE

The promise of a permanent solution to my predicament braced me through the tedium of that night and the next long, long day, when I had to pass the hours with no more visitors and no further updates. At one point I considered calling Carter again and pestering him for news, but he wasn't going to budge until he was good and ready.

"The least he could do is have somebody else call me or come up here to let me know what's going on," I grumbled, but he didn't.

With a defeated sigh, I pulled a romance novel out of the bookshelf and tried to read, but the characters and setting felt flat compared to the situation I found myself in. Everything felt flat. By mid-afternoon, I was going crazy. By evening, I was pacing the perimeter of the room to keep from crawling the walls.

Sometime after six P.M., when the sun was already down, supper was brought to my room. Being bored, restless, and anxious, I ate every bite. My empty plate reminded me of Carter ribbing me about how much food I could pack away.

*Stress makes me eat*, I'd said. I guess it still did.

About an hour after that, the phone rang in my room for the

first time. The noise was startling against the quiet that had permeated the suite all day, and I jumped. When I picked up the receiver, the crisp, professional voice from yesterday was on the opposite end of the line.

"Mrs. Costas wants to know if you would like to join her outside for an evening walk."

I felt a breath of relief. Finally! Something to do.

"Yes, that sounds wonderful," I said.

"Very good. An escort will be sent up for you momentarily."

Escort. Meaning, Mrs. Costas was letting me out of my room, but she wasn't trusting me not to try and escape. She wasn't about to completely circumvent Carter's directives.

A knock at my door heralded the arrival of the escort. I told him or her to come in and heard the key turn in the lock. It was a woman I didn't know, medium height but very athletic looking, wearing jeans and a cropped jean jacket, her short hair dyed bright green.

"You ready?" she asked, tilting her chin towards the hallway.

"Ready," I said, getting off the bed and slipping my feet back into the flats I'd bought yesterday morning before the wedding.

*Wedding.*

I grimaced at the word as I followed the woman out of the room. She hadn't told me her name. I guess being a temporary bodyguard didn't require much conversation from her. She simply led me downstairs, every now and then casting quick little glances over her shoulder as if to make sure I was still following. When we reached the foyer, I looked longingly at the front door, but sighed and walked on. What was the point? This place was crawling with Carter's people, as he'd reminded me. No way could I make it out of here.

The woman led me to the back of the mansion, through elegant French doors, and outside onto the back patio. It was well lit with strings of lights. Beyond the patio was a fountain, lawns, and a flower garden, mostly pruned down for winter. A swimming pool, a tennis court, and a basketball court. Giant old trees were scattered here and there, casting the shadows of their now bare branches over the scenery. The landscaping was beautiful, and I noticed instead of dirt or gravel paths that the walkways were cement, and wide enough for a wheelchair. I couldn't help being impressed with Mr. Costas' obvious devotion to his wife and her needs, even in something like that.

Speaking of Mrs. Costas, she was waiting on the patio, in her chair. She smiled up at me as I approached.

"There you are. How was your dinner, Ellie?"

"Delicious," I told her truthfully. "I ate it all."

"I'm so glad you enjoyed it. I'm sorry you've been alone this long, but my husband and I have some serious issues to consider."

I remembered Mr. Costas talking about Nosizwe recently gaining another Stone, and Nosizwe's own mention of a brief truce and after that...war. From what I'd learned lately of the two shifter leaders and their conflicting ideologies, I highly doubted they could come to a working agreement on the Stones, but that wasn't my problem and nobody would want to hear my input anyway.

I mulled everything over as Mrs. Costas led the way down the cement paths, between gardens and fountains, around the massive in-ground pool with its connected lazy river, and under the dancing shadows of the trees. The bodyguard followed us, not speaking but staying right on my tail. She was so quiet it was easy to ignore her and think.

How much danger was the Costas faction in if Mr. Costas refused his rival's offer? How much danger was Nosizwe in? Clearly, Nosizwe didn't goof around, but neither did Mr. Costas. How much danger was Fort Worth and its surrounding communities in? How about me? My family? I'd heard their threats. I believed every one of them. I'd seen glimpses of what both sides could do.

"You're awfully quiet tonight," my hostess said softly, breaking the gentle silence of the evening.

"I'm sorry," I said, snapping out of my thoughts. "I have a lot on my mind."

"I'm sure," Mrs. Costas said kindly. "Care to share?"

I sighed, toying with a button on the bottom of my cardigan, looking at my feet rather than the beautiful, mild November evening around us.

"Just—just worried about my family, I suppose."

I wasn't sure how much to say in front of the bodyguard.

"You needn't worry over much, Ellie," Mrs. Costas consoled me. "Carter has people watching your home. I know that much."

"Yeah...yeah, he told me."

I didn't want to say I lacked the wholehearted trust in Carter that she and her husband seemed to have.

We'd arrived at the edge of the pool. Most of the grounds were lit either by outdoor lights on poles or else strings of lights, almost like Christmas lights, strung between trees. The pool was no exception, except that half of it was well lit and half deep in shadow. Also, I called it a pool, but it was really more the size of a large pond. Or a small lake. In other words, it was massive. I'd never seen anything like it. The expense of building something like that must have been enormous. We stopped at its brink. Mrs. Costas turned her wheelchair towards me.

"Earlier, I said I'd show you what sort of shifter I am, didn't I?"

I nodded, a little surprised by the abrupt change in topic, but curious.

"Will you help me out of my chair, please?"

"Of course," I said, even more mystified, but I stepped forward and placed one arm around her shoulders, one around her waist. The bodyguard hovering in the background also stepped forward to help, and together we managed to assist her out of her chair.

"Place me on the edge of the pool," she said. We did, and stepped back.

I'm not sure what I was expecting, but it sure wasn't for her to lean over...and deliberately fall in.

I gasped and jumped forward, ready to dive in myself, even though I wasn't a very good swimmer and would probably only wind up drowning us both. The bodyguard grabbed the back of my cardigan in a firm grip.

"Don't," she said. "It's fine. Wait and see."

I stared at her, bewildered, until a splash caught my attention. I looked over at the water in time to see Mrs. Costas' head break the surface of the water. Her long, black hair was unbound, drifting around her. She pulled herself up out of the water, surfacing almost like a dolphin, only to flip, and go under again. My jaw dropped, and suddenly I understood why she was wheelchair-bound on dry land.

She was a mermaid.

That flip had shown me no legs but a long fish tail, complete with fins and shimmering green scales.

Her dark shape whizzed by just underneath the surface. She rose out of the water again, surfaced briefly, flipped backwards this time, bending in an almost unbelievable backwards arc, then vanished in the depths of the water.

I must've been standing there gaping, because the woman next to me chuckled. "She's something, isn't she?"

My jaw snapped shut as I turned to look at the bodyguard.

"She's...she's... I didn't think. I wasn't expecting..."

I didn't even know what to say. That, maybe, out of all the amazing things I'd witnessed, and all of the incredible shifters I'd seen, that this one might be the most astonishing.

"No one expects it," said the woman with an air of practicality. "No one expects somebody living in a wheelchair to all of the sudden change into something magical and powerful and beautiful. Well, Mrs. Costas is always beautiful," she added loyally, "but you know what I mean. Since she lives in a wheelchair, folks feel sorry for her. She doesn't need any sympathy. If she's anywhere near water she's got more power than any of us could ever imagine."

"What do you mean?"

The bodyguard tilted her head. "Wait until you hear her sing," she said mysteriously.

I turned back to the pool, watching the mermaid slip by at a crazy rate of speed from one end of the massive pool to the other, sometimes surfacing, sometimes submerging to where she couldn't be seen at all. She wasn't showing off for me. She was simply enjoying the water and being her truest, deepest self. She was reveling, dancing, glorying in the freedom to move in what must be her natural environment. As I watched her, I remembered all of the stories of mermaids and sirens, selkies and marrows. I didn't know a lot, but I knew some of them, like sires, supposedly had voices that were impossible to resist and could drag humans, especially men, down into the water where they could be drowned, eaten, or held captive in underwater homes.

I could only surmise the bodyguard was implying Mrs. Costas had such a voice, but I didn't get the chance to ask. Footsteps on the path behind us echoed out of the darkness, the thump of shoes on concrete. The bodyguard whirled, hand already touching the gun on her hip.

## CHAPTER THIRTY-TWO

"You're off duty now, Britt. Thanks."

It was Carter. At the sound of his voice, the bodyguard relaxed immediately. So did I, the tension that had flushed my body evaporating.

"Of course. Good night, Carter. Ellie."

She nodded towards me, and before I could even respond she was gone, edging around Carter on the path, walking away as he walked up.

I felt my entire body stiffen as the man I'd fake-married approached. The evening was mild, but still chilly. Despite that, he wore only a t-shirt and jeans. I wondered if he wasn't bothered by the cold like normal humans. Maybe it had something to do with the genetics of his skin, which could alter at a whim from human to bronze. I wasn't about to ask, though. Really, I didn't know what to say or ask, so I kept my mouth shut and tried not to look too nervous when he stopped a couple of feet away.

"Ciara's enjoying her evening swim, I take it," he observed.

By that, I figured this must be a regular thing for her. I glanced towards the far end of the pool, which was overshadowed by the branches of the great tree beside it. I saw a glimpse of pale skin as she momentarily broke the surface. I guess she must have seen Carter. Knowing I was safe, she dove back down into the water and resumed swimming.

"Mmm hmm," I murmured uneasily, wondering what he had in mind.

His hands were shoved in his pockets, and his stance was casual, but I had a feeling he hadn't sought me out for a nice little chat.

He hadn't.

"Listen, Ellie," he began, not looking at me, but gazing off across the darkened lawn, as if this was uncomfortable for him too. "I promised to get you out of this. Granted, you didn't make matters any easier by confronting Nosizwe. On the other hand, it did sort of bring it all to a head."

"What do you mean?" I asked. My voice was faint, barely more than a whisper, as my throat tightened from nervousness.

"I mean, like I mentioned on the phone, I've figured out what to do with you."

"Do—with me?"

"Yeah." Now he did turn to look at me. His dark eyes gleamed out of the shadows dancing over us. Intent. Direct. Brooking no arguments.

"Nosizwe has threatened to turn up the heat if Sean doesn't accept her offer. She's threatening outright war. I don't want you around when that happens."

I noticed he'd said *when*, not *if*.

"I'm not sure what she offered," I said, "although I'm guessing it has to do with the Stones of Fire. Which Mr. and Mrs. Costas explained a little bit, by the way. But aren't Sean and Nosizwe already at war? She tried to kill his family right here on his own property."

"That was her getting his attention, proving what she could do," Carter said grimly. "Threatening what she's going to keep doing if he doesn't accept. And he won't. I know him. Whatever she's going to throw at him, he's going to throw right back. It's going to be ugly. I don't want you here to keep getting caught in the crosshairs. You're too much a target as it is."

A chill snaked down my spine. Underneath the sleeves of my cardigan, goosebumps raised on my flesh.

*A target...*

"Plus this whole police thing..." he went on, rubbing a hand over his head, a mannerism I'd noticed when he was thinking, uncomfortable, or trying to explain something.

"What about it? Have you heard something else?"

"They've pretty much ID'd me from the surveillance video. They haven't ID'd you yet. They may not be able to. They're clamoring to talk to me, though."

With every word he spoke, I felt my anxiety climb. I felt like a net had been cast over me, and the more I struggled, the more entangled I became.

"Are you going to talk to them?"

"My lawyer is. He thinks it's time to send the police a message. They're coming to his office, tomorrow afternoon. I'm supposed to be there, but I'll let him do the talking. Throw up a wall. Remind them who they're dealing with."

"I didn't know the police went to lawyer's offices. I thought people usually came down to the precinct to talk to them."

Granted, my knowledge of police procedures was primarily sourced from TV dramas, which may or may not have been accurate.

"They usually don't." Carter allowed a tiny smirk. "But they're not usually trying to get to somebody high up in Sean Costas' employ, and they're not usually dealing with Miguel Rodriguez. They don't have a case. They're trying to build one out of nothing. At this point, without a whole lot more evidence, they talk to us on our terms, or we don't talk at all. And they know it."

"What are you going to say to them? About...about the Botanic Garden and us being out there? About the whole thing?"

"Miguel will stick to our story. I was out there with my new wife—no judgments, please. They can't even prove we entered the park, so they can't get us for trespassing. We were just walking around the perimeter of the grounds, looking in. Whatever we saw or didn't see, did or didn't do, is covered by spousal privilege. That's it."

It sounded too neat. My life had been so wild lately that I had a hard time believing anything could be tied up quite that prettily.

"What about me?" I faltered. "What if they demand to talk to me?"

"That's the thing," Carter said. "I don't want them talking to you. I don't trust you not to give away more than you should. You're going to sit there and turn red and look guilty. They get one look at you and they'll know something's up. They'll hammer you, you'll get so upset you'll forget you don't have to talk to them, and you'll spill everything you know."

"Hey!"

I couldn't hide the fact that I was offended. Carter laughed.

"Are you trying to deny it? You have the worst poker face I've ever seen. You can't hide anything you're thinking, and you sure haven't learned to keep your mouth shut."

"I can too keep my mouth shut."

"Yes, your conversation with Nosizwe is excellent proof of that," Carter remarked dryly.

I felt annoyance bubbling up. Simmering beneath the surface.

"I was only trying to help my family," I said through almost gritted teeth. "Oh, and by the way, thanks for backing me up with her."

"Backing you up with her? What are you talking about?"

"I'm talking about how I was trying to convince her I wasn't a threat. I told her I wasn't involved with the Costases or any of their dealings. I told her I wasn't even a shifter. Why didn't you back me up on that?"

"I did," he reminded me. "I agreed that you weren't involved with us."

"But you didn't tell her I wasn't a shifter."

"No, I didn't, Ellie. You want to know why?"

He edged a step closer, and it was all I could do not to retreat. To hide my squeamishness, I folded my arms and tried to look strong.

"Why?"

"Because I didn't want her knowing how vulnerable you are. If she thinks you're a shifter, she'll probably think you have some means of protecting yourself. It's not much of a defense, but it's better than nothing. As it stands, you were basically trying to tell her you're helpless. I didn't want her to know that."

"I—"

I opened my mouth to argue, then snapped it shut again.

Okay, what he was saying made sense. Sort of. The logic was hard to counter, since he'd been trying to help me. Again. In his own way.

The heat that had crept up the back of my neck slowly released, subsided. I decided I'd better direct the conversation back on course, and asked, "So, what are you going to do if the police do ask to talk to me?"

"You're not going to be here for them to talk to."

That took a second to sink in.

"What?"

Carter nodded grimly. Behind him, in the background of the shadowy pool, I caught a glimpse of Mrs. Costas in her shifter form surfacing, flipping, gliding back down beneath the water's rippling surface.

"That's right. That's what I came out here to tell you. I want you out of here. Out of here before my appointment with the cops tomorrow. Out of here before the three day window Nosizwe gave Sean to consider her proposal is up."

"By out of here, you mean..."

"I mean people are at your family's home right now. Our people."

My stomach had twisted nastily at the first sentence. It relaxed—slightly—with the second.

"They're giving your family a cover story that explains why you've been absent the past couple of days, why you haven't told them what you're doing, and why they're being packed up and relocated."

"Packed up and relocated?"

"Yeah. Like a witness protection program. Only it's not the Feds handling it. It's us—Sean's people. They don't know that, though. They think we are the Feds."

I stared at him, dismayed, but not knowing how to argue. What he was saying, the solution he'd come up with...it made sense. I didn't want it to make sense, but it did. Still, the idea of leaving my home, where we'd finally settled after Dad left the service, where I was in school, where the boys had friends, not to mention Dad's job with the veterans and even his side business of restoring vintage furniture...

Leave it all? Because of me?

"You're being given new names. A new home will be waiting for you. A job for your father. Your mother, if she wants it. You're going to be taken care of. The only thing you have to do, Ellie, is stick by the cover story we give you."

"Which is?"

My head was swimming. Packing up and leaving...leaving Fort Worth. Forever. No warning. Disrupting my entire family and their lives because I'd been in the wrong place at the wrong time. How could I live with the burden of that?

"That you witnessed a crime. You can't say what, you can't say where, you can't say anything about it. The less you say the better. The more mysterious it sounds, the more plausible to your family that Federal witness protection would step in. That alone will be enough to explain this sudden move, as well as where you've been lately."

"What if my family doesn't buy it?"

"They will. They already have. I'm in contact with the people I have there."

"How? How could you pull this off? How could you pull it off so quickly? I—I didn't know things like this could be done so fast."

Carter winked at me. "I told you with plenty of money and power, anything can be done. Fake badges and IDs, fake documents, fake cover stories...all of it. That's also why you've been alone up there so long. James and I needed the time to get everything in place."

I studied him, wondering what it was like to live your life with that amount of deception, not to mention power. Well, I was about to find out about living life with deception. Maybe not power, but deception, certainly.

"Then...I'll be gone tonight? Is that how you'll keep the police from talking to me?"

"Not tonight. Tomorrow. We're moving your family first, getting them to your new place and making sure they're safe. You'll fly out tomorrow on one of Mr. Costas' private jets. As for the cops? We'll tell them you've already left the US. We're newlyweds. We've got a honeymoon coming up, right?"

"What if they ask why you didn't go with me? You kinda need a bride and groom to make it a real honeymoon."

"Then we'll tell them I haven't left—yet—because of this situation. You went ahead and flew out but I stayed behind to talk to them and clear everything up. We wanted it dealt with so we could enjoy ourselves on our honeymoon."

I know it was dumb, but I was grateful for the darkness. At the mention of enjoying ourselves on our honeymoon, I felt my body temperature start to rise. For some idiotic reason, I was reminded that technically Carter was my husband, and there I was discussing fake honeymoons. All of the sudden it felt incredibly awkward and embarrassing…kind of like the same feeling of being in his shower. Too close. Too intimate.

Thankfully, he couldn't read my mind and didn't seem to pick up on my train of thought.

Clearing my throat, I asked, "Wh—where am I supposed to have gone on this fake honeymoon?"

"Don't know yet," Carter responded, his attention pulled away by a soft splash. "Somewhere with a non-extradition policy to the US, that's for sure."

I looked too. Mrs. Costas had emerged from the water and was sitting on the edge of the pool, gazing up at the stars. Her long tail and delicate fins floated across the surface of the water. She was a fairytale come to life, and she was the most beautiful thing I'd ever seen. A funny thought entered my brain, and I glanced at Carter, trying to judge by his expression if he was looking at her because of how beautiful she was. If maybe he had a thing for his boss's wife. Ciara Costas was a few years older than him, but she was actually closer to his age than her husband's.

He turned back to me, blinked, and the moment passed. Honestly, I couldn't decide if he'd been gazing at her because he was enamored or if he was simply scanning the area, making sure there were no hidden threats. He didn't seem like the type to fool around with his employer's wife, but you never really know what someone's capable of.

Maybe I'd misread him.

"Sorry," he said. "I'm jumpy after last night. Nosizwe's shifters shouldn't have gotten in here. By all rights, Mr. Costas could have ripped me a new one for that happening. Instead, he decided to punish me by sticking me with you."

I think my jaw dropped a little.

*Punish?*

I started to protest, but caught the gleam in his eye.

"Very funny," I said sourly. "I'm sure I'm such a punishment."

"You're a real pain in my a—"

He caught my glare, stopped. "See? That's what I mean. I have to watch my language around you. You also get your feelings hurt and cry a lot. You're a pain to deal with, Ellie."

"I don't get my feelings hurt and cry a lot," I sputtered indignantly.

"Yes, you do."

"I do not." His goading was getting under my skin. "Normally, I don't. I don't cry a lot. I don't even argue a lot. Normally, I can let things go. But this has hardly been normal for me, Carter. Did you ever stop and think about that? I don't live my life on the edge, always worrying about getting killed by a rival gang of shifters. I've been scared out of my mind and worried sick about my family. I—"

"Hey, no need to get all worked up." He held up his hands in mock surrender. "I'm just teasing you, kid."

"It's not funny. None of this is funny."

He sighed a little. "You're right. It's not. Look, I need to get back to the house. There's a million and one things to oversee with this move for your family. James has been tearing it up, getting new IDs and paperwork for everyone, but he still needs help to finish."

"Paperwork?"

"All of you have new names and identities," he reminded me. "You're not Ellie St. James anymore. You're Taylor Scott."

Taylor Scott.

It was so weird hearing him say that, trying to imagine crafting an entirely new identity around this name, this woman, that I didn't know. Trying to imagine casting off Ellie St. James, who I'd been my entire life, for Taylor Scott.

This time, when I fell silent and had no retort, I think Carter did deduce some of my thoughts. Soberly, he said, "I'm sorry, Ellie. Taylor. I promised I'd get you out of this mess, and this is the best way I know to do it. For all intents and purposes, Ellie St.

James is somewhere off on an extended honeymoon, waiting for me to join her. Taylor Scott will be somewhere in the Pacific Northwest. If the police try to track you down, they'll be looking for Ellie St. James, who's out of the country, not Taylor Scott. It's not going to be an easy change, but you're a military brat. You're used to moving and settling in new places. You'll adjust. More importantly, you'll survive, and you'll put all of this behind you. One of these days, life will hopefully get so boring you'll be able to forget that shifters exist or that the past couple of days happened or that you ever even met me."

"That's never going to happen," I whispered, staring down at the ring on my hand. I wasn't sure if I was referring to the last part or all of it.

"What about us?" I asked. "What about this—this marriage? Does the plan change since I'm moving and being given a new identity?"

"No, it doesn't. Name change or not, we're still legally married. Once Miguel is certain the police are done with us and the case is closed, we'll contact you about an annulment. I told you this wouldn't have to be forever. It won't be. If you keep quiet about it, nobody has to know. We changed the cover story, so you don't even have to tell your family," he went on, harkening back to his original idea that I could potentially use the quickie wedding to explain why I'd been acting so strangely. "Hopefully, in a few months it will be like it never happened."

"What about—what about this?"

I'd been staring down at my ring. The diamonds and gold glowed in the soft radiance of the lights strung between trees.

Carter glanced down at my hand.

"That? It was for show. Keep it till after we're separated, I guess, if you think you can keep it hidden. Then do whatever you want with it. Throw it away. Sell it. Give to someone. Hock it. I don't care."

He sounded so cavalier about it.

"I feel like I should give it back," I said, meeting his gaze. "I don't want you to be out any money on it."

He chuckled carelessly. "It was like a thousand dollars, Ellie. No big deal. Don't worry about it."

"Like a thou—"

I shut up when I noticed his expression.

Okay, I knew he moved in different circles than me and earned good money at his job. Maybe throwing away a thousand dollars didn't mean anything to him. It was a lot of money to a broke nursing student like me. Knowing the store where he had to have bought it, it was probably the most expensive set they had, and, judging by the price, wasn't cubic zirconium. Why had he done that? Why not just buy me a sparkling fake ring that cost less than twenty bucks? Or ten bucks? Why go all out?

I stood there staring up at him, my right hand meshed with my left, my right thumb pressing into the ring, wanting to know but afraid to ask.

He might have been right that I couldn't keep my thoughts and feelings hidden. Or else he was simply getting good at reading me.

Gruffly, he said, "It's nothing, Ellie. I guess I just—I guess I felt like you deserved something, if you had to do this. I knew you didn't want to, and I don't blame you. I wouldn't want to be married to me, either."

I choked on a laugh. "You're not that bad, Carter. Well, sometimes you are, but sometimes you—"

I broke off. I didn't know what to say. Sometimes he was frightening and came across as insensitive and caustic and surly, but sometimes his softer side showed, like with this ring, or him keeping his promise to get me back with my family, leaving me confused.

"Sometimes you're really..." I dropped my gaze, forced it back. "You know what? Sometimes you're not half-bad. And I feel like I should tell you that. I feel like I should apologize for some of the things I've said to you. The names I've called you. It wasn't right. Maybe we have our disagreements, but you didn't deserve that."

Carter was Carter, but despite his brittle veneer I could tell this surprised him. He covered it well, replying curtly, "You don't have to apologize. It's no more or less than I ever expect from humans."

That struck a chord somewhere deep inside. A sad one.

Maybe he was uncomfortable with the tone of our conversation. Before I could answer, I heard him clear his throat and say, "Looks like Ciara is about finished. I need to go back. I'll send someone out here to escort you both to the house."

I nodded. "Okay."

Still, he hesitated, almost like he wanted to say something else and was searching for the right words. I felt the same way, but I didn't know what to say or what I even wanted to say. No words sprang to mind. Everything and nothing tumbled about in my brain.

Finally, he said, "Good night, Ellie," then turned and walked away.

"Good night, Carter," I murmured, but he was already gone and didn't hear.

## CHAPTER THIRTY-THREE

"You look tired."
"I didn't sleep much last night," Carter confessed to his boss.

He and Sean were being driven to the back part of the Costas property where the Costas private jet and hanger were located. Ahead of them, Ellie sat in the backseat of the Aston, the same car the police had identified, the same car that had gotten them into this tangle with cops and lawyers and a fake wedding. In the late afternoon light, Ellie wasn't much more than a silhouette, but occasionally the pale autumn sunlight would strike her blonde hair, making it glow. Almost like a halo...which somehow suited the little pain.

"Worried about your plan? I know you, and I'm sure you didn't leave anything to chance."

Carter shook his thoughts away.

*You're being an idiot.*

"Not really," he answered casually. "I triple checked the details. James does good work. So does his team. Her family was fooled. Didn't take much persuasion to get them to go along with it. Ellie's mysterious disappearance had already set the stage."

"Have you heard from your people up there?"

"Only that they're settled. I heard from Blake. I asked him to keep an eye on them. Check in on them periodically. He agreed."

"Sounds like everything is taken care of."

"Hope so."

The car bumped and his focus drifted back to Ellie, being driven by Tracy. He hadn't seen her since last night, out at the pool. In fact, he'd chosen not to. The truth was, he didn't know what to say to her. He had a wife who wasn't going to stay his wife, a human wife, a wife he couldn't touch. A wife who was leaving him, and who he would likely never see again.

Which wasn't a bad thing. There was no need to see her again. Mr. Costas had said to keep her alive, keep her safe. Despite all that Nosizwe had thrown at them, besides even Ellie's best efforts to throw a monkey wrench into his plans, he'd succeeded. She was alive, she was safe, and she was about to fly off across the country to a new life. She'd be okay.

*And so will I.*

He'd be better than okay. She'd be gone, and he wouldn't have to worry about her anymore. He'd get the situation with the cops cleared up, then have their marriage officially dissolved. Afterward, he wouldn't have to think about Ellie St. James ever again. The sooner he got away from that human woman the better, especially considering the way the Talos kept responding to her.

They pulled up at the green and white hangar. The jet was already outside and on the runway, warming up. Their car parked next to the Martin. There would have been ample room for them all in one vehicle, but Sean needed Tracy to drive him into the city after Ellie's departure. Carter had an after hour appointment with the cops at Rodriguez' offices in downtown Fort Worth. Hence two vehicles. Not waiting for Tracy to do her job, Ellie popped the backdoor and climbed out at the same time Carter opened his.

He'd meant to simply walk around and get in the driver's seat.

After all, he'd said goodbye to Ellie last night, out at the pool. No need to draw the thing out. But Ellie was talking to Tracy, a few quiet words Carter couldn't catch. He was a little surprised to see her reach out and give Tracy a hug. With a final goodbye she then approached Sean. Her steps were a bit slower, but she still walked up to him bravely and held out her hand. Even though Carter was hanging back, staying out the way, he heard her say,

"Thank you, Mr. Costas, for what you've done for my family. I'm sorry everything happened like it did. I..."

"Not at all, Ellie. Taylor." Sean shook her hand, offering her a smile. "I'm the one who should apologize to you. I'm sorry your life was uprooted because of us. Please know my people and I are always here for you. If you ever need anything, don't hesitate to contact us. Like I said, you're part of my family, and always will be."

"Thank you."

Sean released her fingers. "Good luck, Ellie."

She nodded. Carter saw her take a breath as she turned to look at him. He steeled himself, waiting for her to say something or hold out her hand to shake his. Instead, after a long moment, she just said quietly, "Goodbye, Carter. Good luck. Let me know about..." She spread her hands. "Us. When you need me to sign papers and everything."

Carter cleared his throat. "I will."

He had the distinct impression there was more she wanted to say. Maybe she couldn't bring herself to do it in front of Sean and Tracy. Either that, or she was finished and he was wrong. Without another word she turned and headed for the steps leading up into the airplane. The flight attendant already stood at the top, waiting for her. Idly, he wondered if Ellie had ever flown on a private jet before, or even first class, for that matter. Probably not, with the way she acted about money. Acting like him dropping a little cash on that ring was some kind of major concern. It wasn't. And anyway—

Ellie had progressed halfway up the stairs when she suddenly stopped. Carter felt his senses rev up. What was it? Was something wrong? Had she heard something?

She turned around. Started coming back down the steps, faster than she'd gone up, picking up more speed as she neared the bottom. Carter quickly scanned the area, searching for signs that something was off. That Nosizwe's shifters had penetrated the airfield's defenses and Ellie had somehow noticed what he hadn't.

He registered no signs of danger. Ellie had stepped off the bottom step. She was still walking quickly, and towards him, actually. Her head was down, almost like she was afraid to look him in the eye. Carter felt confusion swell as she hurried right up to him. She stopped less than an arm length's away, and when she finally raised her face he saw her forehead was puckered and her eyes were intense, yet nervous.

"Carter...Carter, thank you for everything you did for me. I know you were just doing your job, and I know I wasn't always easy to get along with, but you saved my life and you took care of my family, like you promised. I want you to know I'll never forget what you did for us. For me. None of it."

If she'd reached up and slapped him across the face for dragging her through a night of hell he would have been less surprised. As it was, he stood there blinking like an idiot, trying to process the words coming out of her mouth. He'd barely started when she concluded her rushed speech by closing the distance between them, reaching up and putting her arms around his shoulders, hugging him. For a split-second he froze, acutely aware of his employer standing a couple yards away with a raised eyebrow, and Tracy watching with either a smile or a smirk. He couldn't tell. They both knew he wasn't a hugger, but Ellie with her arms around him was impossible to resist, either for him or the Talos. He wasn't sure which he could blame it on as his hands went around her waist, drawing her into his chest.

He locked her in place for a long moment, one palm on the small of her back, pressing her torso gently into his. He could feel her heart thumping, could hear her breathing. As soon as he felt her relax, felt her arms slide away, he let her go. But she wasn't finished quite yet. She stood there, her hands on his biceps, smiling up at him a little sadly.

"You're a good man, Carter Ballis. Better than you think you are. Take care of yourself. Don't let them make you play bodyguard to any more human women."

He fished around for a one-liner, but wasn't quick enough. The next thing he knew she was standing on tiptoe to brush a kiss against his cheek.

"That's for you," she said.

She raised up on her toes again to kiss his other cheek. "That's for the Talos." She winked. "He did a lot too."

For the first time since meeting her, Carter was at a complete loss. She'd taken him fully by surprise. She knew it too. She gave his arms a little squeeze and then stepped back.

"Goodbye, Carter."

Without another word she spun and ran for the jet. This time, she jogged up the steps and into the plane without a backwards glance. The stairs folded in. The door closed. The engine roared to life. Carter thought that was the last he'd see of her, but then her face appeared in a window. He couldn't make out her expression, but he did see the hand that she waved to him. To all of them. Like the others, he waved back. Then her face disappeared. The jet crept forward, making a wide circle, lining itself up on the airstrip. Within minutes, it was rolling down the airstrip, then rising off the ground.

Ellie St. James was gone.

None of them moved until the plane was safely in the air, taking Ellie to a new life and out of theirs. Sean was the first one to speak, saying so only Carter could hear, "Got under your skin, didn't she?"

Carter shifted, giving his employer a sideways glance. Sean had never joked with him about a woman before. Ever. Never tried to play matchmaker. Never said a word about his personal life. But Sean wasn't an idiot, either. He'd seen Ellie's goodbye, and probably heard it too. What was the point in lying?

"A little," he finally said, admitting to his boss what he'd barely admitted to himself.

"Too bad she had to go."

Was it?

"It's better this way," Carter disagreed. "All she wanted was to be with her family and have them safe. That's what she's getting."

"Hmmm."

Thankfully Sean didn't push it.

"I need to leave. My appointment is in forty-five minutes, and it'll take at least that long to get there. Call me after you leave Miguel's. Let me know how your meeting goes."

"Will do."

Sean slid into the backseat of his car and Tracy behind the wheel as Carter got into his own vehicle and started it up. He couldn't resist a final glance in the sky for Ellie's jet, but it was long gone.

He drove into Fort Worth on autopilot, shifting when he needed to, stopping at lights and stop signs, obeying traffic laws because they were ingrained in his subconscious, not because he was really thinking about them. He wasn't. He was thinking about Ellie. About that little speech, coupled with her apology last night. About the fact that she'd run back to him. Hugged him. Told him goodbye. Thanked him. About the way her body had felt, leaning into his. Too good; it had felt much too good.

*It's the Talos,* he told himself again in an attempt to pass the buck.

Couldn't be him.

Nope.

Their brief relationship had been fraught with danger and

death. They'd argued. They'd butted heads. She'd been angry at him more than once over his methods of keeping her safe. He'd been angry at her for being a human, for being his job, his responsibility. He'd wanted to dislike her on the basis of those things, not to mention what he saw as her sheltered upbringing and old-fashioned ideals. But what he'd wanted and what had happened were actually two very different things.

He turned left onto the intersection that would take him to the parking garage by his law firm's office.

In his mind's eye he was seeing her hurrying towards him. In his memory, he was feeling the press of her lips against his cheek.

He saw the red light and put his foot on the brake, slowing for it. His car slid to a neat stop. Carter sat there, waiting to go, idly running her final words through his mind, hearing her tell him he was a good man, teasing him not to let them make him be a bodyguard to any more human women.

He was safe at a red light. He wasn't supposed to have to watch for cross traffic, and he wasn't. Not until the massive dually about to cross in front of him abruptly veered out of its lane. He caught the abrupt motion from the corner of his eye, and glanced up in time to see the truck bearing down on his sports car. Carter stomped on the gas, but didn't react fast enough. The Aston had barely surged forward when there was the sound of an explosion going off. He saw white as the airbag blew up in his face, felt his body whipped to the side as the car went sliding, spinning wildly. He felt his skin itch as the Talos tried to take over in a desperate measure to save his life. But the itch faded. Faded into nothing.

Then there was silence.

# CHAPTER THIRTY-FOUR

"Did you see that?"

Detective Ewing and her partner were nearly to the law offices of Rodriguez, Stanton, and Vern when a red light caused traffic to slow to a stop. Candace was on her phone, checking her texts for messages from the M.E.'s office. She doubted Mavis would have further information before the appointment, but it didn't hurt to make sure. She was scrolling through two or three new messages when they heard a sound like an explosion, or a shotgun going off, or maybe a bomb. Candace's head jerked up as Gary yelled,

"Did you see that?"

"What happened?" she yelped.

"That truck just t-boned a car! Quick, call a bus!"

Gary twisted their car to the side of the road, put on the hazard lights, and jumped out. Candace followed, dialing as she ran, puffing into the phone, "Detective Candace Ewing at the intersection of 15th and Elm, by the law offices of Rodriguez, Stanton, and Vern. There's been a nasty wreck. Send a bus. Send fire trucks. They may need to use the Jaws of Life to get the driver out. Get them here right away."

As they dashed towards the car, the large green truck backed up, tires smoking and squealing.

"Hey, stop, police!"

Gary waved his arms, waved his badge, running right towards the truck. It kept backing, knocking into the little Prius behind it, sending it scooting sideways.

"Looks like it's going to be a hit and run," Candace continued into the phone. "Green F 350. Dually. Driver is..."

She squinted into the windshield, trying to see past the sunlight reflecting on the glass.

"Ah, crap. Looks to be Caucasian and male, but he's wearing a baseball cap and sunglasses. A jacket."

"Can you see the license plate, Detective?"

Gary was still chasing the truck, shouting like a madman, but the Ford finally had room to point its damaged hood the other way. The driver floored it and the vehicle responded, leaping forward with a roar. Smoke billowed out of the tailpipe as it spun off, leaving her partner in the middle of the intersection, hands on hips, panting.

"No. They covered it. Crap." Candace snapped again. "It's headed east on 15th. Notify any cops in the area. I'm checking out the driver of the other car."

She shoved her phone into her pocket and picked up speed as she sprinted towards the mangled sports car.

It looked bad. She didn't see how the driver could have possibly survived.

Smoke filled the air, and she waved an arm in front of her face. She was vaguely aware that Gary was following her, also running over to check on the driver. Other drivers were piling out of their cars, but so far, they hung back. The police were here and they didn't want to interfere. Whatever the case, Candace was the first one to reach the car. She stooped to stick her head into the window frame. The glass was shattered, and the door caved in so far the car had almost wrapped around it, was almost bent in two.

The white airbag had deployed, mostly hiding the driver, but Candace glimpsed what looked like men's jeans, masculine legs.

"Sir?" she called out. "Sir, it's the police. Hey are you okay? Sir?"

"Uuuhhh..."

She heard a groan.

"Sir?"

"Gary, I think he's alive," she yelled over her shoulder at her partner. "I'm going around to the other side."

Gary stuck his head in the window, talking to the man, as Candace nearly jumped across the hood to reach the opposite side of the car. On this side, the trunk had skidded into the concrete wall of the parking garage, but there was just enough room for her to squeeze in. The glass was shattered on this side as well, enabling her to stick her head fully into the vehicle.

"Sir—UUUUUHHH!"

"Candace? What is it?" Gary shouted, hearing her scream. "Candace?"

She couldn't answer. She couldn't speak. Her voice had closed off. Her throat had closed off. Her eyes were telling her what was there, but she couldn't trust them.

The airbag was half-wilted on this side, letting her get her first real look at the driver. His legs in jeans were pinned—no surprise there. His seat belt had kept him from flying out the side window, but the steering wheel was shoved up against him so he couldn't move.

That wasn't what had caused her to scream.

It was the driver himself.

His upper half wasn't human. It was bronze. Bronze, with a smooth skull and a smooth, almost feature-less face. His hands and arms were bronze. He looked like a statue. And yet she saw his chest move with labored breathing. Saw blood pooling on the carpet from his mangled legs....which looked like human legs.

"Candace? Candace, what is it?"

Gary's fierce tones snapped her back to reality. She felt him tugging on her, trying to pull her back through the window.

"For heaven's sake, woman, what's wrong? Are you okay?"

He sounded genuinely worried. Candace let him pull her back.

"Hello? Detective? Hello?"

"Gary—"

She clutched his upper arms.

"Gary..."

"What?"

"Gary—look in there. Tell me I'm not crazy. Tell me you see what I see."

"Tell you—"

"Just look!" she demanded.

She let go of him and he bent to see. Time seemed to freeze. All around her, she could hear the murmuring of the crowd. An ambulance's siren wailed in the distance, mingling with the sirens of the approaching fire trucks.

Slowly, Gary eased himself back out of the window. He looked grim, but he didn't look shocked.

"Did you—did you see it?"

He nodded soberly. "I did. But nobody else is going to."

"What?"

She pushed him aside and ducked back into the window, biting her lower lip to restrain a cry. The bronze skin was gone. A man sat there, pinned. A very human man. A man she recognized from his pictures. Carter Ballis. Head of security for Sean Costas. The very person they were coming to meet. Bleeding from his scalp. His legs. His face. His arms. The bronze was gone. Strangely, he wore no shirt. Just jeans. There was no trace of bronze.

Candace felt her eyes grow even wider as she edged back out.

"But-but I saw it! I know I did!"

Gary said nothing.

"I did, and you did too! You said you did. Tell me I'm not crazy," she begged.

"You're not crazy, but you also don't have any proof."

"Proof. Proof of what? That a half bronze guy was sitting there, that it was the guy we're supposed to meet, that—"

She couldn't have been more shocked when Gary clapped a palm over her mouth, smothering her words.

"Shut up. You're talking about things that you don't understand. Things that will get you killed. You saw it, Candace, but you're going to forget it. You're not going to breathe a word of it, okay? You didn't see a half bronze man. You didn't see anything except the victim of the wreck. Say anything else and I'll deny it. You'll look like you're crazy or an addict. You'll lose your job, your career, your pension, your reputation—everything you've worked so hard to earn."

She reached up and tore his hand away.

"What are you talking about?" she hissed frantically.

"I'm saying you didn't see that man shift into something else. You didn't see him shift back. And if you ever say differently, all hell will break lose. On you. Don't do it, Candace. Don't cross them."

"Don't cross who?"

The wail of the sirens was almost deafening as the bus veered up, pulling to a halt.

"Them," Gary said, and his voice was hoarse, strained. "Sean Costas and his people. His shifters. You play by their rules, or you don't play at all. Because you'll be dead. You're in on the secret now. He owns you."

"Owns me? Nobody owns me."

Gary laughed, but there wasn't any humor in it.

"That's what you think."

Commotion as the fire trucks and ambulances stopped. EMTs, paramedics, and firefighters poured out, approaching the smashed vehicle and the driver inside.

Gently, Gary took her arm, steering her away.

"Come on. Let them do their work."

She was too stunned to resist, but she kept glancing back over her shoulder as Gary walked them to the edge of the scene. She didn't know if she was expecting to see the gleam of sunlight on bronze, or catch a glimpse of a half-monster through the demolished windshield instead of a human man.

She saw neither, but Candace didn't need to see it again to reinforce what she'd already witnessed. The image was stamped clearly in her mind's eye, along with her partner's warning on her brain.

*Play by their rules, or you don't play at all. Because you'll be dead. You're in on the secret. It's over now. He owns you.*

What kind of nightmare had she fallen into?

Continue with Book 2, Down into the Pit. Add it on Goodreads now!

Want to hear *Stones of Fire* brought to life? Discover the audiobook, starting with *Ashes on the Earth*, narrated by Melissa Kay Benson.

For further fun, discover Aerisia, a parallel land to Earth's sunsets, in Sarah Ashwood's portal fantasy trilogy, the Sunset Lands Beyond. Start with Book 1, Aerisia: Land Beyond the Sunset.

# THE STONES OF FIRE SERIES

1. Ashes on the Earth
2. Down into the Pit
3. Fire from the Midst
4. Repairer of the Breach

# ABOUT THE AUTHOR

Don't believe all the hype. Sarah Ashwood isn't really a gladiator, a Highlander, a fencer, a skilled horsewoman, an archer, a magic wielder, or a martial arts expert. That's only in her mind. In real life, she's a genuine Okie from Muskogee, who grew up in the wooded hills outside the oldest town in Oklahoma and holds a B.A. in English from American Military University. She now lives (mostly) quietly at home with her husband and four children, where she tries to sneak in a daily run or workout to save her sanity and keep her mind fresh for her next story.

For a complete list of all Sarah's works and the links to find them, visit her website at www.sarahashwoodauthor.com.

To keep up to date with Sarah's new releases, sign up for her **newsletter**. You can also follow her on Bookbub, or find her on **Facebook**, Goodreads, Pinterest, Instagram, and **Twitter**.

# WORKS BY SARAH ASHWOOD

**The Sunset Lands Beyond Trilogy**

1. *Aerisia: Land Beyond the Sunset*
2. *Aerisia: Gateway to the Underworld*
3. *Aerisia: Field of Battle*

**Beyond the Sunset Lands**

(A companion series to the *Sunset Lands Beyond* trilogy)

1. *Aerisian Refrain* (now available)
2. *Aerisian Waning* (forthcoming)
3. *Aerisian Nightfall* (forthcoming)
4. *Aerisian Dawn* (forthcoming)

**The Sunset Lands Beyond Box Set**
Books 1-3 of the *Sunset Lands Beyond* trilogy

**Stones of Fire**

## WORKS BY SARAH ASHWOOD

1. *Ashes on the Earth*
2. *Down into the Pit*
3. *Fire from the Midst*
4. *Repairer of the Breach*

## Audiobooks
*Ashes on the Earth*, narrated by Melissa Kay Benson

## Standalones
*Knight's Rebirth*

## Novellas
*Amana*

## Short Works

"The Hero of Emoh" in the *Hall of Heroes* anthology

"The Princess and the Stone-Picker" in the *Tales of Ever After* anthology

"Lost" in the *Like a Woman* anthology

Made in the USA
Middletown, DE
30 January 2022